AF243837

TROUBLE IN PARADISE

Also by Cathy Pearson

Family Ties

TROUBLE IN PARADISE

A Cassie Grimes Mystery

CATHY PEARSON

White Dog Books

TROUBLE IN PARADISE. Copyright © 2006 by Cathy Pearson. All rights reserved. Printed in the United States of America. No part of this book may be used or reproduced in any manner whatsoever without written permission except in the case of brief quotations embodied in critical articles and reviews. For information address White Dog Books, 9539 Bridlewood Trail, Dayton, OH 45458.

ISBN 0-9788463-1-1

First Edition: September 2006

Library of Congress Control Number:

Printed on acid-free paper.

Jacket Design: Ron D'Allessandris
Author Photo: Will Shively

To good friends with either skin or fur.

And to my husband, Mark, who is best described
in superlatives.

Author's Notes and Acknowledgements

Thanks belong to Lucy and Kristen Weir and to Karen Notestine for their help with the story and cover ideas, to Sgt. R. Scott Owsley for his tour of a police facility and to Mike Calcaterra, technology wizard.

Ft. Myers Beach, Florida, is one of those places that truly do resemble paradise. Many of its locales and restaurants have provided some of my fondest memories, though they may now have morphed into new incarnations as chain eateries, condos or four lane highways. Yummy. And thanks to the countless variety of sun worshippers and characters there who are so at ease on its white sand. Their lack of clothing and inhibitions are a writer's gold mine.

A special thanks to Small Paws Rescue for their tireless devotion to rescuing Bichons from the most unspeakable circumstances. Robin Pressnall and her army of foster parents, volunteers and supporters are amazingly generous with their time and money on behalf of some of the most loving and trusting creatures on earth. They are the embodiment of the idea of "walking the walk."

To all those kindred spirits who know that our association with animals makes us better people: Bark on!

TROUBLE IN PARADISE

It was only 9:30 a.m., but I was late night weary. I was sitting in front of my PC, dressed in sweatpants and an old shirt of Gene's with a small Bichon snoring on my lap and another stretched out on his back at my feet. I was pleased that the extra treats had bribed Maggie out of the snit she'd been in since her other slave, my husband, had gone to Florida to work on the second phase of a consulting project. My bare right foot slowly stroked A.J.'s exposed belly as I concentrated on the erratic cash flow of my one-woman business. When I moved a foot back into my slipper, A.J. half-heartedly pawed the air before he, too, fell asleep. I stared at the computer screen showing a list of overdue vendor bills and groaned.

The anorexic balance of my checking account embedded at the bottom of the report caused me to whine like a Valley Girl.

"Eeny, meeny, miney, mo," I chanted as I jabbed the screen with my index finger. When our home phone rang, I dumped Maggie to the floor and ran toward the living room. OK, it was probably a telephone solicitor reading a stilted script in an unintelligible accent, but I was grateful to postpone the task of trying to cover ten pounds of bills with five pounds of cash. I grabbed the receiver before voice mail kicked in and said, "Good Morning, this is Cassie Grimes, ah…hello?"

"It's afternoon," Gene said in a low voice.

"Blonde or senior moment, take your pick," I replied. "What a pleasant surprise."

"Not for long," he said. I heard whoops of laughter in the background, but only breathing from Gene.

"Where are you?" I asked.

"Sitting on our front porch. There was an envelope on my desk when I got in this morning. It had a check and letter of regrets from the company's new controller. To quote the little pencil pusher, 'the revised budget has no room for overhauling the sales department.'"

I rubbed the back of my neck where fist-sized knots had suddenly appeared. "Oh, honey," I moaned. "Just when we were starting to see light at the end of the tunnel…"

"...we find out it's a train. I'll call you tonight when the rates are lower," he said and hung up.

My stomach was contributing a few acidic knots to keep the ones in my shoulders company when the phone rang again.

"Gene?" I said.

"It's Sherrie. Sorry to disappoint," said one of my oldest friends. She'd become another Ohio transplant in sunny Ft. Myers and was the reason we'd bought our condo there. But she rarely called me first, especially after she'd begun seeing a therapist for depression a couple of years ago. I pushed my own anxiety aside and asked, "What's wrong, Sherrie?"

"What isn't? I just want to go to bed and never wake up," she said and collapsed into gut-wrenching sobs.

Damn. This woman never, ever, cried. "C'mon, Sherrie," I said. "It can't be that bad." Before she could respond, I smacked my forehead and silently mouthed, "*Lame, Lame, LAME.*"

"Oh, yeah?" she sniffed. "I just spent another two hundred dollar hour with my shrink and can't think of a single thing that I'm contributing by being alive." I kept her talking for another ten minutes as the crying subsided. She finally said, "I'm tired, Cass. Don't worry. I haven't got the energy to walk to the bathroom for the bottle of sleeping pills."

What could I do from a thousand miles away? "OK, Sher. Rest up 'cause I'm on my way down there."

"Don't Cass. It won't make any..."

I cut her off. "Not up to you. Gene and I have a situation of our own. I'll let you know when I get in. Love you."

"Love you more," she murmured and hung up.

I redialed Gene, who was too bummed to ooze excitement at the news, but did manage to sound relieved that I was on my way. Replacing the receiver, I scooped A.J. into my arms and walked back to the office. Seeing A.J. snuggled against me, Maggie deliberately turned her back. There are two drama queens in the Grimes household.

A couple of phone calls and some paperwork and head shots stuffed into a briefcase put my various jobs on hold. Spontaneous travel plans left me without dog-sitting coverage, since my pal, Trudy, was out of town. So, Maggie and A.J. would be visiting Florida for the first time after making an eighteen-hour drive between Middleboro, Ohio and Ft. Myers Beach. But, hey, a road trip with the family pets should pose no larger inconvenience than walks at rest stops with a pooper-scooper, right? Ha. Dental surgery without novocaine would have been less painful for all of us.

Packing was a sullen affair. Gene's being unceremoniously dumped would put our wobbly finances into a tailspin. Even with multiple sources of income, my unpredictable contributions were currently in a lull. He hadn't gotten a regular paycheck for over a year and we were on the brink of fiscal disaster. Our home equity line was maxed out and I'd moved into creative financing with Platinum Master Cards to keep us afloat. The one-bedroom beach condo that we'd owned for seventeen years was our last cash reserve this side of bankruptcy. If selling it was the only way to avoid ruin, then I was by-God gonna spend some time there before we lost it. And I couldn't get Sherrie off my mind. Maybe working through two depressing situations would make both easier? Oh, sure. I'm certifiable.

At nine the next morning, I heaved suitcases into the trunk and back seat of my slightly rusted, decade plus 325 BMW under the woeful stare of two sets of deep brown eyes. "Cheer up, you two," I said in the high-pitched voice you use with toddlers. "You're going, too." I piled a comforter on the front seat and stashed dog food, lidded water bowl and a bag of "filet mignon" treats on the passenger-side floor. When I grabbed a green and a purple leash, A.J. started dancing and Maggie jumped high enough that her little nine-pound body was parallel to the car's windows.

Charcoal gray skies underlined my mood as we took one last tour of the bushes. The dynamic duo strained against the harnesses to continue their normal walking route but I pulled them back toward the garage.

"Not happening. Let's go," I said. They did perfectly matched 180-degree turns and leapt into the car when I opened the door. A.J. stared excitedly from the window, but Maggie was whining before we left the plat, so I started deep-breathing exercises as we headed for I-75 South. After all, I reasoned, I'm the superior human; capable of outwitting mere animals in a test of wills. Hey, a girl's gotta have a dream.

By Cincinnati, the rain was a *fait accompli* and Maggie's crying had been uninterrupted for nearly an hour. I pulled into a rest stop, hoping a brief walk in the rain would make her view the car more kindly. They both jumped across my lap into the downpour when I opened the door. I lunged for their leashes and yelped when a spasm torqued through my side as a reminder of slightly deteriorating flexibility. Maggie's initial enthusiasm morphed into a mule-like tug-of-war as I pulled her in A.J.s' wake. We soon circled back to the car where I struggled to wipe their soggy fur with a wad of paper towels swiped from the public restroom before they did the double doggie shake. Not fast enough. I wiped my own face with a damp, muddy towel as A.J. did two quick circles and sat contentedly on the comforter. Maggie leaned against my arm to resume her whining, now punctuated by several high-pitched yips.

"Damn it, Maggie. Shut up," I ordered as I wrestled my cell phone from the purse I'd stashed behind my seat. "I need to call Aunt Sherrie." I punched in her work and home numbers, only to hear her cheery voice mail greetings on both. Even her cell went unanswered. "Double Damn!" I said, pounding the steering wheel as a sense of dread joined my irritation. I forcefully exhaled my frustration and inhaled the luxurious aroma of wet sheep. Wonderful. As I merged with a steady line of semi's, I cranked up the radio and sang at the top of my lungs, hoping to loosen my tightening shoulders. Whether it was my song or empathy for his pal, A.J. began to pace and howl. With the rain beating a louder staccato rhythm on the windshield, I turned the wipers up a notch and pushed the accelerator down hard. Hey, how long could this last?

The answer was nearly seven hours. I called Gene around Knoxville, Tennessee, after screaming into Maggie's face before hurling her into the back seat. When he answered the phone, I bypassed the usual pleasantries and seethed,

"I'm in a Chevy Chase vacation movie rated "R" because of harsh language and coming violence."

He had the nerve to laugh. Bad move. I unleashed a string of my more colorful hyphenated expletives that caused him to whistle. "Whoa! Sorry! Getting a little frazzled, are we?" I might have heard him smirk if Maggie hadn't started to swear in dog-speak.

"What do you think?" I growled.

"I think that they're lucky to be with you," he said. "If they were making that trip with me, they'd probably be in a camper, headed for parts unknown." I *am* married to a genius. Placate and flatter and you, too, can be a long-time husband.

"Be careful, honey," he continued. "The news is saying there are tornado warnings across Southern Georgia. Maybe you should stop for the night."

"Not a chance in hell," I replied. "What's a little rain compared to the Bichon Banshee?"

"Check in from time to time, ok?"

"You got it. Talk to you soon, Baber."

As we drove through Chattanooga, Maggie finally lay down. A.J. curled up next to her and blissful quiet reigned. Though I was fighting gusting winds that pushed my little car all over the road, my mood lifted considerably. An hour later we were moving past the last lights of Macon when the car was strobe-lit as it rocked with teeth-jarring thunder. Two shaking dogs leaped onto my lap. For the next two hundred miles I gripped the steering wheel with one hand and stroked my terrified sissies with the other as I struggled to see the nearly invisible road over two white heads.

When we finally rolled into the condo parking lot at 4:00 a.m., I barely noticed the star-filled sky or the gentle breezes that pushed against my clothing, still soggy from the inevitable potty-breaks. I stumbled over the pavers sunken into the sand next to our building and climbed the short flight of steps to the porch. Through the screen door, I spotted Gene napping on the sofa. The terrible twosome recognized Daddy and went crazy in greeting. I pushed the screen aside and transferred the leashes to him without a word. My walk to the bedroom was marked with a trail of damp clothes haphazardly discarded on the floor. I sat naked on the blue/green comforter covering our king-size bed, lay back against the peach and beige throw pillows and passed out cold.

****

Consciousness returned at 11:00 a.m. with Gene's side of the bed occupied by two softly snoring dogs. I flipped the extra blanket Gene had covered me with to the floor and reached for the bathing suit and towel laid out on the nightstand. I eased from the bed, tiptoed into the bathroom to change and made a stealthy escape to the private beach between our front door and the Gulf of Mexico. Caressed by the humid warmth, I ambled toward a white plastic lounger sitting in the sand and covered it with my bright yellow towel. A niggling worry about Sherrie surfaced just long enough for me to squash it. I liberally smeared on the sun block that Gene had stuck in the sand next to the chair before I stretched, lay back and quickly nodded off again. Soon, the brightness of tropical sun directly overhead penetrated my closed eyelids. Squinting, I blindly patted the warm sand in search of my sunglasses while breathing in the tangy smell of brine and suntan oil. I listened contentedly to the sound track of constantly blowing wind, water slapping the shore and gulls bleating. Not finding my shades, I raised a hand to shield my sleepy eyes and watched tiny sailboats inching along the straight line between sea and sky with one lone kid, bobbing contentedly in the shallow waters. That's when I spotted the rolling fin, jumped from my lounger and ran into the waves.

"C'mon, baby," I called. "C'mon!" The fin resurfaced, followed by a gray body and I held my breath. About five feet from my half-submerged torso, it surfaced again, veered sharply and flicked its powerful tail. I squealed like a two year old when the splash drenched me and the dolphin sped away.

He quickly turned and repeated the charge. Another wall of water shot in our direction and "Flipper" cut his speed. We stood mesmerized as he circled within a few feet of us, making eye contact. When he lowered his head and swam for deeper waters, I squinted into the sun's glare until it was impossible to track his shrinking form. Giving a small wave to the kid and the dolphin, I turned my back on the horizon and headed for shore.

Junior's parents and some beach walkers shielded their eyes as they continued to stare over the water toward the sun. I shuffled through the water to avoid stepping on the business end of a stingray hidden in the sand. As I looked down to assure myself that the tickle on my legs was a fish, I realized that my left boob had nearly freed itself from the top of my bright yellow two piece suit. The water was murky this close to the land, so I flexed my knees and submerged from the neck down, praying that tickle was benign. I surreptitiously pulled the flap of lemon cloth over the nipple that threatened to expose itself and paddled forward. I stood in thigh-deep water, put a finger of each hand under the fabric in the back of the suit bottom and pulled down in the classic beach butt-cover maneuver that was reflexive to females from puberty to Medicare. Further inland, I saw Gene waving from the porch of the condo. As I raised my hand in return, Gene's arm dropped and he casually pulled aside his swim trunks to flash me. Now that's what I call motivation.

I walked quickly through the thick white sand in an awkward gait. Stopping at the low fence that ran between the private beach and the building, I turned on the shower nozzle mounted two feet from the ground to rinse the sand from my feet.

"Time for a sun-break before we meet Sher and Dave for dinner," Gene called.

"You talked to Sherrie?" I said, hurrying up the steps of the pale beige stucco building. I didn't know whether to be totally pissed or blissfully relieved.

"Yeah. I called her at work this morning while you were in la-la land. You know, I don't think you've really caught up on your rest, yet. We probably need to take a nap," he said, grabbing his crotch in a gesture that was as inherently male as the swimsuit pull was female. I grinned as he pulled the sliding screen aside for me, and two white faces materialized. I bent down to scratch A.J.'s head and extended the other arm toward Maggie. She gave me a glacial stare, turned and walked toward the couch.

"Don't push your luck, princess," I said as I moved down the hall. "I'm heading for the shower, Gene."

"I was counting on it," he laughed, scooping Maggie into his arms. "Daddy will protect you from mean old Mommy." He followed me and stood in the doorway, still cradling a clearly unhappy dog.

She reluctantly allowed me to scratch her ears as I said, "It's all right, baby. Mommy doesn't feel the need to euthanize you any more."

The cool water felt delicious as I soaped the SPF 30 Coppertone from my pinkish, freckled body. Ok, so my skin's variation was really sun damage and/or age spots. And under-wire was definitely one of my best friends. In the middle of this mental whine for lost youth, I flashed on another reality: our finances meant that this oasis might not be ours much longer. If I kept this up, I'd be thoroughly depressed. "Shaddup!" yelled the voice inside my head as I pulled the peach and aqua shower curtain aside. Gene, standing naked in the doorway, took the towel from my hand and dried away the water and the blues.

We awoke in a jumble of sheets to the ringing of the nightstand phone. A ceiling fan pushed cool air across my naked shoulder as I reached for the receiver, smiling at my satiated reflection in the large mirror above the white lacquered dresser.

"Hello?" I said.

"Did I interrupt anything?" said a familiar voice.

"No, Sherrie," I yawned.

"Too bad," she replied.

"You're a little late, and it was anything but bad," I answered, giving Gene an appreciative slap on the butt.

"Quit gloating," she said. "What time are we meeting you for dinner and where?"

The clock on the nightstand read 6:05. "7:30 at the Mucky Duck?" I asked.

"Suits me," she said. "Don't be late, Cassie. You're not going to the prom."

****

When I hung up, Gene and I squeezed into our tiny bathroom and worked on becoming presentable. While blow-drying my hair, I fast-forwarded through the two plus decades of my friendship with Sheryl Marie Walters, who had inadvertently caused Ft. Myers Beach to become our perpetual, travel destination.

After a wild spring vacation, Sher had returned to Dayton, quit her job and packed for the year-round warmth of Florida shortly before Gene and I had our first date. Her first stop was Tampa where, at 20-something and financially challenged, a torrid affair with a wealthy, married man seemed exciting. He didn't have the fatal heart attack in her arms, but the rigors of his double life killed him just the same. Seriously shaken, Sherrie transferred to Fort Myers and took a pledge to date only single guys. Well, they did have to be older and have money, but she vowed that having a wife would be a deal breaker in acquiring the keys to her more than willing panties and incrementally more cautious heart.

But her luck soon changed and she met the man of her dreams. Dave Walters was a recently widowed, attractive 55 year-old entrepreneur in search of the perfect trophy wife.   Hitting the sheets with someone my father's age grossed me out, but Sher swore that it was true love. I adored my friend, but I did believe that she had exercised a more socially acceptable form of the world's oldest profession. The four of us married within three months of each other and embarked on very different life styles. Gene and I spent 75% of our time apart as we crisscrossed the country, climbing the corporate ladder.   Sherrie quickly joined Dave in his business ventures and seemed overjoyed to be in the wrinkly company of her wealthy "Big Fella", 24/7.

For his part, Dave showered his "Sher-Bear" with fabulous jewelry and a beach condo. During a rare break in our frantic schedule, Gene and I dropped in for a visit and put down a deposit on the vacant condo next door to theirs. It was the perfect yuppie investment. It also gave me an excuse to see my friend on a regular basis, since she was too caught up in her new life to spend even one night away from the 'Big Guy', a phrase she swore referred to more than his longevity.

As the years flew by, I waited for verification that my buddy was a garden-variety gold digger, but the sincerity of her adoration never cracked. When I warned that the age gap she trivialized would become significant in Dave's Medicare years, she'd counter with vivid details of the puppy-dog devotion and sexual gymnastics he performed daily. My response was to suppress a gag reflex.

"Ah, honey," I said, during one of our brutally frank girl-talks, "How long do you think the old boy's gonna feel that frisky? And how long do you think *you* can spend genuflecting before your knees get tired? 'Big Guy and his Sher-Bear.' Give me a break."

"Cassie, darling," she replied, "When I've spent a lot of time on my knees around Dave, I usually end up with a diamond bracelet."

I wrinkled my nose. "Now there's a delightful image."

At that point in their relationship, Sherrie's pale blue eyes sparkled whenever she discussed her life. "How many couples are as happy as we are?" became her constant refrain, followed by, "If Dave and I have only 10 years together before he kicks, we'll have had a better marriage than most people I know."

The four of us celebrated our tenth anniversaries watching the sunset over Sanibel Island from our porch on Ft. Myers Beach. By then, I was in business for myself while Gene was rocking from his first corporate downsizing. Sherrie and Dave had sold their condo to buy an enormous house on the most exclusive golf course in the area, but had a key to ours if they needed a beach fix. Whenever we came south, we met at our place. It was microscopic compared to their home, but we had the better view.

During his first physical on Medicare, Dave's doctor told him that non-smoking and exercise had given him the body of a 45 year-old. He shrugged this off as natural since his 87 year-old mother was still going strong. He'd also begun to gradually withdraw from the day-to-day operations of the chain of gourmet bake shops and rental properties that now comprised Davesher Enterprises. After a decade of being the all-knowing Master to Sherrie's compliant student, Dave thought he should be able to direct the company from his deck chair while his Sher-Bear did all the actual work. Unfortunately, his partner started craving recognition for turning a fairly lucrative business into a multi-million dollar success. Sher-Bear may not have needed the ego reinforcement that typical executives require, but Sheryl Walters, Baking Empress, certainly did. In the cause of marital serenity, Sherrie kept stroking Dave's ego and other body parts while complaining to me. I'd like to tell you that I never said 'I told you so,' but I take pride in my honesty – except concerning birthdays, of course.

Soon, we both refused to name the actual number of the anniversaries we'd celebrated. Our condo provided the means for Sherrie and me to cement our relationship, since both she and her overly possessive mate weren't keen on her traveling to see me. Being more flexible, I was in Ft. Myers regularly, with or without my spouse. Over the years, I watched as the wild, impulsive girl who had headed to Florida with big dreams, a sharp wit and an even sharper tongue, morphed into respectability, with a carefully crafted image at work and home. The loyalty and discretion we'd shared for years made me the rare recipient of the unvarnished truth as she saw it and it had become anything but a pretty picture.

****

Sherrie still talked about those 'deliriously happy 10 years,' but in the past tense. Now, her new mantra featured depression, "Big Fella" pejoratives, and a healthy dose of her untenable circumstances. I loved my friend dearly, but it was growing harder to hear my wealthy pal whine about her tough life and tear-filled therapy sessions when Gene and I were busy dodging collection calls. She'd occasionally admit that her problems did seem minor compared to ours, but the escalating depression for which she was being treated, would then slap her back into self-absorbed sadness.

We had talked for nearly an hour last week, when I called to ask if she could lend Gene a car for the consulting gig. "He's coming in on AirTran Flight 498 at 7:15 p.m. Can you still pick him up?" I asked.

"I'm only five minutes from the airport, Cassie. He can drop me off and take my car to the beach. Why don't you join him?"

"Thanks for the loan of the car, honey," I said. I flashed on dodging the question, but replied honestly. "It sucks to be so strapped that we can't get a rental car for even a few days."

"Not a problem. Dave can drop me at the store and pick me up until Gene's done with the car. What else does the old goat have to do?"

The bitter edge to her voice made me wince. "As I recall, lamb-puss, you're the one who wanted Dave to retire."

"Yeah," she admitted, "so he'd quit dropping in and royally screwing things up. Even though the man is so forgetful he can't find his ass with both hands, he still wants to give directions to the employees. It takes me three hours to clean up the messes he makes in thirty minutes."

"Geez, Sherrie, the man is a very senior citizen! It could be a lot worse," I reminded her. In fact, he was just a year younger than my mother. Virginia Marianna O'Donnell was never forgetful, but she was nearly blind, hard of hearing and needed a cane to walk even short distances. I'd gladly trade a bit of memory loss for a valid driver's license and fewer trips to the ER.

"You're right," she said. "Thank God he's not as horny as he used to be." I flashed on a vivid scene involving hot steamy love with a wrinkly septuagenarian and quickly squeezed my eyes to erase it. See what I mean about the picture not being pretty?

"Sher, you had to know that this day was coming," I said. "Just be glad that the wet spots you're cleaning from the sheets aren't of a different nature."

"Yeah, he's healthy as a horse," she sighed. "Who'd have thought the old geezer would still be going strong?"

"*I* would have thought that you'd give up on the rich, young widow fantasy since you're still visiting Dave's mother."

"But his father bit it when he was 67."

"Well, honey, looks like the genetic roulette wheel gave him his mother's genes," I sighed.

"Lucky me," she said.

A flash of irritation shot through me. One of the things that girlfriends do for each other is to listen sympathetically when the other needs to whine about the tough times.   With my friend in a financial position to make any number of changes, this particular song had been overplayed to the point of nausea. Rather than say something bitchy, I walked to the kitchen for some comfort food. After tranquilizing myself with a couple of giant chocolate chip cookies, I said, "You've got enough money to do anything you want. Why don't you travel or set him up in another business?"

"I get air sick and have plenty to do already," she replied. "Why do you think I sleep so much?"

"Massive medication?" I suggested.

"One of the best reasons for therapy," she said. "Otherwise, I'd jump off a bridge."

I could hear real pain rumbling through the phone line. I licked the last crumbs from my fingers and tried a new tactic. "Sheryl, if you're as miserable as you say, why not file for a divorce?"

"And have the whole world talking about me like an ungrateful bitch? No way."

My friend had always been given to exaggeration. "Honey, I think the sphere of interest will be slightly less than global."

"You know what I mean, Cass. Everyone at the club would be so smug about my deserting him when things got rough. And then, there's his kid. Besides, how much longer do you think this can go on?"

"I'd say another 15 or 20 years. He's still hitting the gym three times a week and you tell me his mom is healthy enough to be submitted to Willard Scott's 100th birthday club."

"Thanks for the pep talk," she sighed and added, "I can't be that disloyal to him."

"Uh huh. I'm sure that living with you right now is complete bliss. You just might be doing both of you a favor," I said.

"Probably. Dave says he can't take much more, but my shrink says he's not going anywhere. Hell, the man can't even remember where he puts his glasses. How would he manage without me?" she asked.

I started to reach for another cookie. With a rare surge of self-restraint, I pulled my hand back and filled a glass with boring, distilled water as I answered. "Well, let's see. Half of everything you own would leave him a very wealthy man. He's in great shape, likes to travel and is still somewhat interested in sex. Somehow, I think he'd cope."

"Then why doesn't he just do it?" she whined.

"If you think change is hard for you, Sher, what do you suppose it's like for someone 30 years older? So what are you gonna do? Sit around wishing for a different life or try to do something other than waiting for him to die while drowning in guilt?"

"Yeah, yeah. My shrink talks all the time about the power of change," she said. "It isn't that easy."

"And the prospect of living like this for the next 20 years is?" I asked, shaking my head.

"I hate my life so much, I can't think of anything worth living for," she said.

I bit off a sarcastic reply. It was still difficult for me to distinguish between cloying self-pity and actual depression. Ever the Pollyanna, I replied, "How about exotic destinations, men in Speedos and a friend to keep you company?"

"You and Dave," she sighed, ignoring my witty repartee. "Everybody keeps hoping the old Sherrie will come back. I think she's gone forever."

"Of course she's gone forever," I said. "People change, Honey. When you've stopped, you're dead." I gave myself a mental kick in the ass for sounding so self-righteous.

She sighed more loudly. "Enough. I'm sick of talking about this. Are you still thinking about putting the condo up for sale?"

Now *I* was depressed and equally tired of this conversation. Maggie and A.J. had settled next to me on the couch. I moved a hand between the fluffy ears on each head, counting on the medicinal value of pet therapy to relieve my dreary thoughts. *Little did I know what awaited me on the car trip from Hell.* I looked at a 3' x 4' painting I'd done of the view from our front porch in Ft. Myers and replied, "I don't think we have much choice. Gene's new business just isn't generating enough cash to make up for the uncompensated time I've been putting into my artistic careers. We've max'ed out more Platinum Cards than you can imagine."

"I don't know how you stand it," she said.

"Some days, not very well," I admitted. "We're sitting on some very serious equity at the beach. Selling the condo would help us a lot. As much as I hate having to take my own advice, it may be time for the Grimes family to make some changes."

Sherrie ended our conversation when someone yelled that she had a call waiting. "I've got a customer, so I can't keep flapping my jaws at you. I'll take care of Gene."

She'd picked Gene up from the Southwest Regional Airport in Fort Myers, and handed him the keys to her new SUV. Very shortly, Gene would be unemployed, Sherrie would go quiet after suggesting suicide and I would become the tragic heroine in *The Nightmare on I-75*. Talk about changes.

Mentally returning to the slow rhythm of the present, I was grateful that preparation for a night out on the Gulf was a quick and easy process. Ft. Myers Beach is a place where casual is just this side of naked, so whatever style my short blond hair got came from the blow drier. Since real world make-up in a tropical climate soon looked like Crisco soup, a little powder, mascara and a bit of lipstick were as much as I'd concede to grooming. OK, maybe clean clothes, but that was the limit.

"Are you about ready, Cassie?" Gene called. "It's after 7:00 and Sherrie's always early."

I gave one last squeeze on the eye lash curler and replied, "Putting on my clothes right now."

"Bummer," Gene said, as I reached for my bra, silently thanking the person who'd invented under-wire support. Grooved shoulders were a small price to pay for perky breasts.

I shrugged into a sleeveless ankle-length peach silk dress and tan sandals. "Maybe we'll actually beat them to the restaurant and *I* can nag *her*." Gene locked the sliding door and grabbed my hand as we walked to the car with the surf pounding the shore behind us. The salty breeze and crescent moon hanging in a clear sky tugged my heart toward melancholy. How could we bear to sell this place with so much of our history residing here? Wrestling a sense of sadness, I heard that inner voice dripping with sarcasm. *Hey, genius, how will you bear more collection calls and bankruptcy?*

All right, all right! I answered myself. Carpe diem, and all that shit. God, I hated to be guilty of the same things I lectured Sherrie about. That sort of reality check was usually all that was needed for me to head back toward positive thoughts, but tonight, I just couldn't shake a sense of uneasiness about my pal. Even depressed, she hid behind a razor sharp sense of humor. The pure desperation I'd heard in her voice had catapulted me south. I really was concerned and longed to talk with her. I felt myself slipping into a Sherrie-sized funk, so I squashed my apprehension into a tomorrow kind of box and turned my thoughts back to our pre-nap gymnastics. That put a smile on my face and a tinglin' in my toes as I waved at two forlorn faces watching us descend the steps. Just before turning onto the paver-strewn path to the parking lot, I glanced back to see A.J. chasing Maggie around the condo, in pursuit of the rawhide chew she'd suddenly decided was her personal property. In a dog's world, sadness can be quickly forgotten by chewing dead cow skin into a slobbery mush. Who's the dumber animal?

We were taking both cars to dinner, so that I could return theirs if Sherrie was willing to risk Dave driving at night. I paused next to my Beemer and said, "Hey, sweetie, the Walters' will probably leave early, so how about having dessert at our place?"

"Are you trying to kill me?" he laughed.

"Certainly not. Just want to get in as much beach sex as we can if we decide to sell this place. "

"Keep talking like that and we won't make it to the restaurant."

"Sure we will. A little waiting never hurt anybody," I teased, pressing my left breast against his right arm, as he hit the automatic lock on Sherrie's car.

"Tell that to Mr. Happy," he said.

"Pretty soon," I intoned with a tilt of my head toward his lap. Sadly, that turned out to be a complete lie. That nagging uneasiness became a series of events that left Mr. Happy and me anything but.

TWO

Five minutes later, we pulled into the gravel parking lot of The Mucky Duck. Its faded blue exterior had always looked like it needed a fresh coat of paint because of constant battering by the damp, salty air. Inside, the dimly lit dining room flickered with candles as a steady stream of elderly patrons carefully made their way toward the lobby. Early bird specials were the norm here in Senior-land, so our "late" arrival should guarantee a beach side table. A snowy-haired hostess met us at the door. She was dressed in neon-orange stretch pants and an oversized tee splashed with citrus colors. Smiling through tangerine lipstick, she said, "Welcome to the Mucky Duck. How many in your party?"

Gene answered, "Four of us, with two to follow shortly."

She nodded and checked the laminated seating chart taped to the podium. The marker was poised in the air when I said, "Could you put us at a table by the window, please?"

She turned her head and squinted through turquoise frames that surrounded oversized lenses. When she turned back, she moved the marker toward the top of the chart, placed an "X" over a table, and replied, "Sure thing, honey. Just let me get it bussed before I seat you." She shuffled off as we turned to gaze hypnotically into a huge salt-water tank. Large, sunshine yellow fish and smaller iridescent blue ones swam lazy routes through the decorative stones surrounding a brightly colored house with a bubbling chimney.

Gene interrupted my aquatic meditation with a tap on the elbow, saying, "I think she's ready for us." In the back of the dining room, our hostess waved a stack of menus with the assurance of a traffic cop. We wove our way through the tables of chatting patrons toward a wall of tall windows with the middle panels pushed open. The cool breeze caused some of the blue hair set to pull sweaters more tightly across their shoulders. Since my middle-aged thermostat could quickly flash to sauna, I was grateful for relief from the tropical heat.

My husband was resplendent in a pale olive golf shirt that made his hazel/brown eyes sparkle beneath a tan forehead and sun-bleached hair that was, for the moment, a blonde and silver combo. His mouth was moving, but the noise of wind and surf and the general din of the dining room prevented my hearing him. I leaned forward and said, "Excuse me?"

He smiled. "I said that you're looking very pretty tonight."

"Well, turn up the volume, sweet cheeks. A statement like that should never be missed."

"You got your wish," he said, looking toward the entrance. "We're actually here before Sherrie. She'll never believe it."

"I hardly believe it myself," I said, checking my watch. "They've got five more minutes and then I can ride *her* about being late."

Our glasses were empty and we were nursing our water with the last muffin from the breadbasket. We'd already polished off our appetizers. Gene had eaten a dozen raw oysters to rebuild his stamina. While I agreed with the motivation, I could never bring myself to eat something whose consistency reminded me of swallowed snot. I munched on a jumbo shrimp that did justice to its title and checked my watch again.

"It's almost eight o'clock," I said, scraping the last trace of red sauce from a small bowl with the remains of my shrimp. "I wonder where they are? Do you suppose Sher got our rendezvous point mixed up?"

"Don't have a clue," Gene said. "But it's not like your anal friend to be this late."

"You've got that right," I said and pushed back from the table. "I'll find a phone and listen to whatever lame excuse she can invent." Many of the tables were now empty as I approached the hostess station. Our citrus colored greeter pulled a dangling earring of vividly colored fish from her right ear to answer the phone as I stopped next to her.

"Just a minute, Dearie. I'll see if I can find them," she said into the receiver. She lay it down on the podium and turned to me. "Say, you wouldn't be Cassie Grimes, would you?"

I raised an eyebrow. "Actually, yes."

She picked up the phone and extended it. "For you, honey."

I turned my back on the dining room and said, "Sherrie, what's going on? Did you have a senior moment or just fall asleep?"

"Neither," she replied. "I expected Dave to be waiting when I got home. He's still not here and I haven't heard a word from him. Wait 'til I get my hands on the old fart."

"That *is* weird," I said. "Maybe tonight's his racquetball night, and *you* forgot?"

"No way. I had him make a few deliveries for me in Bonita Springs this afternoon. When I beat him home, I assumed he'd gone further south to Naples to see Tom. But I called there around seven and Susan hadn't seen either of them. I'll bet the old coot started drinking Rum and Tonic with his son and forgot about tonight. I'll kill him."

"Easy, Sherrie," I said. "I know Dave stops to see the kid pretty often, but I thought he always did his serious drinking by your pool while watching the golf channel."

"You can usually set your watch by it," she groused. "And he shouldn't be driving after dark. The last time he was on the road alone after sunset, I had to buy his way out of a police report when he rear-ended a Lexus. If somebody his age gets a ticket they'll pull his license. I'll be damned if I'll become his chauffeur."

That nagging sense of uneasiness was pushing my forehead into wrinkles. I consciously relaxed the tensing muscles and asked, "Have you eaten yet?"

"No, damn it," she said. "And I'm starved."

"Don't despair, lamb-puss," I said. "We'll get dinners to go and bring them to you."

"Geez, Cassie, it'll be midnight by then," she whined.

"Hardly. The place is almost deserted, so I expect to be at your place by quarter to nine."

"You realize that's past my bedtime." For as long as I'd known her, Sher thought the perfect time to retire was before nine. In her defense, she was usually feeding a collection of stray animals before six. I couldn't imagine life without prime-time drama and the Eleven O'clock News.

"Suck it up, Sher," I said, adding a large helping of guilt. "I drove eleven hundred miles to see you, so the least you can do is stay up a little later than usual."

"Stop nagging and drive," she said. "Where do you think Dave could be?"

"Beats me," I said, "but he'll probably get there before we do. Call the gate and tell them to admit us."

"You've got my car, Cass," she reminded me. "Just buzz yourself in." The phone clicked before I could tell her that we planned to return it to them tonight. Sometimes, things have a way of working themselves out. *Welcome to Cassie's Dream World.*

I snagged our waiter on the way back. Gene raised his eyebrows in a silent question when we returned. She'd already told me that we could order everything as take-out while we'd crossed the nearly empty room to our table.

"Dave's still not home," I explained to Gene as I re-opened the menu. "We're going to get four dinners and take them to their place so that we can visit."

"I'll bet your crazy friend is fit to be tied," he said.

"That she is." I turned to our server, whose face suggested Medicare, and whose hair screamed Clairol Brunette #104. "Give us a scampi dinner, an almond grouper and the shrimp pasta. What do you want, Gene?"

"Blackened swordfish," he answered. "How fast do you think you can have this ready?"

"Fifteen minutes, tops," she said, shoving a pencil into the teased pile of way-too-dark brown hair.

"This should be fun," Gene moaned. "Sher'll be bitchin' and Dave'll be drinkin'."

"I know, hon," I said. "But she's pretty worried. Dave is ridiculously predictable and he *is* driving after dark. What if he's actually had a heart attack and crashed?"

"Don't invent disasters, Cass," Gene said.

"You're right," I said. "But you must admit that it's peculiar. I've always told her to call me if something should happen to Dave, 'cause I still don't trust his kid. Who'd have thought we'd actually be here in Ft. Myers?"

"Give me a break, Cassie," Gene said. "They've been married a long time. I'm sure the will is set in stone by now."

"I would think so. But civilized behavior has a way of evaporating when big money's at stake. Besides, I've had a funny feeling off and on all day." Gene smirked at the reference to my sixth sense. He'd seen several examples of its accuracy over the years, but he steadfastly refused to acknowledge anything but factual explanation until he had no other choice. We lapsed into silence while waiting for the food, staring out of the darkened window at the dancing white line that the water's foam made on the shore.

The reverie was broken when our waitress appeared, holding two plastic bags in each hand. "Thirteen minutes," she declared, as she dropped the bill she'd been holding between her pinky and ring finger. Gene dropped his Visa on the table after glancing at me to confirm it would take another charge. She gave us the dinners and scooped up the card. "Meet you up front," she called over her shoulder as she waddled to the register.

Ten minutes later, we crossed the bridge between Estero Island and Ft. Myers proper in the two cars. I was carrying the dinners so the Beemer's new aroma was a heady blend of wet dog and a garlic explosion in an aquarium. We turned right past the always-busy Pancake House onto Summerlin, and headed inland. We were soon turning onto Glengarry Lane, the access road for

Highland Estates, which wound past another country club community and yet-to-be annihilated cypress stand.

A small concrete building meant to resemble a miniature Scottish castle split the road ahead, with wooden gates stretching over both sides of the road. Non-residents had to clear themselves from a guest list and receive a paper pass before the guard would raise the barrier. A small box stood next to the right side to allow residents to raise the arm with a specialized electronic opener. Gene had activated that gate with the remote. I was in the lane behind him, but without the proper ID. I flashed a huge smile and waved enthusiastically to a guard who looked old enough to have been a contemporary of Macbeth. He grinned in return and waved us on our way without leaving his chair. So much for the security of a gated community.

The hour was late enough that Gene sped along Glengarry at 25 miles per hour, nearly doubling the posted limit of 15 MPH. The snail's pace was meant to protect cocktail-toting golf cart drivers that routinely crossed the main roads, oblivious to oncoming traffic.

Even in the dark, it was an impressive neighborhood. Highland Estates sported impeccably landscaped yards of huge palms, surrounded by beds of flowering tropical plants, illuminated by well-placed, decorative lights. The homes were set back on deep lots, with nearly every backyard holding a cage that covered individual pools and, often, a companion hot tub. Fences were forbidden to allow each resident a clear view of the two championship golf courses to which each home abutted. The houses themselves were varying degrees of enormous ostentation. Concrete block and stucco with huge windows were arranged in a variety of custom designs, with contrasting tile roofs slanting toward elaborate entryways of either carved wood and/or etched glass.

Gene pulled Sher's car into the right side of the empty garage of one of the more modest houses on this block. The Walters residence was 4,500 square feet, a comparative midget, when the neighbors' homes sometimes approached 10,000. Perfectly organized tools and yard implements were displayed along the front and sides. A paved extension to the right of the workbench housed a golf cart for most residents. In the Walters' garage, a blue 1970 Mercedes 280 SL convertible in perfect condition was parked beneath a beige car-cover. We walked through the empty space reserved for Dave's Cadillac to the connecting door. After a quick knock, I opened the door and called, "Hi, Honey. I'm home!"

******

A fat, russet-red calico cat blinked yellow eyes at our entrance. "Hi, Scarlette. Where's your mom?" I asked. Scarlette blinked again and lumbered down the hall. We took another step and a gray flash bolted for the patio door. "Sherrie!" I called, "Where are you?"

"Out here," came the reply. Walking down the hall of sparkling white tile, we heard a yowl from the dining room. A rectangular Italian marble table held an array of red silk tulips. Nestled in the midst of them was a large Siamese, whose icy blue eyes watched us warily.

"Swell," Gene grumbled. "And I do mean that literally."

"Head for the pool enclosure," I directed. "Sherrie and I will dish up supper." I am an equal opportunity animal lover. Gene, unfortunately, has a severe allergy to cats. If he didn't get into the open breezes, his eyes would soon be swollen shut along with his good mood.

He plopped the sacks onto the counter, giving Sherrie a hug in the open doorway that connected the kitchen to the enclosed pool. As he headed for the padded peach rockers on the deck, several flashes of gray bolted through the open door of the pool cage. Sherrie shuffled toward me with open arms, dressed for the evening in long, pale green shorts and a matching shirt and sweater vest that were the required country club golf chic. She kissed me on the mouth and hugged me fiercely. I returned the embrace with enthusiasm, and stepped back.

"Nice," I said, sweeping my eyes over her ensemble and toward the pool. "Aren't you a little young to be playing the crazy cat lady? How many did I just count?"

"Two live-ins and the five strays that I feed," she answered. "When Dave's not home, I open the pool cage door and coax them in.

They'll let me pet them, but when anyone else walks in, they run for their lives." Sheryl Walters: Society Matron and Animal Trainer.

I smiled as I rooted through her cupboards for plates. "How many species are currently dining Chez Sheryl?" She waved a fist full of silverware as she calculated. "Not counting the residents, there are five cats, scores of birds and squirrels, a family of raccoons and one large possum."

"You've got to be kidding," I said. "Is there any creature you've missed?"

"Well, I used to feed an alligator that lived in the water hazard behind the house. Two days after I threw some left over chicken in the pond, the next door neighbor almost lost her poodle. I decided if I didn't knock it off, the kitties would become the next snack."

"What's the menu for this bunch?" I asked.

She reached into a drawer for pale green cloth napkins. "Twenty pounds of peanuts a week, several loaves of day old bread that I bring home from the stores and boxes of Vanilla Wafers from Sam's Club," she answered. "Oh, and several bunches of grapes and bananas from the farmer's market."

"It's a good thing you're loaded," I said. "You're running Dr. Doolittle's soup kitchen here."

"Not a problem," she said. "Besides, it comes out of the cash reserve."

"Are we going to eat, or are you two going to jabber all night?" Gene called from the patio.

"Keep your shirt, on," I answered. "Yours is being nuked as we speak." While I waited for the timer to ding, I smirked at my eccentric friend. OK, if her quirks were trees, she'd be a forest. After delivering Gene's dinner, I came back for ours. "Sherrie, you're not still squirreling away cash at home are you?" This little twist had been inherited from her father, who didn't trust banks or his wife with his cash. The old coot had actually said he'd take it with him or let it rot in the ground where he buried it in coffee cans.

"Of course, I am," she said. "It's my private escape fund. Listen, when you own a cash business, why let the IRS take more than they already do? Besides, if I want something that Dave might wrinkle his nose at, I get it and then claim it's been here for a year and he's just forgotten."

"What's the total up to?" I asked.

"Somewhere over a hundred grand."

My plate fell with a loud clatter. "Are you nuts? What if you had a fire?"

She clicked her tongue at my reaction. "In a house built with concrete block? Not likely."

"And you don't think Dave will ever stumble onto it?"

"Even more unlikely," she smiled. "It's tucked away in my shoe closet."

"You're right, Imelda," I agreed. When she said shoe closet, that's what she meant. In addition to the walk-ins, there was a second large closet in the master suite that was floor to ceiling with footwear. Scores of shoes were lined up side by side on the lower shelves, with stacks of boxes for the coming season on the upper ones.

"Still no word from Dave?" I asked.

"Not a peep. I'm stunned since he usually has his nose so far up my ass I think I've got extra nostrils. I could just kill him."

"Are you that worried?" I asked.

Dropping the protection of sarcasm, her face clouded as she answered. "Yeah, I am. If he hasn't called by the time we've finished eating, I'm calling the cops."

"I'm sure it's nothing," I lied. As unlikely as it seemed, people his age keel over unexpectedly all the time. "Let's eat this fish before it's not fit for anything but cat food."

THREE

For the next hour, we sat in the warm breeze, eating and chatting. Well, Sherrie and I talked. Gene grunted agreeably from time to time. We were winding down with three slices of blueberry cheesecake in a roasted macadamia nut crust when we heard scratches against the pool cage. Fourteen gleaming black eyes stared enviously from the bandit masks of raccoon faces.

"Hey, we've got company," I said.

"They're after dessert, too. Dinner was at the usual time," she replied. When the wild things saw Sherrie stand, three of them stretched up on their back legs and peered intently through the enclosure. Sherrie opened a cupboard door under the grill on the patio and grabbed a box. She quickly tossed several handfuls of Vanilla Wafers through the door and said, "Ok, gluttons, dessert for you, too."

"I'm surprised you didn't offer them cheesecake," I said.

"We'll see how much is left," she answered, unfazed.

Mom raccoon and the kids were busily eating while Dad stood guard a few feet away. Suddenly, he reared up and all seven fled into the night. Headlights swept into the drive a moment later.

"Dave must be home," I said.

Sherrie rose from her chair, grumbling, "He'd better have a damned good reason for not calling." She continued to gather the dessert dishes as she called out. "It's about time!"

I looked at Gene, who grimaced at the anticipated fight we were about to witness. Sherrie clanked the dishes in the sink to audibly underline her hissy-fit, but the connecting door from the garage failed to open.

"What the hell is he doing out there?" she asked, returning to the patio for another load of dishes.

I shrugged and followed her into the kitchen with the place mats and napkins. I dropped them on the counter as the front door bell rang. Stepping into the hallway, I could see the drive through the dining room window. A Ft. Myers Police car was parked behind my Beemer. My heart sank as I called out. "Honey, I think you'd better come out here."

Sherrie's beaded sandals clicked across the tiles. Her angry eyes followed my arm sweeping toward the driveway. The implication hit her and her eyes flew open wide. I watched as fear replaced anger and nudged her gently forward.

She flipped on the porch light and opened the door to a cop dressed in the dark green uniform of the Ft. Myers police. He looked between us and asked, "Mrs. Collins?"

Sherrie didn't move as she squeaked, "That's me."

"May I come in?" he asked.

She stared at the man in silence. I took her hand, gently pulled her aside and replied, "Of course." Still holding her hand, I led him into the living room and gestured toward the white linen furniture.

He perched hesitantly on the end of the larger couch. I took Sherrie to the love seat and sat with my arm thrown over the back, hugging her without touching. Gene walked into the room and leaned against the stucco archway. The officer removed his hat, revealing a white flat top, as very steady hands flipped open a small notebook.

"Mrs. Collins, does your husband drive a red, late model Cadillac Seville?" he asked.

"Yes, he does," she replied. "Has...has there been an accident?"

"I'm afraid so," he said. "We found his empty car at Lover's Key Wildlife Preserve in south Ft. Myers Beach."

"Empty? But where was Dave?" she asked.

"I was hoping you might have some idea."

I looked at Sherrie, who was staring open-mouthed at the officer. "What are you talking about? I've been right here, waiting for him."

"Are there any witnesses to that?"

I moved my arm from the back of the couch and squeezed her shoulder. "You're looking at two of them."

"And you are…?" he said, swiveling to address Gene.

"Long-time friends," Gene answered with a frown.

"Your names, please," he politely demanded.

"Grimes, sir. And you are Officer…?"

"Logan. How long have you been here?"

Color me suspicious, but I didn't like the way this conversation was going. "A few days," I interjected. "What's this all about, Officer Logan?"

"Just trying to get a few things straight. How long have you been with Mrs. Collins this evening?" he asked.

I leaned around Sherrie to check my watch.

"About an hour and a half," I replied.

Logan scribbled in his notebook, looked up and addressed his next question to Sherrie. "And where were you prior to Mr. & Mrs. Grimes arrival?"

"Here. I got home from work around 5:30 and was waiting for my husband. We were supposed to meet Cassie and Gene on the beach for dinner," she said, fidgeting and twisting the six-karat diamond solitaire on her left hand.

"So, you were here alone from 5:30 to 9:00. No witnesses?"

I leaned forward and re-positioned myself to place a restraining hand on Sherrie's knee. "Just what is this about? You found Dave's abandoned car south of here and we've told you that we've all been together here, waiting for him. He's missing and his wife is clearly upset. Should we be filing a missing person's report?"

"That's up to Mrs. Collins," he said. "I'm just trying to get a handle on how long he's been missing. When was the last time you saw your husband?"

"This morning, when he dropped me at the Pinebrook Store."

"And you claim to have been here since 5:30?"

Sher nodded as a worried frown wrinkled her forehead. She held the officer's steady gaze for a few seconds and dropped her eyes. After several moments of uncomfortable silence ticked by, Logan asked a pointed question in a flat voice. "Then how would you explain your car's engine still being warm?"

I leaned forward and said smugly, "Because Gene drove it here. We came to Ft. Myers separately and she lent him the car until I arrived." His expression flashed disappointment as he jotted this last tidbit in his notebook and returned my gaze with a lifted eyebrow. Feeling I had the advantage, I gave him my indignant authority voice. "Why are you asking all these questions?"

He ignored me and continued to address Sherrie. So much for my commanding the situation. "If Mr. Grimes had your car, how did you manage to get home by 5:30, Mrs. Walters?"

"One of my employees dropped me off."

"I'd like his name to confirm that," he said.

"Impossible," she said. Logan raised his eyebrow again and waited. She clicked her tongue impatiently and continued, "He dropped me on the way to the airport. Andy was headed to

Wyoming to hook up with a friend for two weeks of wilderness camping."

"How convenient," Logan said. "So you really don't have anyone who can corroborate your whereabouts for a large part of this evening."

"I guess not," she said. "Since we had plans for dinner, I was waiting for him to call on the cell phone with a reason for not being here on time."

"And you have no idea how his car got to Lover's Key?"

"Of course not," Sherrie replied. "You said you found his car. But not Dave?"

The stare that Logan turned on my friend was stone cold. "That's correct, Mrs. Walters. By the way, do you own a gun?"

"Whoa!" I said, holding up my hand. "What does that have to do with finding her husband's abandoned car?"

"I'll ask the questions, if you don't mind."

"Sherrie," I said, glancing at her and then back to Officer Logan, "I don't think you should answer any more questions without calling your lawyer."

She raked a shaking hand through her short brown hair. "It's ok, Cassie. Yes, Officer, I have a gun. I got it after a woman was robbed in the parking lot of one of our stores. But Dave, and a few of my friends," her head turned to throw a withering glance toward me, "thought it was a bad idea. So it stays locked in the safe."

"Could you get it, please?" Very polite, that Logan.

"Sure," she said. Sherrie walked to the bedroom, shaking her head. Logan followed her. Gene and I followed him. She went to the middle of a sectional dresser of lacquered bamboo and moved a huge silk floral arrangement of Birds of Paradise and other exotic imitations to the larger section on the left. As she tugged at the middle section, a drawer stuffed with multi-colored silk scarves slid open and fell to the floor.

"Damn it," she muttered.

"Need some help, Sher?" I asked.

"You think?" she replied, trying to hold the dresser section with a hip while snatching at the scarves.

I grabbed the drawer, stuffed the scarves back in haphazardly and sat on the bed. Gene righted the wobbling dresser section and asked, "Where do you want this, Sherrie?"

"Just move it out of the way," she said, flicking a wrist to the side.

Gene lifted it about four inches from the carpet and set it down in front of a larger section. Logan was leaning against the curved archway that connected the master bedroom with a bath and dressing area that could have accommodated a basketball team. His face had a flat expression, but his eyes were constantly moving. Sherrie stooped in the empty space and peeled back a corner of the carpet at its seam. Beneath it lay a safe that was embedded into the concrete slab of the house. She sat on her heels, spun the combination lock quickly and opened the top. Bending forward, she pulled out jewelry boxes and several large manila envelopes from the safe, tossing them haphazardly aside. Finally, she sat back on her heals and frowned. "I don't understand," she said, moving exasperated eyes between the three of us.

"Something wrong, Mrs. Walters?" Logan asked.

"It's not here."

"Really," he raised his eyebrows. "And how would you explain that?"

"I don't have an explanation," she said. "I put the gun in here months ago."

"Who else would know about this safe?" Logan asked.

"I dunno," she said. "The company that installed it and a few girlfriends. They're pretty standard in this neighborhood."

"And who has the combination?"

"Just Dave and me, though the old fart always calls me to open it since he can't remember what day it is."

I stood. "Shut up, Sherrie."

"Well, it's true," she pouted, rattling off a familiar refrain. "He calls me every fifteen minutes to help him find something he's lost again."

"Are you deaf? Shut the hell up!" I said through gritted teeth and turned to Logan, whose face was creased with a smirk. "You find the deserted car of her missing husband and all of a sudden, you're asking questions about her gun. What else did you find?"

"Nothing much," he said as he snapped his little notebook closed. "Just a shattered windshield with a bullet hole in the middle. Oh, and blood on the front seat."

"Oh, my God!" Sherrie moaned as she wrapped her arms around her sides and began rocking back and forth. I stooped and gathered her into a hug, waiting for the unconscious movement to subside.

"Let's continue this discussion in the living room where you'll be more comfortable," he said. Logan, Mister Courtesy.

"Not necessary," I said. "She won't be answering any more questions without her lawyer." Cassie Grimes, Mother Bear.

Logan moved between us, grasping Sherrie's elbow. "Perhaps it would be better if we went directly to the station." He was pulling her toward the door. Too numb to resist, she started to follow until I stepped forward and took her other elbow. She stopped abruptly and turned frightened eyes toward me.

Looking at Logan over her shoulder I said, "Better for whom? Tell him, Sherrie."

"Tell him what?" she said, shifting her gaze between us.

"That you want a lawyer."

"Step back Ms. Grimes," he said.

"Tell him now," I insisted.

"I want my lawyer," she whispered, all the color draining from her face.

"You heard her, Officer Logan. She wants to talk with her lawyer."

"She can call him from the station."

"Oh, for Christ's sake," I said, losing my patience. "This isn't a scene from some television cop show. Unless you're arresting her, she doesn't have to go anywhere."

"It would look better if she would co-operate."

"And she will co-operate, with the help of her lawyer, right Sher?"

She nodded.

"So why not make this easier on everyone," I said. "I'll just put this stuff back into the safe."

"Don't touch anything," Logan said. "This home is now connected to a possible crime scene and you're leaving."

"Not with all of her valuables lying about in an empty house. You can call the lawyer to meet us here and get someone from the department to guard this place if we go to the station with you. We'll also want a detailed inventory of everything that is returned to the safe or taken as evidence."

"Is that so? And just who do you think you are to be giving me orders?" he asked.

"The one with Mrs. Walters's best interest in mind," I answered pleasantly, "and a witness to her asking for her attorney.

Now what's it gonna be?" I hoped I was masking how nervous I'd become. From the corner of my eye, I saw Gene perched on the arm of an overstuffed chair, absently swatting at a gray tabby making repeated attempts to jump on his lap with one hand and rubbing irritated eyes with the other. Was the scowl on his face due to this line of questioning or the feline onslaught? Hard to tell.

Logan stood for a moment considering his options without releasing Sherrie's elbow. She seemed content to quietly wait, staring blankly into the space. Finally, Logan said, "Ok, call your lawyer."

My friend didn't budge. I gently pulled her toward me, but Logan stopped me with an icy look. Everyone stared without uttering a word. Gene finally broke the silence. "Sherrie, where do you keep your address book?"

"My purse," she said.

"Where is it?" Gene pressed.

"Credenza by the laundry room," she replied.

Gene moved from the bedroom, with the three of us following. Scarlette leapt from the top of the credenza and bolted for another room as Sher dumped the entire contents of a purse the size of a suitcase onto the table's top. Sifting through the small mountain of personal clutter, she eventually found an address book, crammed with notes and cards. She flipped through it and pointed a bright pink, squared off nail to an entry and looked at Gene. He nodded and pulled the phone hanging on the wall of the laundry room from its cradle. Gene briefly described the situation to the lawyer, with Logan occupying himself by shooting optical venom toward me. Clearing his throat, Gene smiled and held the receiver to Logan. "He'd like to speak with you."

Logan took it and grunted a few responses. After he banged the phone into the wall holder, he turned and said, "Let's wait in the kitchen."

I tried, rather unsuccessfully, I'm afraid, to wipe the smug expression from my face as we silently trooped into the kitchen, and settled onto the high stools surrounding a long, narrow table perpendicular to the door. There was nothing much to say, now that I'd insisted on silence. I rose and pulled a few cans of soda from the fridge, thinking for an instant of excluding Logan out of loyalty. I passed out cans of Diet Coke to everyone, giving the last to Logan in a show of good manners. He nodded his thanks and Sherrie absently pushed hers aside. We sat, sipped and fidgeted in absolute quiet until a loud scratching sound resounded through the house.

"What the.....!" I yelped, knocking over my stool as I jumped up.

Logan was also up and moving. Sherrie remained motionless. He'd drawn his gun and looked cautiously around the door between the kitchen and pool cage. We peeked through the window over the sink and saw several pair of gleaming eyes just beyond the cage.

I let out the breath I'd been unaware of holding, "Looks like the raccoons are back."

Sherrie bent her head and started sobbing for the first time. Through gasping breaths she said, "Who'll feed my babies? They'll think I've deserted them, too."

Logan looked at her with renewed interest and shook his head. I reached for her hand and squeezed it. "I doubt that you're going anywhere. Besides, I can take care of them in a pinch." I threw Logan a belligerent look. His response was to raise the corner of his mouth and one eyebrow about a quarter inch each. We were saved from any more of the non-verbal pissing contest by a car door slamming. I threw a "Stop me if you can" look at Logan as I headed for the door. A silver-haired man dressed in a pale gray golf shirt and darker gray pleated slacks was walking from a silver BMW 725 sedan, whose metallic paint sparkled in the reflected landscape lighting.

When I opened the door, piercing blue eyes surrounded with deep laugh lines appraised me with amusement. "Take me to Mrs. Walters, please, " he said.

"Boy, am I glad to see you," I replied.

"As you should be," he said. A sparkling white smile that must have cost a bundle flashed brilliantly from his tan face. He extended a perfectly manicured hand toward me and said, "Arthur Goldman, attorney at law. And you're…?"

I took his hand and replied, "Cassie Grimes, long-time friend. Thanks for coming so quickly at this hour." He gave a short bow and waved for me to lead on. Sherrie was still frozen on her stool, staring at nothing, with Gene's arm hugging her protectively. As Goldman approached, Gene rose, shook his hand and introduced himself.

Sherrie continued her imitation of a statue with leaking eyes until Goldman lay his hand on her arm. She jumped as if electrocuted. He tsked and said, "My dear Sheryl, Arthur's here now, so don't worry about a thing." She blinked twice and mutely nodded. At last, Goldman addressed Logan. "Officer Logan. Always a pleasure."

"Counselor," Logan responded. "Anything but." The air crackled as they held each other's gaze. Goldman's smile was pleasantly expectant while Logan fought to drop a mask of neutrality over a scowl.

"Now, what's this business about wanting to take my obviously distraught client to the police station?" he asked. "That's hardly standard in an hour old missing person situation."

"Evidence at the scene suggests violence," Logan replied.

Goldman's hand remained on Sher's arm, intermittently patting it. He turned sad eyes toward the cop and sighed.

"How awful. Are you suggesting that this poor woman's husband has been forcibly kidnapped?"

"That's one possibility," he said.

"Then shouldn't we wait by the phone for a possible ransom demand?" Goldman suggested, the picture of happy cooperation.

Logan pressed his lips together, drew an exasperated breath and exhaled. "Mrs. Walters has no explanation for her whereabouts over the last several hours and seems reluctant to answer even basic questions."

"Hey," I interjected. "She was completely cooperative until he started treating her like a criminal." I was tired of all this phony civility.

"Officer Logan, I'm sure this lovely lady is mistaken," he said, nodding toward me. "I know you'd have politely explained her rights to Mrs. Walters if you were about to arrest her based upon any evidence you might have found at the scene."

"I wasn't arresting her," Logan replied.

"Ah, then. You've done your duty by informing Mrs. Walters of this tragic circumstance. As you can see, she's clearly upset and in need of some privacy while we await word on what might have transpired." He reached into his pocket, withdrew an embossed business card and extended it toward Logan. "I'll be leaving soon, myself. I'm sure she'll be fine in the capable hands of her friends while you continue to investigate the disappearance of her dear husband. You will call me as soon as you've further information, I trust?"

"Sure," he grunted. "Mrs. Walters, don't leave town."

"Why on earth would she do that?" he said, patting Sher's arm again.

"Can't imagine." Logan rose from his stool and walked toward the front door. "I'll be in touch, Mrs. Walters."

"With my constant oversight, Officer," Goldman said. "Do be thorough."

"You can count on it," Logan replied as he stepped through the door, closing it with a slam.

Gene had been slouching against the door throughout this exchange. He pushed himself erect and walked toward Goldman. "Is there a little history here, Counselor?" he asked, raising an eyebrow.

Goldman shrugged, chuckling softly. "It really is quite a small town, Mr. Grimes. Officer Logan and I have both been practicing our chosen professions for many years from the opposite point of view. I'm afraid the lopsided tally of my victories versus his has tainted his manners. And it's Arthur."

"I see," Gene said with a blank expression. This must have been a real dilemma for Gene since his definition for wasted space was a bus full of lawyers at the bottom of a lake. But his sense of decorum was bone deep, so he replied, "Call me Gene."

"Quite right," Arthur smiled. He patted Sherrie's arm more forcefully to get her attention and said, "Now, my dear, please tell me what's happened to your husband?"

She made a small mewing sound and covered her face with her hands.

I was vibrating with the need to detail the last hour to Arthur, but Sherrie's shaking shoulders reminded me of my first priority. "Gene," I said, "Why don't you tell Arthur what we know and I'll try to get Sher composed enough to participate."

"Excellent idea, Cassie. That's acceptable, since we're being rather informal, yes?" Arthur asked.

"Of course, Arthur," I replied. "Come on, honey. Let's get rid of the raccoon eye make-up and then we'll rejoin the guys." She allowed me to lead her into the master suite and deposit her on the waterbed. I closed the door to the house and, then, crossed the room to latch the French doors leading to the pool deck.

Sitting next to her, I hugged her and said, "I'm so sorry, Sherrie. You must be out of your mind with worry." Her eyes flashed and I said, "Sorry, bad choice of words."

She absently bent to pick up a silk scarf of dazzling yellows and greens that probably cost more than my entire outfit. After wiping her eyes, she blew her nose, wadded her expensive handkerchief into a ball and tossed it in the direction of a wastebasket. When she spoke, her voice was dripping with sarcasm and composure. "So, Cass, when are you going to say 'Be careful what you wish for?'"

I was stung. "Geez, Sherrie. I *can* be a cold-hearted bitch, but not that cold."

"Hey, Cass," she said. "It's crossed my mind, so why not yours?"

"Ok, sweetie, I confess," I replied. "But I wouldn't have said it out loud until this mess was behind you."

"Well, thanks for that. I guess I should pull myself together."

"Hurry, will you? There's something else you've got to do while it's just us." The corners of her mouth dropped in a confused frown as I pulled her to her feet. "C'mon, Sherrie, I'll explain while you put on some ridiculously expensive make-up in an attempt to look 30." That earned me a prolonged, wet raspberry, as she walked purposely into the huge bath.

****

I perched on the edge of a dusty blue Jacuzzi tub the size of a small swimming pool while she swabbed her face with cleanser soaked cotton balls. She reapplied under-eye concealer, baby blue eye shadow and dark brown mascara while looking into a brightly lit magnifying mirror hanging on the wall to her left.

"Nice touch," I said of the mirror. "So far, I'm still able to use the big mirror, but that won't last forever."

"Lucky you," she said. "I've got reading glasses in several colors to match various outfits, but they don't work for make-up. Aging sucks."

"Beats the alternative," I said and winced as I saw pain flash across her reflection. "Sorry. I just can't get used to the idea that something's happened to Dave."

"Tell me about it." She pulled a container of loose powder and a sable brush from the vanity drawer. She quickly dusted her face and reached for a blusher compact. Finishing off with pale pink lipstick, she turned to face me and asked, "Better?"

"Much," I nodded, as Gene tapped on the windows of the French doors. I motioned for Sherrie to wait and walked to the bedroom, opening the door a crack.

"How much longer?" he asked.

"Almost ready," I replied. "Why don't you fix Arthur a drink or some coffee?"

"Whatever," he said. "We're running out of things to say."

"Be there in a jiffy," I said as I reached out to tweak his nose. He was mumbling something about women and vanity as he returned to Goldman. I pushed the door shut and returned to my surprisingly composed friend. "There's something we should do before rejoining the guys."

"Like what?" she asked.

"Sherrie, your situation could get really messy before it's over."

"God, Cass, you're starting to think like me. Innocent woman goes to jail to pay karma debt for poisonous thoughts. Hell, this could turn into a regular soap opera."

"I don't know, you might get lucky," I suggested. "Arthur seems pretty calm."

"Arthur would be calm in a hurricane. But something's on your mind. Spill it."

I rubbed a hand across my brow. While she'd been calmly cleaning up, a thousand scenarios had flashed through my head, most of them grim. I'd even given a moment's thought to her having hired Dave's demise before quickly banishing it. *I knew my friend better than that, didn't I?* I gently nudged her toward the bedroom. "Sherrie, Arthur will certainly have several legal options for you. But I'd like you to have a contingency plan."

"Like…" she said, moving her long hand in a circular motion, causing a kaleidoscope of color to flash from her monster ring onto the walls.

"Well, Logan seemed pretty eager to lock this place down as a crime scene. Who knows when he'll be able to fabricate enough suspicion to pull that off?"

"No way."

"Yes, way. So, how do you think he'd feel about $100,000 in cash stuffed into your shoe boxes?"

"Oh shit! I've got to get that out of here."

"No you don't, Sher."

She was pacing and waving her arms in frustrated energy. I put a finger to my lips to remind her that we had company in the other room. "But you just said…" she hissed.

I held up a hand. "I said that <u>you</u> shouldn't take it out of here, but I didn't say anything about me."

"Huh?"

"Sherrie, there's no telling how much of your life they'll be digging through. That cash would look suspicious as hell, but it's a safety net you may need. Let me keep it for you until this blows over."

"Aw, Cass, I don't know."

Why was she hesitating? I could see her vacillating on what to do while I was watching the clock, knowing that Arthur and Gene would be getting curious. "You trust me, don't you?"

"Don't be stupid," she said. "How would you get it out of here?"

I'd been wrestling with that while she'd been beautifying. The solution was an oversized peach beach bag decorated with silver conch shell appliques. We stuffed more $100 dollar bills than I'd ever seen into the bottom and covered them with a tennis outfit. Three pair of sandals went on top and I lugged it to the patio. When Gene spotted me, he took one look at the bag and rolled his eyes. "I'm afraid to ask, " he sighed.

"I talked to the talent agency down here before I left, but I didn't pack enough clothes. Sherrie loaned me a few things." This was a plausible enough explanation since I could whip out my union card if pressed. Last year, Sherrie had introduced me to the aging beauty queen owner of a local talent agency. So far, I'd had only one four-hour print shoot for a country club brochure, but it guaranteed that Gene wouldn't be overly suspicious.

"You're shittin' me," Gene shook his head. "With all that's happened here tonight, you two are talking about wardrobe possibilities. Women." I looked at Arthur and shrugged. His face wore the same inscrutable smile that it had since I'd opened the door, so it was impossible to read his thoughts. Gene's were pretty clear. He thought we'd both lost our minds. We'd cleared the first hurdle.

Sherrie, who always needed to have the last word, added, "Look, Gene, this situation with Dave has made my thoughts jump around like heating popcorn. I remembered the glamour queen, saying she might get work while you're here and I wanted something…" she paused dramatically, and continued with, "*anything*, to distract my morbid thoughts. So give me a break, will you?"

Arthur seemed to accept this explanation, since he launched into the vagaries of the female mind. Gene added a few anecdotes that had the two of them smiling and the two of us stifling yawns. Sherrie slouched against the counter and yawned pointedly. The male bonding finally took a break when Arthur said, "Forgive the ramblings of a lonely widower. Sheryl Marie, you look as if the events of the evening are taking their toll."

"I'm exhausted, Arthur," she agreed.

"Then we should all leave you to your rest," he said, including us with his glance. "I doubt that Officer Logan will try to interrogate you without me, but do be vigilant. Call me any time, dear lady. The enormous retainer that I'll require should alleviate any qualms you might have about our speaking frequently."

I stuck out my hand to Arthur in a good-bye gesture. He responded by taking it and raising it to his lips for a quick kiss. Either this guy was caught in a time-warp or he was 100% pure baloney beneath that carefully groomed exterior. He did a longer replay with Sherrie and I started leaning toward the time-warp theory. When he turned to shake Gene's hand, I hugged Sherrie and winked conspiratorially. Lugging the bag to the car without grimacing required some effort, but I did so after declining Gene's offer for help. He opened my door and extended his hand for the bag. I pretended not to see it and placed the bag between my feet.

We saw Arthur's tail lights flair at the stop sign and turn right. So, he was a neighbor. I was wondering how much business he'd gained just by having drinks in the Club House, but I kept those thoughts to myself. The bag of loot between my feet was a presence so vivid, it might have been alive. Gene was lost in his own musings, so I was momentarily spared the ordeal of elaborating on our cover story. I hated having to lie, but I really didn't know Arthur at all. I fully intended to come clean with Gene, at the right moment, of course. I rationalized that this wasn't being dishonest, exactly. By delaying the conversation until the time was right, he might not explode like Mount St. Helen. But then again, he might.

62

FOUR

Ah, the benefits of dog ownership. Of course, I'm referring to being owned *by* your dogs if your relationship is anything like mine. Maggie and A.J. provided another reprieve by demanding a walk when we got home. We got them in leashes, kicked off our shoes and dutifully followed as they surged toward more solid sand at the water's edge.

My Northern dogs had to make serious adjustments to beach life where there are no fire hydrants and few trees. The sparse palms near the buildings were surrounded by sand spurs that painfully imbedded themselves between the pads on their little paws. As such, we walked near the surf where the tide and beach strollers smoothed a path. But my Yankee barkers needed upright objects against which to lift a leg. That left driftwood, dead fish or sand-castles. Since there wasn't a kid in sight, I let them demolish several construction sights that were built too near the incoming tide. With luck, the surf would erase any evidence of our cavalier treatment of the little tykes' efforts.

We could hear distant laughter coming from the end of the beach that housed the hotels and restaurants. Our end of the barrier island held only condos, so we were alone. Maggie and A.J. paused to investigate a foot high castle after smashing its turreted moat. I laughed at their determination and squeezed Gene's hand. "What a night, huh? I *almost* feel guilty about enjoying this so much while Sherrie's suffering."

"Hate her luck," he said. Maggie and A.J. were straining to move on. He looked at A.J. and then turned a question to me. "It's just us. What do you think about letting them off the leashes?"

"Why not? It's still pretty unfamiliar territory, so I doubt that they'll go far." While Gene freed A.J., I bent to undo Maggie's harness, gathering up my long skirt to protect it from the elements. Both dogs shook vigorously, looked at each other and took off at warp speed toward the north end of the island. "Aw, shit," I said as I hiked my skirt and loped in the direction they'd taken. If I were running full out, which you could clock with a sundial, I wouldn't have a prayer of catching them. Yelling seemed more efficient, but I hadn't counted on the ambient noise of the surf. Worse still, their white fur blended perfectly with the pale sand. Add a helping of mid-life diminished night vision and I realized that if they didn't want to be found, I was pretty well screwed.

I'd stopped running and was turning in circles yelling their names when Gene caught up, put a hand on my shoulder and said "*Your* dogs are so well trained."

"Oh, now they're *my* dogs, huh? Geez, Gene, can you save the 'I told you so's' until we locate the little shits? Maybe your voice will carry better than mine."

He turned his back to the water and did his best fog-horn. "Maggie! A.J.!" Instantly, a blur approached from the direction of a pine stand at the end of the island. Seconds later, A.J. stood panting and wagging at our feet, as I bent to re-harness him. "Ah, the good, *male* dog," Gene said

I responded with a loud raspberry and said, "A.J., where's Maggie?" His nose went down and he trotted back toward the pines where we heard a yelp. We found Maggie standing at the edge of the preserve. I scooped her up and ran a hand over the bottom of her feet. "Ouch!" I squealed as a sand-spur nicked my fingers. I carefully extracted two that were buried in her right front paw. "It serves you right," I added.

I took Gene's hand again as we turned for home. "So, Baber, what do you think we can do to help Sherrie?" I waited patiently for a response. After several beats of silence, I tried again. "Honey, about Sherrie?"

"What about her?" he said.

"Is that a real question, or were you on 'wife mute' when I asked the first time?" I said.

"Probably both," he replied. "Honestly, Cass, we can't do anything right now except hope that Dave shows up."

Not the icebreaker I was hoping for, but he did have a point. Arthur Goldman would shield her too-quick mouth from getting her into trouble and the police had nothing but suspicions. The moon's position over the gulf told me that we'd probably already passed into morning, so I decided to hold my tongue. The tide was moving closer to shore, forcing us into deeper, uneven sand that made walking difficult for us and nasty for the dogs who sank past their knees with every step. The temperature had dropped enough that gooseflesh erupted on my bare arms. I shivered and turned for home. "Guess we'd better call it a night."

"Yeah, I'm pooped. Let's dust off the dogs and go to bed," he said. Simultaneous yawns followed. We trudged home, stopping to rinse the sand from our feet.

"Guess Mr. Happy will have to take a rain check, huh?" I said, as I held onto his arm, balancing on one foot while holding the leash.

"He could use the rest. Is there anything else that can't wait until morning?"

Except for that bag full of money stuffed in the closet, I couldn't think of a thing. "Nope," I said as I stooped and extended a wiggling Maggie to Gene before picking up a consistently patient A.J. We patted and fluffed and carried them into the condo. They bolted toward the kitchen as soon as their feet hit the carpet. They rounded the corner and we heard a sharp, insistent clattering of china against tile. I quickly followed and found an indignant Maggie dragging her empty water bowl across the tile floor. A.J. stared expectantly at the empty food dish and moaned under his breath.

"Ok, ok, I'm a terrible mother," I said. "Call the Humane Society in the morning." I refilled both, saluted and headed toward the bathroom for my pre-bed rituals.

By the time I'd washed my face and brushed my teeth, Gene was out cold on his side of the bed and two satiated Bichons were stretched out on mine. I climbed over them and slid beneath the covers in a space that would accommodate a broom handle. *Shouldn't Paradise be a little more comfortable?* As if reading my mind, the dogs rolled toward the edge of the bed, opening a human sized space. When I adjusted a pillow, Maggie woke and re-positioned herself against my side. I lay a hand over her back and listened to the sounds of A.J. and Gene softly snoring. Dreams of my own quickly followed. Wonder what the significance was of sea gulls flying in formation, carrying Ben Franklin's instead of fish?

****

Light filtering through the translucent aqua curtains caused me to wake earlier than I'd have liked. I lay listening to the sound of the sea with my eyes closed, hoping it would lull me back to sleep. The images of dolphins frolicking in the waves played across the movie screen of my mind. Suddenly, pictures of blood splattered white upholstery and Sherrie in prison orange were superimposed, as if my head was channel surfing. I exhaled and opened my eyes to find four dark brown ones staring back. Admitting defeat, I left the bed and grabbed a ratty pair of khaki shorts and a navy tank top from the dresser. I pulled them on without underwear and headed for the leashes. Remembering how cool last night had been, I returned to the closet for a jacket and saw that damned beach bag, accusing me of keeping secrets from my husband. "Later," I said aloud and shut the door.

"Coffee ready yet?" asked a sleepy voice from behind me. "And if it is, why don't I have some in my hand?"

I re-opened the closet door and grabbed Gene's robe. Before I closed it, I gave the bag a good kick. Gene was still in bed, so I tossed the robe on the foot of it and went to the living room where Maggie and A.J. were moaning beneath the curtain as they watched the beach come to life. "Gotta take the dogs for a walk," I said, stooping to attach the harnesses. "Why don't you go back to sleep and I'll put the coffee on when I get back? That is, unless you want to go with us."

His reply was two snorts that were the wind-up for serious snoring. The three of us were at the bottom of the steps when I realized I'd forgotten a plastic bag. I dragged two protesting dogs back to the condo and into the kitchen for a grocery sack and a paper towel. *I would never again take for granted the advantages of a fenced back yard.*

By the time we started the return trip from early morning potty patrol; my mood was as calm as the morning waves. Several yards out in the Gulf, old ladies in sweatshirts and sun hats were bent toward the sand bar that the receding tide had exposed. One by one they'd bend, scoop and stand again to examine a shell or blue-green sand dollar. Then they'd drop their treasures into a grocery bag or, determining them to be sub-par, toss them back into the shallow water for the next tourist to discover. One of them spotted us and raised a rattling, bag in greeting. "Shelling's pretty good this morning, isn't it?" she chirped. I grinned in response and waved my bag in a cheery two-dump salute.

Insistent tugging on the arm holding both leashes got me moving again. The dynamic duo had spotted Gene on the front porch. One of the nice things about dogs is that every greeting feels like a reunion. They bounded across the sand as if he'd been gone for a year, with me jogging clumsily behind. While the celebration was in full swing, I went to the kitchen for the dogs' water bowl and a cup of coffee. Gene had looped the leads through the slats on the guardrail around the porch. A.J. was panting at his feet with Maggie hanging between two rails to get a better view of the shell crew. I sat in a plastic chair next to him and said, "Honey, we have to talk."

"Now there's a phrase every man learns to dread."

"Isn't it a little early for female bashing?" I asked.

"Just pointing out the obvious," he said. "I can't remember a single time when that phrase was followed by good news."

Oh, shit. So much for all the carefully crafted explanations I rehearsed on the walk. "I'm worried about Sherrie, Gene."

"With good reason," he said. "But about what this time?"

"I've got this bad feeling that last night was the tip of the iceberg," I said. "And, you must admit, my premonition of disaster was right on the money."

Gene sighed and looked at the view. Is this something they teach male children in secret session? To lapse into silence after hearing a statement that screams for a response? When the acknowledgement wasn't forthcoming, I plunged ahead. "Speaking of money," I began *(Ok, not the most clever segue)* "this could get pretty expensive before it's over."

"Uh-huh," he replied.

I chose to interpret an audible answer as encouragement and continued. "And if something terrible has happened to Dave, probate court could tie up her money when she needs it the most."

Gene turned his head to look at me. "True. But, Cassie, we're in no position to help."

"That's not exactly true," I said, dropping my eyes like a kid caught with a hand in the cookie jar. When I looked up, his eyebrows were raised over a disgruntled expression. "You remember me telling you about Sherrie's Dad burying coffee cans full of cash?" He nodded without comment. Damn. For someone in sales, he seemed to have real problems with communication. "Well, Sherrie's version of this family trait involves shoe boxes, so she does have a small safety net."

"She may need it," he said. "When Mom died, one of the first things that Dad did was hit the bank for cash. Wait a minute, if Logan should get suspicious enough, he may come back with a search warrant. Shit, Cassie, you'd better warn her."

I decided it would be too showy to jump up and do a victory dance, so I reached over and patted Gene's cheek. "Now there's one of the real benefits of being married forever. We really can read each other's minds." A smile flicked across his face and quickly morphed into suspicion. I pushed ahead, ignoring his changing expression. "In fact, I told her that last night, so we're holding that safety net for her.""

He gave me puzzled. "But how...? Of course, the beach bag."

"See, I knew I married a genius," I gave him the million dollar, suck-up smile.

A frown was his reply. "Just how big a safety net are we holding?"

I looked away again, so I didn't see him take a long drink from his coffee mug. I took a deep breath and turned to face him. "Around a hundred thousand dollars."

Good thing I was wearing old clothes. I wiped the coffee he'd spit from my face and bare shoulders and smiled weakly. He wasn't smiling. "You're as crazy as your nut-cake friend. You walked away from a possible crime scene with that kind of cash and left it in an unlocked condo while we did our little beach stroll last night?   Jesus, Jumped-up Christ, Cassandra.   What were you thinking?"

"Who said anything about a crime scene besides that snotty Logan?"   I'd turned defensive.   "You can't possibly believe that Sherrie had anything to do with whatever happened to Dave."

"Let's just say that I don't think Sherrie's motives for anything she's done in her marriage were purely from love. You're a good friend, Cassie, but your loyalty can make you blind."   There was that mind-reading thing again. Ok, I'd had my own doubts about Sherrie's gold digging and a possible part in Dave's disappearance. But, hell, I'd known her longer than my cynical husband. She may be spoiled rotten, but I knew in my heart that she wasn't criminal. I shook my head and mutely waited for him to continue. "One thing for sure, Cassandra, is that we will NOT be keeping that cash here."

"But, Gene," I interrupted more loudly than I'd intended. He held up his hand for silence. I pursed my lips and nodded for him to go on.

"The banks should be opening at nine. Get dressed. We're going to get a safety deposit box, if they have one that big."   All righty. The ass-hole was gone and the genius was back.

"Good thinking, honey," I said, pushing up from the chair.

"And your point would be...?" He stood and said, "Say it loud and with feeling: 'You're right again, Gene, and I'd be in deep shit without your help.'"

****

The beach's only bank, First Florida, was a few miles south of us at mid-island. We pulled into a surprisingly deserted parking lot at 9:10 and learned that this branch kept vacationer's hours, opening at 10:00 and closing at 4:30, Monday through Friday. Rather than fight the northbound traffic headed toward the bridge, we looked for an outdoor restaurant so that we could keep an eye on our imitation Brink's truck.

The gods of Marital Bliss were sympathetic on this sunny morning. Just two blocks away, we found the Rustic Café, situated in the lower level of some rickety beach shacks that formed a "U" around a brick courtyard. We had a clear view of the car since a few low shrubs were all that separated it from the sandy strip that swerved as sidewalk and parking lot. I nonchalantly tossed the beach bag into the trunk and locked it, taking a last, paranoid glance in its direction as we entered the open door of the shop. Dressed like an ad for *Gentleman's Quarterly,* a young man with dark hair and olive skin was reading the morning paper alone at a small table.

"Good Morning," he said in heavily accented English. "I'm Antonio. Welcome to the Rustic Café."

"Just coffee, please." Gene said.

Antonio rose and laughed. "You'll need to be more specific." He pointed to the chalk- board above a counter crammed with electronic devices. It was the hand-written menu for what could be described as Starbucks Goes Bahamian. I ordered a mild concoction of coffee with hot milk, cinnamon and whipped cream. Antonio was detailing the finer points of coffee beans and a drink called the "Eye-opener" to an interested Gene. This combination of an exotic blend and expresso would have kept me awake through next week, but its description was putting me to sleep. I nabbed a lemon poppy-seed muffin the size of a boulder and walked through the connecting door to the patio while Gene waited for our drinks. A canopy of palm and eucalyptus trees shaded an uneven brick patio with a dozen wrought iron tables and chairs. Only two of the tables were occupied, so I sat directly in front of the Beemer and opened the plastic wrap on the muffin. I was making an effort not to swoon as Gene and Antonio approached, each carrying mugs with a capacity normally reserved for root beer floats.

I waved a chunk of muffin at our host. "If the coffee's as good as this muffin, we'll be back, even though you have a serious problem with portion control."

Antonio laughed as he placed my mug in front of me. "Since we serve only the finest coffees, our prices reflect it. We want our new customers to feel they've gotten their money's worth."

Gene took a sip and said, "Well." Considering the time of morning and our mission, he was positively gushing. My coffee was as sinfully rich as the muffin. Some serious time in the pool would be required to atone for this little outing. Our host left us when Gene took the seat next to mine. He drank in silence for a few moments before a small smile appeared. "So, tell me, wife-of-mine, just what did you have in mind concerning your ditzy friend?"

"Nothing specific," I said. "The amount of cash she had in that house was insane, and I'm not sure I got all of it. I just wanted to get it out of there in case things went in the shitter. With any luck, Dave will come wandering in today with an explanation and we'll have to drive back down here tomorrow to cancel the box and have some more of Antonio's coffee."

"I hope you're right," he said. "It'd be nice if Sherrie was only guilty of gold-digging and tax evasion."

"Hey, after all these years, I know her pretty damned well. She can do some really outrageous things, but she'd never hurt Dave."

"Maybe. She's lucky to have a friend like you," he said. "How many people do you know that could resist this kind of temptation?"

"What are you talking about?" That comment had come out of left field. Besides, if I were all that good at resisting temptation, there wouldn't be a pile of muffin crumbs on the table.

"I take it she knows more of the details of our finances than I'd like," he said.

"Yeah, so?" I couldn't imagine why this would be an issue. The sun comes up. Girlfriends talk.

"So, Cassie, what kind of a difference do you think that bag of nice, untraceable cash would make in our lives?"

I hit my forehead with my palm. "No wonder she hesitated. But that honestly never crossed my mind."

"I know, sweetie," he said. "But believe me, it crossed hers."

I unconsciously looked at the car, baking in the sunlight. Had my pal really thought me capable of stealing from her? I vacillated between anger and self-doubt as I drained the last of my now cold, but still delicious coffee. A great deal of debt and stress would evaporate with that kind of money. But I'd always thought that honesty was a bit like pregnancy. You can't be kind of pregnant, either. Of course, withholding information that might create marital duress was in the same category as fudging your age. Ok, sometimes I played a bit loose with the truth, but not on the important stuff. "Well, let's go set her mind at ease," I said, rising from the table. "Your idea of a safety deposit box looks even better now."

****

We accomplished our mission with little notice from the banking personnel. Maybe they were used to tourists toting in bags full of unidentified goodies that needed a secure home. When they told us the cost of a three-month, minimum rental, I was sure they'd mistakenly moved a decimal point. That explained the ease of the transaction. Vacationers who'd watched one too many Travelers' Check commercials would pay a ridiculous amount for a little piece of mind. We joined the cue of crawling traffic, heading for the only bridge that gave access to the city proper and to the north end of the island. Snowbirds found the siren song of shopping malls and restaurants irresistible enough to suffer the sweltering traffic jam. The next three and a half miles took fifty minutes and seriously overheated the Beemer's ancient engine. When we finally pulled into our parking lot, we were as fried as the car since we'd been forced to kill the air conditioner.

The usual earsplitting, canine greeting followed. I left Gene to deal with them while I quick changed into a bathing suit. We harnessed them for a potty break and I stepped through the door. "Don't be long," Gene called. "You'll be toast without any sun-block."

"Back in a flash," I called as they pulled me down the stairs toward a picture-postcard day. A clear blue sky with mid-day sun hung over the gently undulating waves of the Gulf. The beach was now crowded with sun-bathers and walkers in a variety of shapes and sizes, many of whom reacted to my bouncing fur-balls like fraternity brothers to a beer keg. We halted frequently for animal lovers, whose pets had been left behind, to get a fix of hot doggie lovin'. My shoulders were starting to tingle when a woman with a suit identical to mine bent down, exposing pendulous breasts to me, and a mega-plus size derriere to the beach behind us. For some inexplicable reason, even Maggie was submitting to her cooing and petting.

"Oooh, Babies, what are your names?" she said, addressing them directly. "I bet you'd like to meet my little, Snookie, wouldn't you? But she's locked in the lanai at home." Well, that explained the reception. They must have smelled donuts and dog. I tried not to stare at how much of her body sported an even coffee-colored tan on surprisingly smooth skin. She started pointing between our suits and exclaimed, "Hey! We're twins! Except, of course, there's a whole lot more of me to cuddle."

Talk about a terrific self image. I caught her infectious giggles, and finally pointed an introduction. "Maggie and A.J."

"Well, hellooo, Maggie! Hellooo, A.J.! Nice to meet you!" she gushed and, finally, stood to address me. "Hellooo, Dearie! What's your name?"

"Cassie," I replied. "I'm afraid I'm cooking in this sun."

"I'm Madeline. You'd better scoot until you get a better base," she warned.   "Maybe Snooks can meet Maggie and A.J. later."

"Maybe so," I said, trying to guess her age, but the sunglasses and smoothly stretched skin made it impossible. "Well, see you, Madeline," I called as I tugged the dogs back toward the safety of a shaded porch. I expected to pass Gene stretched on a lounge in the sand, but there was no sign of him. When I'd de-beached the dynamic duo, we walked into the condo, which was pleasantly cooled by sea breezes and two humming ceiling fans.

Gene sat on the sofa, still dressed in real-world clothes, with a plate of sliced strawberries, melon and fresh veggies balanced on his lap. "Yours is on the kitchen counter," he said, popping a large piece of cauliflower into his mouth.

"Thanks, sweetie," I replied. I unhooked the dogs, who tagged along behind me to the kitchen. I took a cold diet root beer from the fridge and pressed it gratefully against my forehead. The dogs were lapping at the water dish as I picked up the waiting plate and headed for the living room. The first bite of ripe cantaloupe in my parched mouth was nearly orgasmic. "Heaven," I sighed. "How come you're not in your suit?"

"I checked for messages while you were walking," he said. "What took you so long?"

"Doggie Fan Club," I explained. "Anything from Sherrie?"

"Yes and No," he replied.

I frowned. The Gene *I* knew and loved should have been giving me some lip about my delay and his gallantly making a meal. Instead, he put his plate on the glass and wicker coffee table in front of us and took my hand. A shiver of dread ran through me as he met my questioning expression with sorrowful eyes. "What?" I demanded.

He grabbed my other hand and squeezed them both, holding my gaze. "Cassie, I'm afraid I've got some bad news."

My heart sank. "They found Dave," I said, aching for my friend.

"No, honey. The message was from Arthur. They've arrested Sherrie."

My mouth dropped and I exhaled a sharp breath, pulling my hands away. "For what?"

"Murder," he said. "There are new developments."

"Like what?" I demanded.

"He didn't say. Just that Sherrie had asked him to call you. He wants us to come to his office as soon as we can."

"Then, let's go," I said, forgetting the lunch as I headed for the closet. "I've got a really bad feeling about this."

"For once," he said, "I agree."

FIVE

Arthur's office was on the tenth floor of Building #2 at the University Center Business Park, a modern complex of blue-green glass cubes surrounding a large cement pond and fountain, with the requisite palm and floral landscaping. The local government saw it as a testament to progress. I remembered the lush cypress stand that had been leveled and filled to build something similar to any large city in the north and it pissed me off. Lee County had "enjoyed" unprecedented growth in the late 80's and early 90's. It was now home to more golf courses per capita than anywhere else in the country. Marshes that hadn't fallen to the need for rich retirees to chase little white balls had succumbed to office complexes full of insurance companies and financial planners. Joni Mitchell was right: they were paving paradise and it sucked. Those same city planners shook their heads and shrugged at the steadily climbing temperatures and perpetual drought of recent years. Let's see, which would create more rain: forested swamp or asphalt parking lots? I wanted to punch them all.

Still doing a green fume, we entered the office of Goldman, LPA. We stepped from a hallway of beige and peach into another era. Wingback chairs in heavy brocade clustered around dark cherry furniture on a carpet the color of a good cabernet.

A woman with salt and pepper hair pulled into a smooth pony-tail by a large silver clip looked over black-rimmed reading glasses as we approached a huge desk, also in cherry.

"May I help you?" she asked.

Gene answered, "Mr. and Mrs. Grimes to see Mr. Goldman."

She nodded and held a finger in the air as she buzzed the inner sanctum. After announcing us and gaining approval, she cleared her computer screen and rose. "I'm Miss Lanahan. Please follow me." Miss Lanahan was paper thin, dressed in a beautifully cut silk sheath that shimmered between gray and silver in the subtle office lighting. She opened a set of heavy oak French doors leading to a plush office that screamed 'old money,' and waved us toward an over-stuffed cordovan leather couch. "Would you like coffee or tea?"

Iced beverages are the norm in the tropical heat of West Coast Florida and we were clothed in warm weather garb. But, the temperature of Arthur's office was in the vicinity of meat locker, so we both requested coffee. Miss Lanahan withdrew as Arthur stepped from an adjoining door and crossed to the couch.

"Cassie, Gene, thank you for coming," he said.

I understood the room's temperature when I saw Arthur. In a part of the country where long pants and a Ralph Lauren golf shirt were considered dressy, our host was clad in a navy three piece suit. His heavily starched white shirt had French cuffs that extended just far enough from the sleeves of the suit to reveal gold and diamond cufflinks. He unbuttoned the jacket as he sat in a matching leather chair that faced us.

I had quickly tired of the pleasantries and was drumming my fingers on the supple skin of a long-dead cow when Miss Lanahan re-appeared, carrying a silver tray that held a delicate decanter of white china with matching cups and saucers. She placed the tray on the table, poured three cups and lay a silver spoon in each saucer. "Will that be all?" she asked, addressing her boss.

He nodded. "Thank you. Please let me know when the courier from the prosecutor's office arrives." Miss Lanahan dipped her head in acknowledgement and silently withdrew.

As soon as the doors closed, I put my cup on the tray and leaned forward. "Arthur, what's happened in the last few hours?" I asked. "Last night, we were expecting a ransom call and now Sherrie's in jail?"

"Unfortunately, yes," he said.

"What's this new evidence?" I pressed.

Arthur leaned back in his chair and exhaled as he tugged at the cuffs of his shirt. "The police received a video that Dave made some months ago."

"And something on it was damning enough to arrest Sherrie?" Gene asked.

"So it would seem, though I've yet to view it. All they would say was that it changed the terms of Dave's will and suggested his wife should be interrogated if he disappeared. Naturally, I immediately demanded a copy of the tape to prepare an informed defense. The courier should arrive any moment."

Questions flooded my mind, so I began with the most obvious. "Where would they have gotten the tape?"

"From his son," Arthur replied. "Sheryl called him this morning with the news of his father's disappearance. A few hours later, Officer Logan arrived, handcuffed her and took her to the county holding facility."

"Why would his son have the tape?" I asked. "I thought you were his attorney."

"As did, I," he said. "Apparently, he'd had a change of heart without informing me."

"Let me guess, the kid is now a major beneficiary of the estate," I said.

"I've no idea, dear lady," he replied. "We won't know the specifics until we've had a chance to see it for ourselves."

"But can't you do something in the meantime?" I asked. "Poor Sherrie." Shaking my head to erase the image of her in handcuffs, I fell silent, waiting for a reply.

Arthur sighed. "I'm afraid not. I've filed for bail; though I've been informed it will be hotly contested. With her means, the prosecutor views her as a flight risk, and this has been upgraded to a murder investigation."

"How could that be?" Gene asked. "Have they found Dave's body?"

"No, they haven't. But Officer Logan has convinced the District Attorney's office that the circumstantial evidence is compelling enough to place Sheryl in custody. I must admit that my curiosity has been greatly piqued."

"And Tom Walters just happens to be holding the tape that puts the screws to Sherrie? How very convenient." I said. Dave's only son was one year older than his "step-mother." I clearly remember her describing his disenchantment with his father's new wife in the beginning of their marriage. But she was sure that he'd mellowed as they stacked up the anniversaries. Of course, setting Tom up in a related business and showering his children with an avalanche of extravagant gifts might have convinced him to keep his objections to himself.

Sherrie was adamant that her devotion to his father had made bosom buddies of Tom and his wife, Susan. I had my doubts. The Senior Walters were certainly generous with their growing wealth, from interest free loans to amazing vacations for Tom's brood, but money can do strange things. What if he never really got over his father's new wife being the beneficiary to the cookie dynasty? *I* knew that the family fortune would have been much smaller without Sherrie's efforts, but it was quite possible that Dave and his offspring still believed that the "Big-Guy" created the cash and "Sher-Bear" spent it.

"I take it you're of the opinion that Dave's son isn't your friend's best advocate," Arthur said.

"Cassie's always said she'd fly here the instant Dave passed away to protect her from his kid trying to grab the estate," Gene said. "Truthfully, I thought she had a point at first, but after this many years, I doubt it's an issue anymore."

"Stranger things have happened with less at stake," Arthur mused.

"And now, instead of the police trying to find her missing husband, Sherrie's in jail, thanks to a tape that Tom just happens to have?" I turned to Gene. "Say it loud and with feeling: 'You're right again, Cassie.'"

A rap on the door allowed me to have the last word. Miss Lanahan walked quickly from the French doors to a dark walnut armoire in the corner. She opened the doors to reveal a large television attached to the electronics for either VCR or DVD usage. She inserted the video and brought the remote control to Arthur.

"I assume you'll be busy with the tape," she said. "Would it be all right if I went for a brief lunch?"

"Of course," Arthur responded. "Perhaps the Grime's would like something as well?"

I started to decline, but remembered the plate of shriveling produce I'd left untouched at home. A quick glance at my watch showed 1:30 and, right on cue, my stomach growled. "A salad would be nice," I said.

"Mr. Grimes?" she asked.

"Nothing, thanks," he replied. Before I could be more specific with my request, Miss Lanahan turned and quickly left the room. Salad? Considering what we were about to watch, I should have asked for a giant slice of French Silk Pie. Chocolate and whipped cream would have been infinitely more calming than lettuce.

"Shall we begin?" Arthur asked.

I nodded and reached for Gene's hand as Arthur pushed the remote and the TV screen turned royal blue. An arrow at the bottom flashed expectantly to the right and the blue faded, dissolving into a portrait of Dave, clad in a sports coat and silk tee. He nodded once to someone in the background before looking directly into the camera.

"My name is David Allan Walters. Being of sound mind and body, I do hereby revise my last will and testament in the presence of my attorney, who will transcribe the statements made and register them with the Clerk of Courts as the legal addendum to any previous documents that address the settlement of my estate."

Involuntarily, I sucked in a breath and held it. Sherrie had been supremely confidant that her aging husband was too addled to suspect her growing antipathy. The firm voice and steady gaze of this self-assured man were a far cry from the feeble-minded geezer that she had described. I knew that whatever the speaker on this tape had to say would be given serious consideration.

****

For twenty minutes, we watched in morbid fascination as Dave explained the changes he was making to his will and why. The new primary beneficiary of his estate would be a company called Davtom Enterprises, a limited partnership to be jointly held by him and his son, Thomas. He explained that he'd tired of his wife's depression and hostility and had decided to file for a divorce based on irreconcilable differences. He further accused her of having an affair, mishandling their finances and, for good measure, consorting with a known felon.

As the tape drew to a close, Dave looked into the camera with sad eyes and said, "It's terrible to have to admit that I was betrayed by my ego and a woman I gave everything to. Years ago, my son tried to tell me that she was only after my money, but my vanity made me believe that she really loved me. I hope my folly won't cost me my life. She's so disturbed that a psychiatrist is prescribing several types of strong medication.   When she's not withdrawn, she's verbally abusive and I can't take it any longer. If anything happens to me, search the house for her gun, her passport and large sums of cash. Thomas, I'm so sorry that I didn't listen to you. I hope I'll be able to spend however much time that a merciful God allows with you and my grandchildren before I leave this earth."

The video quickly panned to an average guy behind a light oak desk. Dressed in a navy golf shirt stretched over a chunky frame, his heavy lidded blue eyes stared from designer glasses into the camera. "My name is Gregory M. Kowalski, Attorney at Law. This statement was taken in my presence, and I verify the sound state of mind of my client and his ability to fully understand the ramifications of these changes to his estate. I further confirm having had preliminary conversations concerning divorce proceedings and the impact that action would have on the assets jointly held by the couple." Kowalski then gave the date and time of the recording, placing it just ten days before Dave's disappearance. When he finished speaking, the screen went to black. Arthur hit the stop button on the remote and began to rewind the tape. He leaned back in his chair and stared at the ceiling, lost in silent thought.

The shocking VCR left me temporarily speechless. "My God, I can't believe what I just saw," I finally said. Gene unwrapped the fingers whose nails were digging into his hand.

He shrugged his agreement and exhaled forcefully. I turned to Arthur, hoping for a miracle disclaimer and saw a small smile spread across his face. "It certainly complicates my original defense strategy, but the challenge of finding the truth should prove quite stimulating."

"Stimulating!" I cried. "That's a hellova strange way to describe an accusation of adultery, theft and murder. You can't possibly believe that load of shit!" Arthur raised an eyebrow at the profanity and I muttered, "Geez, sorry."

"What I am willing to believe will require a great deal of investigation," he continued. "Trust me, my dear. I am a formidable advocate for your friend to have in her corner."

"So you say," I replied. "What do we do first?"

Arthur calmly walked to an antique cabinet in the corner and withdrew a legal-size yellow pad. Stopping at his desk, whose top was clear except for a phone and the gold pen that he picked up, he hit the intercom button on the phone and said, "Miss Lanahan, would you be so kind as to refresh the coffee?" He crossed to us as Miss Lanahan opened the door. In her left hand, she carried a plate with a delicate spinach salad. In her right, she held silverware wrapped in a linen napkin and a stainless steel coffeepot. I muttered thanks as I took the plate and set it aside. Arthur leaned back in his chair and gave his cuffs another reflexive tug, the picture of patience as she refilled the decanter. "Thank you," he said as she silently retreated to the outer office.

"For God's sake, Arthur," I said. "Don't we have more important things to do?"

Gene leaned toward him and said, "Forgive her, Arthur, she can be a little high-strung."

I gave Gene's knee a loud smack and said, "Hello! I'm right here and I'm just fine. It doesn't change the fact that Sherrie's in jail while we're sitting here having a lovely snack and polite conversation."

Arthur reached for the tablet and pen that he'd placed on an end table beside his chair. "Let's start by reviewing the tape. Cassie, I assume you know the family dynamics better than your husband does. Please give me your impressions of what you just saw."

"My first thought was that Dave didn't look anything like the addled senior citizen that Sherrie's been bitching about – sorry – in our phone conversations."

Arthur made a note as he said, "So your discussions with her made you feel that she was not entirely enchanted with her husband?" I looked at him and hesitated. Girl-talks contained a lot of venting that to the uninitiated male might sound like incriminating intention. Taken out of context, my side of our conversations might sound less than flattering to Gene. Arthur held the pen motionless as he persisted. "Cassie, my dear, I'm sure you're aware of the concept of attorney/client privilege. It would be a true betrayal of your friend's confidence if you didn't help me to defend her."

I nodded. "You're right. She was less than happy with her marriage, but determined to stick it out. And yes, she was being treated for depression. As for that bullsh…ah, baloney, about her mishandling their finances, Sherrie was very instrumental in building Dave's little business into a huge success. He'd never acknowledge

91

that because she worked so hard at stroking his ego, but, without her, they wouldn't have nearly as many zeroes behind their bank accounts. For the last several years, Dave's only real contribution was acquiring property with the profits that Sherrie generated from the business."

"Interesting," Arthur replied. "Of course, so long as Mr. Walters remains missing, divorce proceedings can't move forward, so we only have Kowalski's word that he'd intended to file." For the first time, I saw a small crack in the unwavering courtesy that was Arthur's persona. The look that flashed across his face told me that he held Kowalski in anything but esteem. " I take it that you also had reservations about the relationship between your friend and her step-son?"

"Damn straight – sorry," I said again.

"My dear lady, rest assured that in my line of work, cursing is the last thing I'd find disconcerting. If we're to work together, you must stop apologizing and begin to speak freely."

Gene smirked, "Be careful what you ask for."

"Ok," I said, "I don't trust him any further than I can throw him. Sherrie told me he'd tried to talk his father into a pre-nuptial agreement that, fortunately, never materialized. I've always expected him to behave like a starving vulture when his old man kicked, but this is even worse than I imagined."

"Could you elaborate on 'known felon' and 'large amounts of cash?'" Arthur continued.

I dropped my eyes to the hands I was unconsciously wringing in my lap as I shrugged and prayed that Gene wouldn't mention the safety deposit box. I frowned and then said, "I wonder if he was talking about the guy that does occasional deliveries for her. I seem to remember her saying he'd spent some time in the big house, but with Sherrie's penchant for exaggeration, that could have been a DUI. There's so much on that tape that could be distortion or plain fabrication that I don't know where to start. The whole thing smells like …" I paused in an attempt to find a better way to phrase it and then gave up. "It smells like shit."

"There is one other thing the tape mentioned that you failed to address," Arthur said

"Like what?" I sighed, holding up my hand. "Dave sounded perfectly lucid," I said and dropped my index finger. "She was gutting it out in an unhappy marriage and contributed mightily to their financial well-being," I continued, dropping two more fingers, leaving only the pinky and thumb extended. "And her delivery guy might have an unsavory past," I said and dropped my thumb. I refused to look at Gene when I saw little dollar signs appearing on my outstretched pinky.

Arthur smiled indulgently. "You failed to address the point about your friend having an affair."

Several beats passed as I considered the possibility. I finally answered. "I suppose it's possible, but she told me she sleeps most of the time that she's not at work. I can't imagine her having the will or the time to work in a clandestine horizontal mambo."

He looked at Gene and asked, "Does your wife always use such colorful metaphors?"

Gene answered, "You're just seeing the tip of the iceberg."

"Honestly, Cassie," Arthur said and held my eyes. "Are you sure that she didn't confide in you?"

"Honestly, no, she didn't say anything about a supposed affair. I can't imagine something that big happening in her life without talking to me about it. Girlfriends share everything," I asserted. OK, there was the tiniest doubt that she might have kept this to herself, but it was very tiny. "If I could just talk to her face to face, I could tell you more. Can't we go to see her now?"

"Sadly, not today. There are several things I need to attend to," Arthur replied. "My first order of business will be to prepare what I fear will be a futile attempt for bail. I'll need to quickly investigate the extent of their holdings and in whose name they reside. Unfortunately, I expect reticence from Mr. Kowalski in the sharing of whatever information he has and Sherrie can't easily access her documentation. What a time for my research assistant to leave."

I was pretty sure that a light bulb didn't flash over my head, but it felt that way. "Arthur, have we got a deal for you!" I said as I jumped from the seat and started pacing.

"What do you mean 'we,' Kemosabee?" Gene asked.

"Ok, ok, I'm sort of putting this together as I go, so bear with me." Gene slouched deeper into the leather couch and groaned as I continued. "Gene has some unexpected free time. I'm sure there are all sorts of regulations on private investigators, but if he were to be hired as your new research assistant, he could do a lot to help. And neither Tom nor Dave's friends know him, so he may be able to snoop around undetected. That would leave me free to help out in other areas."

Gene was rubbing his forehead, as Arthur responded. "I wouldn't presume to impose on your vacation time, but, if he were willing, it would save precious time I'd have to spend interviewing someone else. I don't want to sound insulting, but that position usually pays only $100 a day and expenses." I fought down the urge to jump in the air and give a war whoop. Ok, it wouldn't put a dent in the massive debt we had, but it would at least allow us to keep the dogs fed and the lights on, since helping Sherrie would probably dry up the puny revenue streams that were my contribution to the family coffers. I looked at Gene, who was still silently rubbing his head. I knew he was trying to squash the desire to pinch me until I screamed for dragging him into another "stray rescue", but Arthur must have interpreted the gesture as a negotiating ploy since he continued. "However, in view of the circumstances, I'm certain that my client would be willing to double that rate."

Gene finally looked up. "All right, Arthur. If it will expedite this situation, I'll be glad to become your temporary employee. It will certainly help me avoid the water torture treatment from my wife." Arthur raised an eyebrow. "How long have you been widowed? You may have repressed the particulars of your wife 'suggesting' that you do something."

"How can you say such a thing?" I asked innocently. "Now let's talk about what I need to do. With Sherrie in the slammer, someone needs to pick up the slack. I doubt the cops will be worried about feeding the animals, but it will be one of the top things on her mind. Unfortunately, Logan saw us return her car and Gene's going to need ours to work for you."

Arthur gave me the benign father smile. "I think I have a solution, dear lady. My late wife's car is parked in our garage, complete with a resident sticker and guard gate remote. We'll need to notify the police, but I'm sure they'll be fine with your being the feline food service."

"Thanks, Arthur," I said, "Let's hope that Dave shows up soon. I don't mind filling in for a while, but we do live in Dayton." *Where there's a nice fenced yard waiting for the dogs. Between the beach bags and litter box duty, Florida and feces will be forever linked in my mind.* I frowned and added, "But who'll be watching her back with the business?"

"That could get complicated," Arthur said. "I will do my best, of course, but, clearing your friend of the charges leveled against her will have to be my priority. If your suspicions are correct,

I expect Dave's son to become very much involved with the business."

"That's what I'm worried about," I replied. "Would a Power of Attorney allow me to act on Sherrie's behalf?" I knew a little about P.O.A.'s since I had two for my mother's affairs.

"I'm sure that it would," he said. "But it would require a great deal of trust on the part of your friend to turn the reigns of the business over to you."

I remembered the hesitation she'd shown when I took the cash from her house. This wouldn't be easy, but she had few other options. Maybe there was already a contingency plan in place. Maybe Sherrie was as hands-on as I thought so that she'd have access to the cash that ran through the doors of her main store and wouldn't trust any employee with too much authority. And, did I really want to get this involved? Of course! I'd already proven my ability as a sleuth by helping to solve the double felony involving my family last year. Permission to look through her P & L would feel like being left alone with your best friend's unlocked diary. The good angel on my right shoulder was telling me not to snoop into Sherrie's life. The bad angel on my left looked at it like being in her bathroom. What harm could it do to open the medicine cabinet for a quick look? Thoroughly rationalized, I said, "It can't hurt to ask her. But I'd like to do that in person."

"We'll see," said Arthur, looking at his watch. He stood and gathered his notes. "I've got to see two more clients this afternoon.

If it's not too inconvenient, Cassie, could you meet me here at five o'clock? I'll drive you to Highland Estates to pick up the car. In the meantime, Miss Lanahan will have made arrangements for you to care for the pets. I'll also have her draw up your employment contract, Gene. Assuming that's in order, could you start tomorrow morning?"

"I'd be glad to, Arthur, but I'm afraid I'm here without business attire," he said.

"Not to worry, old chap. You may be involved in some fieldwork that should be done as discreetly as possible. I'm afraid that I'm a bit of a dinosaur concerning business dress. Though, in all candor, my wardrobe is selected as much to make a statement as out of long-standing habit," he smiled. "A casual appearance will certainly blend more effectively with the natives."

Gene silently shook his hand and I waved my goodbye as I said, "All right, then. I'll see you at five."

As we stepped into the elevator, my stomach growled loudly enough that the caftan clad woman in the back said, "Miss your lunch, Dearie?" I realized that the salad Miss Lanahan had dutifully purchased on my behalf was wilting untouched on Arthur's coffee table. I smiled and shrugged in reply as the doors opened and we waved her out on the next floor. As the door re-closed, my insides growled again and Gene laughed. I adopted a southern twang and said, "Well, golly, Pa. I guess I could use some vittles."

"Okey,doke, Martha," he drawled back. "If we find the right restaurant, bet we could be the first ones in line for today's early bird special."

I poked him in the ribs. "Sounds good to me."

He reverted to the King's English when he said, "And we can talk about your latest bout of temporary insanity."

I swallowed a pithy reply and kissed him on the cheek. "Ah, my love, I'm so lucky to have an indulgent husband. Perhaps you'll allow me to go completely crazy and get a wedge of lemon in my water."

"If your behavior warrants it," he said, holding the door.

"Don't push your luck, Bubba," I said, "or I might be withholding more than lemon."

****

By 5:30, Arthur and I were cruising down South Ft. Myers main traffic artery, Route 41, a.k.a. Tamiami Trail. Before the days of Super-highways, this road had been the main thoroughfare between coastal towns from Tampa to the southern tip of the state. It was also known as "the strip" because of the wall to wall businesses and restaurants that stretched for several miles on either side of Morgan Field. Thanks to the influx of development money, the old airport had been converted into a home for smaller private and charter aircraft. Their constant arrivals and departures added to the general din of the slow-moving cars on the six lanes of Tamiami Trail. Though only a few miles inland, the lack of Gulf breezes and miles of asphalt caused different weather patterns and much higher temperatures. I was grateful for German efficiency as we drove along in the icy comfort of Arthur's Big Beemer past a large sign that alternately announced the time and present temperature of ninety-six degrees.

I listened to Arthur chat about the weather in an Old World accent that sounded almost British. Somehow, it didn't fit with my stereotype of a guy with the last name of Goldman, though it did match the suits. "Hey, Arthur, where are you from, anyway?"

"Why do you ask?" he replied.

"Typical lawyer," I said. "Never answer outright when another question will do. I've been trying to place your accent. Your speech reminds me of my favorite aunt. She worked for the United Nations her whole life and developed a sound that was so grammatically correct it had a British flavor. So, what's your story?"

He tipped his head back and laughed, uncharacteristically, aloud. "Always this direct, Cassie?"

"You see?" I said, pointing out another question as answer.

"Touche'," he said through what, for him, amounted to a belly laugh. "I'm one of the Long Island Goldman's. Before beginning the studies for my law degree, I convinced my father to fund a year's sabbatical in jolly old England. When I returned to take up the family mantle of barrister, as the Brits would say, the accent came with me.   It proved as effective as wine or flowers during my frivolous youth.   Another perk," he said, reverting to Brooklyn-ese, "was that it drove my Jewish mother out of her mind." Who would have thought? Arthur Goldman: Comedian.

"You cad," I pulled the vowels in my best imitation of Brooklyn chic. "Charmed the pants off the goils in New York, eh?"

"I was no Casanova, but I did have my moments. My late wife, God rest her soul, found it attractive enough to listen to my postulating for thirty-five years." The British flavor had returned.

That would put him in the 60-something range. Just about the age for what Sheryl called her "Next ex." I was dying to learn more about that relationship, but we were turning onto the road leading to Highland Estates.

"So, Arthur, you said that Miss Lanahan would try to arrange my visiting the menagerie. How'd that go?"

"Well enough," he said. "Officer Logan agreed to meet us at the Walters' residence."

"Why don't we stop there first?" I suggested as he zapped the guardhouse gate with his remote. He nodded and we crawled down Glengarry Lane, stopping once for two carts to cross the road, carrying a merry foursome, dressed in colors resembling a fruit plate. The driver of a white van lettered with the green and gold seal of the Ft. Myers police on its door was waving to Logan as he backed from the drive. We waited for the van to move away and pulled into the spot he'd just vacated.

Stepping out of the refrigerated confines of Arthur's luxury sedan felt like walking, fully clothed, into a steam bath. I was glistening in seconds, wondering how long my deodorant would hold up to this kind of abuse. Logan's dark green uniform was sticking to his back, with dark circles of perspiration peeking from his underarm. Arthur looked like he'd just stepped from the elevator for a Board meeting. He extended his hand and said, "Officer Logan. Thank you for agreeing to see us."

"I've been here most of the day, anyway," he replied. "The lab guys just finished up, so I guess it's ok to talk inside where it's a little cooler."

"Thanks for that," I said and hurried into the connecting door from the garage that Logan was holding open. I paused in the hallway, feeling like something was out of kilter, but what that was eluded me. Well, let's see. We were standing in Sherrie's house while she was in jail. Duh. As we walked down the hall, things weren't scattered, but it was obvious that they'd been moved around. No, that still wasn't it. I stopped at the long table next to the kitchen, frowned and said, "Damn it."

"Something bothering you, Ms. Grimes?" Logan asked.

"It's a fairly long list," I sighed. "Something just doesn't feel right and I can't put my finger on it." Shifting from one foot to the other, I drummed my fingers on the table and struggled to get an image of what felt weird. "Shit!" I exclaimed and turned to Logan. "Where are the cats?"

"Haven't seen 'em for a while," he yawned.

I stepped to the doors leading to the pool. The screen door of the pool cage was propped open, revealing peanut shells beyond, but no movement.

"Just great," I muttered as I walked back into the heat that dripped with tropical humidity. I kicked off my sandals by the open door and walked into the wet grass, yelling, "Scarlette! Scooter! Here kitty, kitty!" I walked around the back yard for five minutes calling for the house cats, hoping they'd respond to their names. But hey, they're cats.

Widening the grid of my search, I'd forgotten about one of the delights of dusk in the tropics – mosquitoes and no-see 'ums in a blood sucking frenzy. I slapped my ankles and legs between shouts for the cats as my particular body chemistry sounded the dinner bell for those little suckers. I knew better than to go out at dusk without being covered in bug repellent. But here I was, walking barefoot through a converted swamp with decorative blobs of standing water, being eaten alive. To make matters worse, I was doing this for a couple of cats who were probably hearing me call and taking sadistic pleasure in ignoring me. I was a dog person for a reason.

But Sherrie was my friend, and these fur-balls were important to her, so I persevered. The closer I got to the water hazard at the end of Sherrie's property, the more often I smashed a bloated insect into a bloody spot on my legs In the pond's middle, ripples appeared around a branch floating a few yards from the algae cloaked edges of this mosquito breeding ground. I looked at it for a few seconds, wondering why that was the only place in the pond that had waves. The branch suddenly did a ninety-degree turn and started moving toward me. "What the...oh shit!" I screamed, and hurled myself backwards. I was in a dead run when I looked behind me and watched a four-foot long alligator slowly pull himself onto the bank for a nap in the waning sun.

A few feet from the house, I bent at the waist and expelled a large breath in an attempt to lower my wildly thumping heart. What if Sherrie's favorite two felines had become dinner? The strays were used to the wild outdoors, but the two house cats were as pampered as Maggie and A.J. A wave of nausea swept through me as I flashed on an image of a white furry body clamped in the teeth of that monster, screaming in pain as it was dragged to the bottom to await being eaten. What a tasty morsel Scarlette's fat ass would make. With a top-speed of waddle, she'd be an easy target.

When I straightened up, I saw Logan and Arthur grinning in a rare moment of male bonding at my expense. I clenched my fists and blew a blast of exasperated air from puffed cheeks. "Sons of bitches," I fumed, marching back to the house to wipe those silly smiles off their faces. I had worked up a jumbo-sized huff when I heard a yowl from the shrubs just outside the pool cage. Squatting down, I moved the thick foliage aside, to find yellow eyes blinking back from a russet face. I cooed to her with open hands as she stared back without moving.

Kind words failed to move her, so I took a more direct approach. "Enough of this shit. Come out of there, Scarlette," I said as I stuck both hands under her fleshy forelegs and dragged her out. I was rewarded for my rescue with a sharp bite on the web between my thumb and forefinger. "Ow! You bitch! Do that again and I'll throw you to the alligator, myself."

I lifted a flaccid twenty-five pound cat that began purring the moment I had her in my arms. She hadn't held a grudge for very long. I was a bit less charitable. I wrestled her into one arm as I walked through the cage door, pushing it closed before I released her. The acid look I shot toward the men was designed to instill enough guilt to convert smug into humble sympathy. Instead, Logan pointed to a flowerbed inside the cage and laughed out loud. It was shaded more than the rest of the pool and sported a thick mound of multi-colored impatiens, overhanging the bricks of the pool deck. As I watched, the flowers moved and a gray paw with a white stocking extended from beneath the flowers to swat at an unsuspecting chameleon. The chameleon zipped to the opposite end of the pool and the paw withdrew. I stooped beside the bed and pulled the flowers aside, causing a gray blur to shoot past me into the house.

"Fabulous," I sighed, scratching the red welts on my ankles before standing. "Glad I could give you two a little comic relief. The house cats are accounted for."

I walked to the cabinet beneath the grill and started pulling out supplies for the soup kitchen. I closed the doors to the house to prevent another escape and began tossing handfuls of peanuts, birdseed and crunchy cat food into piles outside the cage. When I'd heaved the sacks under the grill again, I headed for the house with Logan and Arthur following.

Logan quickly returned to cop-mode. "Goldman's secretary contacted me about your feeding the cats. We've got what we needed here, so you're free to come and go. We're keeping the keys, but you can use the garage opener from Ms. Walters' car after her attorney has made arrangements with the guard."

"Are there any additional security codes?" I asked.

"Not to my knowledge," said, Arthur. "Sheryl gave me a few telephone numbers of neighbors that might be able to help with the feeding."

"I think I can cover it for a while. So, Officer, is there anything else you need?" I asked. Cassie Grimes, ever helpful. I was anxious to do some serious snooping on my own without the cops or Arthur looking over my shoulder. Logan shook his head and gave me a blank stare. He started to leave and then turned back. "There is one thing that puzzles me," he said. His mouth was twitching with the same kind of expression my baby brother used to wear following a *'nah-nah-na, nah, Nah, na'* when he'd been about to rat me out to our mother. "I assume you've seen the tape."

I nodded and walked to the cupboard that I knew held the food reserved for the housecats. My back was to him as I snagged two cans of Gourmet Tuna Dinner and carefully peeled back the lids as he continued.

"We found Ms. Walter's passport and, as you know, the gun is missing. She had about $800 in her purse and a little over $3000 in a make-up bag under the bathroom sink. That's a lot of money to me, but in this neighborhood, it doesn't sound like the 'large sum' her husband mentioned in the tape. Got any idea what happened to the rest?"

My hands were shaking in the silverware drawer, as I took a slow breath. I made a show of clanking utensils as I tried to recover my cool. *Wait a minute, I am an actor.* I rearranged my expression into a mask of indignant innocence and turned to face him.

"Of course not," I replied. "Dave told so many lies on that tape, what makes you think he's not lying about a bunch of cash just laying around?"

He held my eyes for an uncomfortable moment and said with a smirk, "We'll see who's lying." *God, don't let me blush!* He turned to Arthur and said, "We'll be in touch when the lab guys are done. Lock up when you've finished." He tossed the house keys in the air, caught them and left without further comment.

I spotted Scarlette and Scooter watching us beneath the dining room table as I retrieved empty dishes on a mat beside their water bowl. I scraped the gooey contents of the cans into the dishes, amazed that this foul smelling stuff would be considered 'gourmet.' The very ends of both tales flicked as I set the dishes on the floor, but neither approached. I shrugged. "It doesn't get any better than this, you two. Maybe they'll eat when we're gone," I said to Arthur. "Considering how much time they've spent outdoors, I'm going to forego the litter box."

"Then, let's be on our way. I'm sure your husband's waiting, and I need to make several calls this evening," he said.

Goldman lived three blocks away in an enormous Tudor home. The garage door eased upward to reveal a forest green BMW 330 convertible with cream-colored interior and a beige ragtop. This was a shiny new, souped-up version of the relic that I was driving. When it hit me that this was to be my 'loaner', I got dangerously close to having an orgasm right there. Grinning like an idiot, I pictured myself downshifting through a tight curve with my hair flying in the wind. My eyes were glued to this dream-mobile as I followed Arthur up a short flight of steps, into the "mud room" just inside the garage. Yeah, right. Like muddy shoes had ever walked across the spotless garage floor, let alone into the house.

I automatically swiped my feet on a small throw rug that covered the first few feet of white marble tile leading to plush gray carpet at the end of a long hallway. The side of a black lacquered baby grand piano peeked from the doorway straight ahead with white cabinets and charcoal countertops showing through a large opening to the left. Arthur lifted a set of keys from a pegboard next to the light switch and held them toward me.

"I'd offer you a glass of wine if things weren't so pressing," he said. "I'll have a plan for Gene by tomorrow. What's on your schedule?"

"I was hoping to see Sherrie, if it's possible. And I'll take a rain check on the wine." Truth was, I was dying to walk through this monster house. My nosy friend Trudy, who made a hobby of going to real estate open houses, would give her left boob to go through this joint. I always acted above all that, but I was feeling like a mouse on the set of *Lifestyles of the Rich and Famous.*

"Both can be arranged, I should think," he said. "I'll be able to devote some time after lunch to Sheryl's case. Would two o'clock be convenient?"

"That'd be great, Arthur. How's she holding up?" I asked.

"Remarkably well," he said. "She talks as if she's been dropped into a legal thriller, playing the part of the wrongly accused. She's being held in the new facility our burgeoning tax base has just built as their first and only female prisoner. Except for the cramped quarters and paper thin mattress, she'll be safe and quite alone with the occasional check by the officer on duty."

I wondered if claustrophobia was part of the myriad neuroses for which she was being treated. Having never seen the inside of a jail, I had no reference other than television drama for the experience of incarceration. Assuming Arthur's description was accurate, the largest risk she faced was sore muscles.

I still felt itchy to do something, but it was no longer from fear. "Well, I guess there's nothing I can do for her tonight. Thanks for everything, Arthur, including the car loan. I'll take good care of it."

He smiled knowingly as he watched me back from the garage. I was vibrating from pent-up energy and Sherrie's lawyer had just given me the keys to a totally hot ride. I made a quick turn into a Shell Super station and parked next to the mini-mart housing the cashier. I started pulling levers and hitting buttons until the automatic convertible top on the Beemer had disappeared into its compartment behind the back seat, wrapping me in a blanket of warm, humid air. I flipped the sun visor down to adjust my mirrored sunglasses and headed west toward a sky that was a tapestry of gold and orange. The glasses concealed enough of the telltale laugh lines around my eyes, that I was drawing some serious attention from passing male motorists. I smiled and waved at a 30-something in a Mercedes SL when we both stopped at a light. He gave me a thumbs-up and went forward, while I turned left on Summerlin, grinning like a teenager. Hey, on a day like today, I had to get my jollies where I could find them.

SIX

I pulled into the parking lot, put up the top on Arthur's loaner and locked the car. As I walked toward the front of the condo, I spotted two dark brown, button noses poking through the porch railing outlined with the last rays of the sunset. Shades of magenta and dusty blue had replaced the vivid oranges of the drive, coloring the gentle waves a shade of granite. "Hi, luvvies. Did you miss me?" I called to the dogs, assuming that Gene was with them and would feel included in this mushy catch-all. A crescendo of yipping and barks shattered the calm, no doubt endearing me to the strollers and porch-sitters on sunset patrol. Tough noogies. Only a stone wouldn't love that much excitement for simply showing up. Today, though, it had an added quality. The reason poked a skinny brown nose through the slats and woofed at my approach.

As I walked around the corner of the building, I saw that Gene had company.

"Hellooo, Cassie! Snooks and I were headed out for our sunset walk and we spotted your kids and their Daddy on the porch, didn't we Snookie-Wookie? We've been having the best time!" Gene silently rolled his eyes. "Come on up and meet my baby,

Cassie," Madeline said as she pried herself out of the plastic chair. Tonight she was wearing a bright pink, terry cloth tube top, matching shorts and a pair of pink sandals with giant pink daisies on the straps over her puffy, pedicured feet. When she bent at the waist to snag Snookie, I got a view of mountain-sized cleavage while Gene was treated to bare thighs and receding pink terry cloth that threatened to disappear thong-like into her amble bottom. He squeezed his eyes shut as he quickly turned his head. I swallowed twice to stop the guffaw erupting at the back of my throat.

Madeline cradled a rusty brown Dachshund that looked like ten pounds of sausage stuffed into a five-pound casing. Her skinny tail beat expectantly against her mother as twin ebony buttons watched a potential petter approach. "Hello, Snookie," I cooed. She sighed contentedly as I stroked her velvet ears. "What a *BIG* baby you are," I said, hoping her mama wouldn't take offense at the emphasis.

"She is, aren't you Snookie-Poo," Madeline replied. "And just full of surprises tonight."

"How so?" I asked.

"Snooks can take a while to warm up, but she took to your dogs and husband like ants to a picnic," Madeline said. "She seems to like you, too."

I plopped down on the top step and was immediately assaulted by the dynamic duo. Maggie climbed onto my lap and A.J. draped himself over my shoulder to furiously lick my ear. When

Madeline put Snookie on the floor, she walked to my side and nudged her pointy nose under my arm to be included in the petting. I expected Maggie to do a Werewolf imitation at the intrusion, but she just sighed and snuggled closer. "Well, I'll be damned," I said to Gene. "The princess is actually being civil."

"Go figure," he replied.

"We're neighbors," Madeline gushed, "so Snookie can see lots of her new friends."

Gene didn't share my penchant for strays, regardless of the number of legs. He was watching me closely for a reaction. "Where are you staying, Madeline?" I asked. Gene made a lemon-bite face.

"Right next door at the Westward Arms," she said, pointing to the ten-story high rise. "I can see your porch from mine. My girlfriend, Gladys, talked me into this trip. She likes to cruise the outlet malls for bargains but Snookie and I would rather walk the beach, work on our tan and make new friends."

"What are your husbands doing while you're away?" I asked.

She sighed. "We're widows. Jack and Arnie spent over 40 years with the Akron Police. The four of us had such plans for retirement. We were gonna see the world since Gladdie and I could finally stop worrying about a knock on the door in the middle of the night. But both of them died within the first year of leaving the force." She lapsed into silence, staring wistfully at the gray sky and water as she absently stroked Snookie. Then she puckered her mouth, shook her head and continued in a firm voice, tinged with sarcasm and punctuated with giggles. "Gladys and I acted like zombies for the longest time until we got hammered together at a wedding and decided we were going to start living again. And, Honey, we are havin' a ball! Tonight, we're gonna check out the local Bingo game for men whose hearts are still pumping well enough to handle a couple of hot chicks."

"Take an oxygen tank along, Madeline," I laughed. "The two of you loose on the senior circuit could be lethal."

"But the old farts will die happy," she leered. Gene just widened his eyes.

"Yoohoo!" rang out from our left. The three of us looked toward the Westward Arms. On one of the screened-in balconies, a woman dressed in a flowing purple caftan waved enormous shopping bags. "It's cocktail hour, Maddy!"

Madeline patted the brown rump of her wiener dog. "Say good-night to your friends, Snooks. Mommy's got to get the blender started and I'm sure these kids have plans." Snookie waddled over to Maggie and A.J., who were now lounging at their father's feet. The three of them did a quick nose-to-nose sniff and tail wag before forming a nose-to-butt-to-nose circular, doggie Conga line. After a few rotations, Snookie broke ranks, walked to the top of the stairs and waited expectantly for Madeline to follow her.

Both eased their considerable bulk down the five steps and headed for home. "Have fun, Maddy. See you in the morning," I called, watching them cross the path cut in the sea oats atop the sand dune between our properties.

"Toodaloo," she called with a wave and giggle. It was nice seeing you and meeting your silent stud-muffin."

Gene was rolling his eyes again. More time with Madeline would have caused a vision problem. "Well, that's one of your more interesting finds. Where did you pick her up?"

"Walking the dogs," I said. "She's just lonely. I'll try to keep it in check. "

****

We spent a quiet evening, relaxing with the dogs and cashing in on the rain check for Mr. Happy. Gene was on his way to Goldman's office by eight o'clock the next morning. I intended to be a beach slug in the morning before having my virgin experience visiting a jail.

By nine, Maggie and A.J. were chugging along at a leisurely pace. We'd quickly walked the quarter mile to the north point of the island and paused to watch a family of dolphin follow a shrimp boat through the channel. The dolphins submerged and we headed for home, stopping frequently for the prince and princess to be admired and petted. As we neared our condo, I saw Madeline and her friend positioning lounge chairs on the sand next door. Gladys waved a bag and split the air with her trademark, "Yoohooo!"

We bypassed our building to chat with the old girls. Snookie was curled on a beach towel at the bottom of Madeline's chair, watching our approach through half-slit eyes. Gladys had returned to the building and was dragging another chair over the sand for me. I handed my leashes to her roommate and quick stepped through the deep sand to help. Maggie joined Snookie on the towel to sunbathe. A.J. found a spot shaded by the chair where he panted as he pawed a beach bag tucked beneath the lounger.

"Stop it, A.J." I said and turned to Madeline. "Sorry about that."

"He probably wants some breakfast," she said as she rubbed #4 Coppertone liberally over the large expanse of her stomach which partially revealed an "outty" navel. Maddie wiped her hands on the towel beneath her and reached for the bag. "We hit the Bagel Café first thing. Normally, I'd get the Breakfast Special with bacon, sausage and egg, but I'm starting a diet today. If I'm gonna catch the eye of the cutie-pie I spotted last night, I've gotta look my best." She pulled a bagel with a half-inch of cream cheese oozing from its middle and extended it to me. "Feel free. I got Lite cream cheese, so it won't do any harm to *your* skinny butt. You never know what life's gonna throw at you, so, drink, EAT and be merry."

I lived in the land of permanent diets and food guilt, but Sherrie's predicament had served up a large helping of 'Carpe Diem.' I saw that our pool was deserted, so I could do some laps before driving into town. And the cream cheese had a pink tint, hinting at strawberry. Party On.

"Thanks," I said. When I accepted the bagel, I became the focus of all three dogs' attention. "So, you girls found a couple of live ones last night?"

"Cute, but no stamina," Gladys answered. "I won $100 at Bingo and invited them for a drink. After one teensy-weensy Mai-Tai, they headed for home."

"We looked hot, last night, Gladdie," Madeline said. "They probably had to rush home to check the Viagra supply."

"Oooh. It's too early in the morning to get me all tingly," Gladys laughed. *And it's way too early to view that particular X-rated movie, I thought.* "So what kind of excitement are you planning for today, Cassie?"

I pulled off pieces of cheesy bagel and fed them to the dogs. "I'm not sure I'd call it exciting, but it will be a new experience. I've got to visit a friend in jail."

They sat forward so quickly, their chairs rocked precariously. A.J. jumped to safety as Snookie and Maggie were dumped into the sand. "Now this sounds like a story!" Madeline said as she snagged the wiener dog and reinstated her on the chaise. "C'mon, Cassie. Take pity on a couple of old ladies. We're walking on the wild side when we buy green bananas. Tell us everything!"

I turned my head and held the rest of the bagel to the side to avoid the flying sand that Maggie discharged when she jumped onto my lounger and shook. A.J. saw his opportunity and leapt into the air. He grabbed the bagel from my outstretched hand and scooted beneath the chair to munch his prize in the shade. "There's *my* diet," I laughed and leaned back in the chair. The sun felt great and I had time to kill. Maybe if I talked about Sherrie, I could figure out a way to help her. "Well, ladies, to use a Florida metaphor, I'm afraid my girlfriend is up to her ass in alligators."

I retold the events of the last two days to the rapt attention of the humans and the bored indifference of the dogs. "Well, now, Honey, this could be your lucky day," Gladys said.

"How do you figure?" I asked.

Madeline hefted a leg over Snookie to recline in her chair. Snookie nervously watched her mistress' enormous thigh hover overhead. When the threatening appendage was safely on the other side of her body, Snookie sighed and closed her eyes.

"That's my girl," Madeline patted the top of her silky head. "Sweetie, between the two of us, we spent nearly a century being sounding boards for a couple of pretty good cops. And if I do say so, myself, we were a big part in solving many a tough case. We'd be glad to give you the benefit of our years of experience."

"Ah, Geez, Madeline, I appreciate the offer, but I'm not sure what you can do," I said. Gene was right. I needed to stop running my big mouth.

"You never know," she replied, stretching her arms over her head before leaning back. "Help often comes from the most unexpected places."

A patronizing reply was about to slip out when the image of Virginia Marianna O'Donnell flashed through my mind, mouthing "I'm old but I'm not stupid." Now this was a record. My mother was heaping guilt on me telepathically from 1100 miles away. Squeezing my eyes together and frowning, I mumbled, "Dammit."

Madeline raised her sunglasses and said, "Something bothering you, Honey?"

"Nah," I lied. "The sun has me glistening like a pig. Hey, Madeline, would you mind keeping an eye on my two while I grab a few laps in the pool?"

"Glad to, Dearie," she said. "You see? We've already come in handy."

I quick-stepped across the hot sand and hotter cement surrounding the pool. Dropping gratefully below the water's surface to shove off, I glided a few feet before beginning the steady rhythm of a crawl stroke. The condo's pool was smaller than the Olympic one at the Rec. Center back home, so I figured a mile here would be about 100 laps. The stresses of the last few days were melting away after lap 50. By 75, my muscles were stretched and loose and nearly 40 minutes had passed.

Holding a hand over my eyes, I saw the old girls pushing out of their lounges as the three canines stretched and yawned. I trotted the short distance and said, "Thanks, Ladies. That was fabulous."

Madeline smiled as she extended Maggie and A.J.'s leashes toward me. "It was our pleasure. Gladys says it's time for lunch. And since Vitamin C is important for us senior citizens, we'd better fix a batch of Mimosas to go with it."

"Sounds like good advice," I replied. "I'm headed for the shower and town."

"Can't wait to hear about what happens with your friend. We'll be waiting for your orders," Madeline said, adding a snappy salute.

I returned the gesture and said, "10-4. Enjoy the afternoon." The three of us jogged through the sand, washed our feet and ducked into the breezy condo. Maggie and A.J. made a beeline for their water while I pulled a can of Lemon Diet Coke from the fridge. I popped the top and luxuriated in that first blast of fizz ripping icicles down my throat. "Mommy's gotta take a shower," I said, carrying the instantly sweating can to the bathroom. A small jolt of anticipation shot through me, immediately followed by guilt. "You're a sick puppy, Cassandra," I muttered as I adjusted the shower's water temperature. My best friend had just spent the night in jail and I was jazzed about seeing one for the first time. Rationalizing as I scrubbed, I decided that my twisted emotions were like seeing a horrific automobile accident.

You're simultaneously repulsed at the sight and elated at not being the victim. While not exactly sympathetic, it seemed perfectly understandable.

****

The ceiling fans were turning at hurricane speed, but they were no matches for the mid-day tropical sun. My furry kids were belly up on the bed beneath the whirring blades with their tongue's protruding from their mouths. I padded naked through the condo, cranking the windows closed and turning the air-conditioner to a temp that would allow the dogs to nap in comfort. I gazed into the closet, debating the appropriate attire from my limited wardrobe. I'm a clothes junky, but I'd come to Ft. Myers with more bathing suits and shorts than "big girl" clothes. The radio in the background announced a temperature of 90 degrees inland, so long pants were definitely out. I settled on a sleeveless raw-silk shift of pale blue with serious side slits and clunky sandals. Not exactly power dressing, but better than cut-offs and a tank top. When I'd finished dressing, I returned to the bedroom to retrieve the keys from the dresser and found the dogs in the same position, but with no tongues in sight. "Bye-bye, Babies," I whispered as I eased out of the door.

Even with a breeze, the sun beating on the asphalt parking lot had turned the car into a sauna. My make-up was starting to melt before I turned onto Estero, but the little Beemer's air conditioner blasted ice, so I was comfortable by the time I crossed the bridge. I called Arthur's office on my cell phone and confirmed directions with Miss Lanahan. At 1:45, I parked the baby BMW next to Arthur's silver one at the Lee County Police Station. Transplanted palm trees, whose branches were motionless, surrounded the lot. The still air blanketed the shimmering streets like a hot, moist towel just a few miles inland from the breezy beach. But Floridians knew how to do air-conditioning. I approached the tinted glass doors of the station as an electronic eye caused them to part, expelling a whoosh of cool air.

I stepped into a huge atrium filled with several islands of tall palms surrounded by brightly colored birds of paradise and other exotic plants. A heavily padded, circular beige vinyl bench was centered in the rotunda, allowing visitors to wait in comfort or examine one of the multiple paintings by local artists that were suspended from the walls. I spotted Arthur studying a bouquet of irises whose vibrant tones of purple and gold sparkled in the afternoon light.

"This is a jail?" I said as I joined him. "It looks more like the lobby of a Hyatt Regency."

He leaned toward the neatly printed card next to the painting and noted the artists' information in his Daytimer. "Lovely, isn't it?"

"Not exactly what I imagined," I replied.

He laughed softly as he snapped his planner closed and turned toward me. "I meant the painting. It is pleasant here, but the décor becomes quite a bit more Spartan as we enter the working part of the building." I turned in a slow circle, noticing several doors leading from the lobby, but no other people. Except for the display cases filled with uniforms of past and present officers, there seemed to be no hint that this was actually a police station. Then, I noticed the receptionist housed behind an oval of thick bulletproof glass with only a tiny slotted tray at the bottom and a round metal speaker imbedded above it. Arthur bent to return the planner to his briefcase and said, "Come along, my dear. I'll announce our arrival."

I stood next to him at the window as he talked with a woman about my age. A microphone apparatus with a long cord looped behind her ear allowed her to move about the room. Her voice was muffled but clear as she replied, "Officer Malloy will be with you shortly."

Moments later, we heard a buzzing sound and the first door to our left opened. A tall man in the now familiar green uniform of the Ft. Myers police was standing in the doorway, arms casually at his side. As we approached the door, he extended his arm and Arthur gave him his briefcase. "Good afternoon, Counselor," he said. "and M'am."

"Officer Malloy," Arthur acknowledged. "How's the new baby?" I guess it *was* a small town.

I expected to move into the pale yellow hallway that stretched behind Malloy, but he remained rooted to the spot as he answered, "Fine, sir. The only bad part is that he's a night owl. It's rough on me when I've got the early shift."

I moved nervously from one foot to another, giving Malloy a courteous smile, trying to hide my irritation at the cordial small talk. "That will soon pass," Arthur replied. Both men looked expectantly at me. Now what was I supposed to add to that? I shrugged and shifted my weight again as I looked questioningly between them. "Sorry," Arthur laughed, again addressing Malloy. "It's her first time. Cassie, please give the officer your purse."

Blushing, I shrugged the strap from my shoulder and held the purse toward him. We stepped into the hallway far enough for the door to slowly close. When it audibly clicked, Malloy placed our bags on a small table, and searched their contents. Arthur's attache held very little and was quickly closed and returned. He unzipped the top of my crème colored Sak purse and pulled first wallet and then make-up kit from it. He felt around the interior of the main bag and examined the numerous necessities of middle-age camouflage. In moments, he nodded, dropped the contents into the bag and handed it back to me. Mounted on the wall next to a door were six small rectangular compartments with numbered keys in each slot. He opened one, pocketed the key and placed his revolver inside.

Malloy announced, "Three to area six." A whirring noise was followed by a click as he reached for the handle and opened another door into a bare area that smelled heavily of fresh paint and cleanser. Three doors with windows led from the passageway. The glass in the first door showed a room with a bench that faced another window to the hallway we'd just left. A telephone hung next to the outside window, looking exactly like the ones you see on TV. The second door revealed a small room with a narrow table bolted to the wall, two chairs on either side of the table and an adjoining door on the back wall. The third was unmarked and closed. I had begun to unconsciously tap my foot as we stood silently, the only sound being the slight whoosh as the door we'd just entered slowly closed. "We have to wait until the outer door locks before any of these doors can open," he explained.

"Then, what?" I asked.

"Then a light on the dispatcher's control panel will indicate the lock down. She'll then make visual confirmation and buzz the access door allowing the prisoner to enter the interview room." Looking up, I spotted the overhead camera slowly panning the waiting area where we stood. Another muffled buzzing sounded and the door opposite the desk in room number two opened. Sherrie stepped through and took a seat on the opposite side of the desk. She turned expectant eyes toward us as the door she'd just exited was closing. Malloy pulled his key ring away from his belt along a cable that extended from the holder. He passed a feature-less chunk of black metal across the keypad on the wall. A green light flashed and he pushed the door open for us. "I'll be right here if you need anything," he said as he pulled the door closed.

"Oh, Sherrie," I cried and started around the table. Arthur's hand caught my elbow and held it as he took a chair facing her, glancing down pointedly at the one next to him. "Ah, Geez," I sighed, "Can I at least hold her hand?"

"Of course," he said to me while looking at Sherrie. "I trust that you're doing as well as can be expected under the circumstances?" I reached across the table, lacing my naked fingers through her manicured ones and held on.

She squeezed my hand reassuringly and grinned. Surprisingly clear eyes twinkled through black smudges of mascara and eyeliner, making her look like a bulimic raccoon in drag. Her clothes were crumpled, but her attitude resembled a kid at a carnival. "It's just like being a character in a John Grisham novel. In a warped sort of way, I was even looking forward to a strip search. When you're married to an old fart, you have to take your action wherever you can get it." My jaw dropped in disbelief. She leaned forward to pat our intertwined fingers with her other hand. "Hey, Cassie, ease up. They'll soon figure out they've made a mistake and I'll be the star of the juiciest story to ever hit the Club. Right, Arthur?"

He smiled at her and sighed. "I certainly hope things work out in the manner you've described, dear lady. But resolution will come with difficulty and, therefore, not necessarily soon."

The corners of Sherrie's mouth twitched downward in a scowl. "Because of that ridiculous tape? I can't believe anyone would take the ranting of an old coot seriously."

I squeezed her hand again, released it and leaned back in my seat. "Sherrie, anyone watching the calm, articulate person on that tape would not describe him as 'ranting.'"

"Hey, I thought you were on my side," she said, her blue eyes clouding with anger.

"I am, honey. But you've got to know what you're up against. Either Dave was having a rare burst of lucidity, or you've been carefully, methodically set up."

She shook her head in dismay. "It's not possible. I'm sharper than the average knife in the drawer and I know my husband. There's no way he could have figured out anything this slick by himself."

"Maybe he did have some help," I suggested.

"Tom," she spat. "After all we've done for him and his family. It was never enough. He was always hitting Dave up to join some sure-fire, get-rich-quick scheme. Of course, they all failed and Dave and I would have a big fight about throwing more money down that rat hole. I finally made Dave cut him off and Tom was some kind of pissed. But he'd never harm his Dad."

"Money can cause a variety of aberrant behaviors," Arthur interjected. "And Thomas did stand to gain the most from a change in the will."

"And where in the world did he find this Kowalski?" I asked. "He reminds me more of the East Dayton thugs I grew up with than a lawyer."

"That load?" Sher sighed. "He was a concession to Dave. We were setting up the wills about the same time that we set Tom up in his first store. Dave thought that his son's affairs should be handled by someone different than ours, to protect my interests." She ran her hand through short dark hair that was more squished than spiked. "God, that was ages ago. Anyway, just about the time all this is happening, this old buddy of Dave's gives him a call. He's sick of Akron winters and is relocating to Florida. Could Dave help him out with a few references when he gets his Florida license and relocates? So, good old boy that he is, Dave tells him he even has his first client in mind. Guess who?"

"Number One Son," I said. "Did Kowalski know how you felt about him?"

"Nah," Sher waved her hand. "You know me and old men. I used to tell him that if his Winkie was half as big as his mouth, he'd be next on my list when Dave started dining on dirt sandwiches."

"Yeuuww! Yeuuww! YEUUWW!" I said and scrunched my face into the expression being sprayed by a skunk would cause.

"Ladies," Arthur interrupted with an indulgent sigh. "We still have business to conduct. We'll be appearing in court to request bail tomorrow morning."

Sherrie squealed, "Oh, God, this is exciting! They'll let me clean up, right?" Arthur nodded. "Cassie, I've got a new crème pants suit that's still in the Jacobsen's bag. Matching shoes and one of those useless little bags you like should be hanging next to them. And throw together some make-up and hair stuff."

"Yes, master," I replied. I turned to Arthur and asked, "I assume I'll be able to bring those back here today, right? And they'll let me talk to Sherrie again?"

"You will and they will, though not in this room without my presence," he explained. "You'll have to hurry, though, since visitors' hours will soon be over."

"No problem," I said. Sherrie started to rise, but I reached for her hand saying, "There is one more thing."

She dropped the few inches she'd risen from the chair. "What?"

"Who's running the stores in your absence?" I asked.

"Mary Lou," she replied. "She's been with us for years and talks to the stores daily. I've called her from here a couple of times. Evidently the grapevine has kicked in and my new celebrity has actually caused a surge in business. We've been thinking of adding a new bread to the menu: Nail-file Nine Grain. What do you think?"

"That you're nuttier than the Peanut Butter Cookies you sell," I said. "Does she sign checks, deal with suppliers, all that?"

"No," she frowned. "Oh, man, this is shaping up to be a real pain in the ass."

"Honey, how would you feel about giving me Power of Attorney? It would allow me to keep things rolling and give me a legitimate reason to look over Tom's shoulder."

Sherrie responded by folding her arms and closing her eyes. We sat for a couple of uncomfortable moments in silence until she opened her eyes and hugged herself more tightly. "I'm not crazy about the idea. You don't know shit about the baking business."

"You're right," I conceded. "But I do know business in general. I assume Mary Lou can do the day-to-day stuff and I'll just keep an eye on the financial end."

"Isn't there another way, Arthur?" she asked.

"Perhaps," Arthur replied. "But I've taken the liberty of drawing up the POA with certain fiduciary restrictions that will accomplish what we want: maintaining a friendly presence as we prepare a defense," he said, reaching into his briefcase and sliding a two-page document across the table.

"Shit," Sherrie exclaimed. "I can't read all this fine print without my reading glasses. Net it out, Arthur."

"The document gives Cassandra check signing authority to known vendors with a limit of $2000 per check. She'll have access to all records but will be unable to enter into any new contracts without my agreement. Rudimentary, but sufficient."

"Fine," she huffed, reaching for Arthur's proffered pen and scratching a signature on the second page.

"Well, excuse me all to hell. I'm supposed to be here on vacation. The last thing I want is to take on another job," I snapped, more irritation than I intended. "I'll do as much as necessary and not a thing more. Gene's helping, too, so we're spending what might be our last time in the condo bailing your butt out of a jam. Try acting the tiniest bit grateful."

"Oh, Cass, you know I'm grateful," Sherrie acknowledged. "It's just hard for me not being the one doing the helping. It's a control thing."

"Hey, sucks to be you, right now," I said as I rose from the chair. "Be back soon."

Arthur rose as I did, but didn't move. "I'll be staying for further legal discussions with my client, though I'll be gone before you return. It would be helpful to let the dispatcher know you'll be returning." He turned and rapped on the glass window in the door.

Malloy pushed off the wall of the waiting room and waved his thingamajig across the keypad. The door buzzed open and I joined him. While we waited for the door to close, Malloy looked at the camera and said, "Returning one visitor to the front." A metallic voice said, "Go ahead. I'll buzz you through."

Malloy held the outermost door for me as I re-entered the atrium. I walked to the dispatcher's sealed window and rapped on the glass to get her attention. She looked away from the console and leaned closer to the glass. "Yes?"

"I'll be returning shortly with clothes for Mrs. Walters," I said. "I'd also like to speak with her again."

"My shift's ending," she replied. "But I'll leave a note for the next girl."

"Thank you," I said to the back of her head as she walked to a file cabinet, the umbilical cord of her headset trailing behind. I reached into my purse for sunglasses as I stood before the electronic eye of the outside doors. They separated and I stepped into the sauna of a springtime day in Southwest Florida, paused and pulled in a lung-full of humid air. Funny. On my way in, the air had felt stifling. Standing on the sidewalk, I watched the heat rise in waves from the blacktop, opened my mouth and inhaled deeply. As I released my breath, I decided that ambrosia wouldn't taste as sweet as free, unsupervised air.

SEVEN

Traffic was light and I was soon buzzing through the gate at Highland Estates. I passed a small caravan of golf carts stopped on the path where it met the main road. One player reached surreptitiously into his golf bag, withdrew a silver flask and beckoned with his finger for the others to join him. Several heads dipped toward the floor of their own cart, emerged and scanned left, right, left. They did a combination senior tip-toe/shuffle toward the shade of a large tree and extended their mugs toward the ringleader. Smiling, I watched six gray heads huddle up and pass around the flask like teenagers on prom night. Ah, the intrigue of Country Club life.

I pulled into Sherrie's drive and hit the garage door opener. As soon as the Beemer could slide safely beneath the still-moving door, I hit it again to close it, hoping to be less conspicuous than the rolling speak-easy I'd just watched. It was a safe bet that some of the neighbors might recognize Arthur's car and feel the need to investigate, adding more fuel to the raging gossip fire. I wanted to snatch the clothes and get back to the jail quickly. Thousands of questions that I wanted to discuss with Sherrie away from Arthur's well-meaning supervision still whirled through my head.

"Hey, Kitties! Anyone interested in some food?" I called as I opened the connecting door. I expected a feline flurry at the sound of any human voice, but only silence greeted me.

"Where *are* you guys?" I raised the volume a notch and walked to the dining room expecting to find Scooter hiding in his usual spot amidst the silk tulips. Fake flowers were strewn across the marble surface of the table, but the vase looked empty. "Come on, you spoiled fur-balls, enough of this! I've got better things to do than play hide-and-go-seek with your silly butts."

I leaned over the side of the table to see if Scooter was snoozing on one of the chairs. At the other end of the dining room, I could see the mirrored entryway through the stucco arch, and spotted a man step quickly from the kitchen. My heart leapt into my throat as I threw myself backward and shouted, "What the hell…?" I banged hard into the marble and glass china cabinet whose doors flew open as crystal glassware cascaded around me.

"Poke in your nose where it don't belong, and you're liable to pull it back bloody," he said through a snarl that exposed yellowed, uneven teeth. His grin widened as he slowly stalked toward where I was sprawled on the floor in the midst of broken glass. Suddenly, Scooter leapt from his hiding place behind the curtains and launched himself toward the freedom of the hall.

The intruder turned his head as the cat sailed past. I wrapped my hand around a lead crystal vase that was still in one piece and pushed to my feet. Adrenaline must have caused temporary insanity because I hissed back at him, "You're the one who doesn't belong, ass hole. I'm calling the police." I backed slowly around the table with my body concealing the vase clutched in my right hand.

"Ooh, I like it when they play hard to get," he laughed as he followed me around the table. My heart was hammering so loudly, I shook my head to clear the drumming in my ears. "Come to Daddy," he said, curling fingers encased in surgical gloves. Suddenly, he stepped from a chair to the table and launched himself toward me.

"Like hell!" I yelled as I lurched backwards and his momentum carried him crashing into the wall, jamming his outstretched fingers into stucco. He roared in frustration as I wrapped both hands around the vase and slammed it into the side of his head. I reprised his chair-to-table leap, flung myself toward the open door and hit the button to open the garage. I dropped to my knees, crawled through the slowly opening space and ran, screaming, "Somebody, Help me! Heeellp me!" A golf cart was pulling from the drive across the street. I pumped elbows and knees in my pathetic version of a sprint.   It felt like dragging my feet through quicksand.

The cart's driver turned in his seat as he backed down the drive. His face flashed from consternation to disbelief as he stomped on the break and leapt from the cart, grabbing a golf club from the bag in the rear. "Run, lady! Run!" he yelled.

I looked back and nearly fainted. My assailant had closed the gap to within a few feet, his blood-covered face twisted in a mask of loathing. He looked over my head at Sherrie's neighbor, whose spiked golf shoes clicked audibly on his drive as he ran toward me, brandishing his oversized putter in the air. The creep was only an arm's reach away when he veered to the left, crashing through the palm fronds and roses that lined the Walter's drive. Seconds later, he jumped into a red Taurus parked at the curb next door and roared down Glengarry. I met my savior in the middle of the street where we watched the taillights of the Taurus flare as it swerved to miss a golf cart crossing the street. His wheels sunk into one of the mechanically soaked lawns and spun there, trying to gain traction. Golf paraphernalia and curses flew from the cart toward the Taurus' trunk before it finally lurched forward and sped away.

"Are you all right?" Sherrie's neighbor asked.

"FFFine," I stuttered. I started to shake uncontrollably as it hit me and to pray that the sudden urge to vomit would pass.

"What's going on?" he pressed.

I looked at the ground and shook my head from side to side. Taking a deep breath, I said, "I'm a friend of Sherrie's. I came by to take a few things to her and to feed the cats."

"I'm really sorry about what's happened. I like Sherrie a lot. Anything I can do to help?" he offered. "By the way, I'm Bruce Addison."

I attempted a weak smile. "Be careful what you ask for, Bruce. If you're serious, I might need some help with the cats." Bruce was a 40-something, tall man whose buzzed brown hair showed beneath a Marlin's baseball cap. "You seem a little young to be retired."

He shook his head and grinned. "I wish. Actually, I'm a pilot for Delta. You caught me on a home rotation."

"Lucky for me. Listen Bruce, as much as I'd like to chat, I should call the cops while I'm gathering the things I promised Sherrie."

"I understand," he replied. "Let me give you our phone number just in case." He jogged back to the cart and returned with a score card and pencil. He drew an "X" through the scores and wrote his number in the right corner. "Claudia and I would be glad to help."

I took the card and turned to go. "Thanks for everything, Bruce. I may be calling you."

"Do that," he called to my back.

Scooter and Scarlette were sitting on the hood of Arthur's BMW when I re-entered the garage. Bored expressions were fixed on both faces when I offered, "Hey, you two, want to have some dinner?" Except for flicking the end of their tails, they were statues until the overhead door started rumbling down. They beat me through the connecting door and vanished. I pushed it closed with my hip and leaned against it for several beats before walking down the familiar hall that now held an aura of menace. It was reassuring to see Scooter watching from the marble table until I remembered the broken glass just beyond.

"Ah, shit, Scooter, you've got to get out of there," I grumbled as I opened the door to the pool and found the cage door open. After pulling it closed, I headed for the kitchen to grab two saucers and a couple pop-top cans of kitty-chow. I opened the cans on the patio and dumped the stuff onto the saucers with Scarlette and Scooter watching from the door. When I set them on the bricks, both cats ambled forward to investigate and I locked them in the enclosure.

Now what? I checked my watch and swore as I realized how much time had lapsed. The deadline for visiting hours was minutes away and I had a mess to clean up and the menagerie to feed. I gazed longingly at the liquor cart as I tried to calm my jumbled thoughts. Shuffling toward the laundry room on wobbly knees to get the vacuum, I was plagued with a nagging sense of forgetting something important.

"This is no time for a senior moment, Cassandra," I said aloud. "You should be telling someone...ah ha!" It had finally hit me that I was standing in a crime scene. Calling Logan would not only be the right thing to do, but might help me bend the rules for an after-hours conversation with Sherrie. "Purse, purse," I mumbled as I turned in circles. Logan's card was in the wallet, but where had I left the damned thing? Remembering, I hustled to the garage to retrieve it from the front seat of the Beemer. I grabbed the phone from the wall, but quickly returned it. OK, I was going to be a good citizen and call the cops, but not before I took a quick look around. That creep had been after something. Maybe I could find out without messing things up too badly. Since surgical gloves weren't part of the collection in the bottom of my bag, I dropped it on the credenza, grabbed a bunch of tissues and started through the house to investigate.

The attack had come from the hall leading to the kitchen, so I started there. But the countertops were empty and the cupboards closed. I opened the drawer on the small desk beneath the cupboards with two tissues and found the usual jumble of junk in such disarray that it would be impossible to know if anything was missing. The pool cage door had been opened before I closed it. Maybe that's where he…damn. I hadn't used the protective tissue to close it or the doors to the kitchen. So much for protecting the crime scene. Logan would not be pleased.

In the wing of the house that held the guestrooms, I thought I'd struck pay-dirt. Papers were strewn across a pale oak desk, pictures were askew and the drawer to a matching oak file cabinet stood open. I plucked two more tissues from the box on Sherrie's desk and carefully flipped through the files, hoping for an empty space to indicate a missing file. Nothing. The office looked disturbed, but if anything had been taken, I had no way of knowing.

Frustrated, I continued down the hall. I leaned through the doorway to the last bedroom and the connecting bath with my hands clasped behind my back to avoid touching anything. The rooms were tidy, smelling of furniture polish from the housekeepers' last visit. "Duh!" I exclaimed, as I froze with a foot in mid-air over the carefully raked beige carpet in these rooms. Had I walked in to further investigate, my size 8's would have been the only footprints in the plush. Back on the safety of the tile, I retraced my steps and took one last glance at the disarray in the office. Either that slime ball was the neatest criminal alive or I'd interrupted him before he had a chance to move further into the house. Or the office had been his only destination. For what?

I stomped back to the garage and grabbed my purse from the Beemer's front seat, tossing the wad of tissues into a convenient waste can. I slammed the door and stood there trying to remember why I'd needed my bag in the first place. Pacing back and forth while slapping the back of my head, I mumbled, "Think, Cassie, think." Memory lapses. Either I was getting older or I should have done a Clinton and not inhaled. Finally the fog lifted and I pulled Logans's card from my wallet as I walked to the phone on the bamboo nightstand in the master bedroom. I pulled a beige tissue from the box beside the phone, wrapped it around the mobile headset and called Logan as I headed for the walk-in closet. A half dozen

Jacobsen's bags were neatly aligned on the top rack. "Sherrie, my love, you are a shop-a-holic," I tsked as I lifted the opaque beige plastic in search of the crème suit she'd requested.

A brisk voice barked into my ear, "Logan, here."

"Officer Logan, this is Cassie Grimes, Sherrie Walters friend."

"Yes?" he replied. That Logan. What a conversationalist.

"I came by to feed the cats and pick up some clothes for Sherrie and was jumped by a guy hiding in the house. Thought you'd want to know," I said.

"You were just assaulted *inside* the Walters home?" he turned up the volume a notch.

"Just a few minutes ago."

"Damn it. Are you ok? Stay there and don't touch anything. I'm on my way."

"I'm fine," I said and realized I was speaking to a dial tone. I pushed the off button, extended the receiver and addressed it like a person. "Thanks for the concern." I resumed my inspection of the latest assault on Jacobsen's and found the crème pantsuit with a bag of accessories looped over the hanger. I lay it carefully across the bed and pulled a pale pink set of lingerie from the top dresser drawer. Pushing the drawer closed with my hip, I spotted a couple of diamond rings and some earrings lying in the open next to the vase holding a huge arrangement of silk Birds of Paradise. "Not very thorough, were you, bubba?" I muttered. I found a make-up bag beneath Sherrie's sink in the bathroom and began loading it with an assortment of goodies. While I was debating which color eye shadow would look best with the ensemble, the doorbell rang.

Logan walked with me through the house as I explained what had happened and what I'd concluded. He called for a crime scene tech when we'd finished the tour and followed me into the bedroom.

"Ok, let's review what you've told me. The broken cabinet happened when you fell into it. The blood was the perp's from your braining him with a vase though you escaped unhurt. The neighbor, a Bruce Addison, scared him away when you ran from the house and will corroborate your story. You found the pool cage open, but closed it, playing hell with any fingerprints we might have recovered. Then you stomped through the house and found only the office disturbed, and, in your infinite wisdom, concluded that he hadn't been in the house for long before you arrived. So, tell me, Cagny (or is it Lacey?) why do you assume that?"

I stopped by the bed and turned. "It's Cassie…oh, very clever. Would you believe I'm too young to know what you're talking about?"

"Not for a minute," he said, his mouth twitching in either a smile or a smirk. With Logan, it was hard to tell the difference.

"Hey, be nice," I said. "Here's why I knew that either he wasn't here long or wasn't your garden variety thief." I waved a hand toward the glittering array on the dresser.

He picked up several karats of stones in platinum settings, rolled them in his hand and dropped them. "Point taken. Did you find the clothes on the bed like that?"

"No, no. This is the outfit that Sherrie wanted me to take to her for tomorrow's court appearance."

He tsked. "Swell. Anything else you've pawed through?"

"Nothing except her make-up drawer, but I'm sure he wasn't in there."

"Well, as long as you'r*e sure*," he replied.

Ignoring the sarcasm, I went into my pitch. "C'mon. Gimme a break, huh? The guy scared the crap out of me. And, I still need to clean up the glass and throw out some food for the strays." Giving a worried look at my watch, I continued babbling. "And, visiting hours are over at the jail by now. Could you get them to make an exception and let me see Sherrie, anyway? She really ought to be allowed to wear clean clothes to her hearing tomorrow. If you could do that for me, I'll leave and you guys can take your time here and with the neighbor. Oh, by the way, he was heading for the golf course when he helped me."

The doorbell rang and Logan excused himself to admit the tech and his bag of crime-fighting toys. I stuffed a sandy bronze eye shadow into the bag with the other war paint, picked up the clothing bag and walked toward the kitchen where I dropped Sherrie's civies on the table. Logan snapped the cell phone closed as I approached. "They're expecting you at the jail. Now, get going."

"Thanks. But I'm not done with my chores, yet."

He held up a hand. "We'll clean up the glass when we finish. The housecats bolted inside when we opened the door to the pool and, if I remember correctly, the food for the strays is under the grill on the patio."

"Good memory, but I wouldn't want to impose."

"I'll bet," he snorted. "Now, good-bye." He double-flicked his hand in a wave toward the garage. "We'll be in touch if we have any questions."

"OK, I'm going. Oh, yeah. Bruce Addison volunteered to help with the cats. If you still have a key, you might want to take him up on the offer."

"Fine. Now, maybe if I say it slowly. G..oooo..d Byyyeee."

I shrugged and smiled as I picked up the clothes from the table. "Thanks again, Officer Logan." He stared silently at me, so I turned and left.

I heard a muffled ring from my purse as I turned onto the entrance ramp for I-75 to head back to the jail. I managed to extract it from a zipper pocket before voice mail kicked in and said, "Hello?"

"Hey, Cassie, where are you?" Gene asked. "Arthur thought you'd be home by now and I wanted to tell you that I was on my way."

"No such luck. There's been a delay and I'm just now heading for the jail with Sherrie's stuff. Why don't you head for home, let the dogs out and meet me in a couple of hours at the Fishmonger? We can relax and catch up without cooking."

"That works for me. How was your trip into the land of crime?" He asked.

"Interesting," I hedged. "How was your day?"

"So,so. See you about eight?"

"It's a date. Bye, honey," I said and hung up. Oh, boy. Gene was not going to be a happy camper when he heard about my day. I flashed on the image of a bloody face chasing me down Sherrie's drive and a jolt of acid hit my stomach, making me shudder involuntarily. I clutched the steering wheel with white knuckles and felt the chill of panic turn into red-hot anger. "Oh, hell no," I said aloud, then squeezed my eyes shut as I vigorously shook my head and inhaled through clenched teeth. A horn blared and my eyes flew open as I exhaled and pounded a reply on the steering wheel. In keeping with my sunny mood, I glared through the window and extended the middle finger on my left hand. When a wrinkly claw returned the gesture with the embellishment of a wet raspberry, I burst out laughing, realizing that I'd just seen a very probable future self.

****

The public parking lot of the jail was deserted. With Sherrie's clothing draped over my arm, I moved back and forth under the electronic eye over the not-so-automatic glass door to the lobby until a female metallic voice squawked, "May I help you?"

"Cassie Grimes to see Sheryl Walters," I said, looking upward as I raised my arm to indicate the reason for my after-hours visit.

"Just a moment, please," she answered. I passed the time by flapping the arm that held the plastic covered clothing at the squadron of mosquitoes diving at fresh meat. Out-maneuvered and out-numbered, I dropped my purse and squished the ones landing on my exposed skin into their next incarnation, puzzled that I was slapping the length of my legs. As I twisted around, I realized the slit in the skirt that had previously reached to a couple of inches above the knee had been ripped in my fall. I was now vented to my upper thigh. "Freakin' great," I murmured, shifting Sherrie's outfit to the other arm in a belated gesture of decorum.

"Ms. Grimes?" called a voice to my right.

Startled, I leapt to the left and stumbled on the purse I'd dropped to the ground. I heard the fabric of my damaged dress rip again and wheezed, "Geez, you scared me to death." I stooped to retrieve the purse, hoping I wasn't exposing my French-cut cotton Jockey's to the officer who opened a small metal door in an alcove to the right of the main entrance.

"This way, please," he beckoned. I stepped around him and waited for him to close the door. "Please," he said again and extended an arm for the plastic bag that was draped over my arm. I passed Sherrie's clothing to him and followed his quick steps down a brightly-lit corridor. Our steps reverberated on the polished linoleum as we wound around the quiet station. We stopped at a glass window extending up from a small ledge embedded in the wall with a pale green upholstered chair resting beneath. "Have a seat and I'll get Mrs. Walters for you."

"Thanks," I replied and, remembering my earlier gaff, extended my purse.

"That won't be necessary. Please, have a seat," he repeated. I draped my purse over the back of the chair and sat, trying to smooth the fabric of my ruined dress over my exposed thigh. He stepped in front of the door and said, "One to area six." The now familiar whirring noise followed and he stepped through the opening, leaving me staring at the wall and empty table on the other side of the glass.

I fidgeted in my seat, turning my head in both directions and saw only empty hall. Several minutes passed before I saw the door from the locked waiting area open and Sherrie step through into the cubicle. She snatched up the phone as she was seating herself and waved it toward me to do the same. I picked up my receiver and heard, "Well, you certainly took your sweet time."

"Lighten up, girlfriend," I replied. "You're not the only one having a tough day."

"What could possibly have happened to you that would compare with cooling my heels in the big house?" she asked, drumming her fingernails on the metal table.

"Oh, I don't know," I said, looking at the ceiling and tapping my abbreviated nails in rhythm with hers. "How about..." I paused dramatically and leaned closer to the glass and snarled, "...being mugged in your house?"

"What!" she screamed as she jumped from her chair. Behind her, a guard placed a hand on her shoulder and gently pushed her back toward her chair. She flinched like she'd been slapped, dropped the receiver and gave him a withering look. He responded by smiling until she was seated again. She picked up the phone, straightened her back and said in a controlled tone. "What are you talking about, Cassie?"

I briefly detailed what had happened since I'd left her, including the lucky coincidence of Bruce's appearance. "What do you think he was after?" I asked.

"Who knows? What'd you think of Bruce? He's a little young for my taste, but he's a hotty. Bet you'd like to wrap your legs around *his* ears, eh, Cass?"

The guard shifted his gaze over Sherrie's head and raised an eyebrow toward me. I rolled my eyes and mouthed, "Diarrhea of the mouth." I turned back to my friend and continued. I'm glad to see your prescriptions haven't killed your libido altogether, Sher. But let's try to focus here."

"Ok, ok," she conceded. "I've got no idea what he was after, especially in the office. I occasionally pay bills from there, but all the real work is kept at the office. Dave uses it to play around with real estate listings or to watch our stocks on the Internet. I keep hoping he'll find a porn site so that he'll leave me alone all together."

"Focus, Sherrie."

"Sorry, Cass. Honestly, I've got no idea what he could have been after, especially if he didn't take the jewelry. Pretty stupid thief."

"Or not a thief at all," I said. "There is one other thing I'd like to do, if it's ok with you."

"Such as…"

"I'd like to spend some of your cash-stash," I said. On the way to the jail, I'd given myself a pep talk about how well I'd handled the assault. Truthfully, I was a wreck. The more we became involved with this mess, the less I liked it. And I liked being threatened with bodily harm least of all. I lowered my voice to a whisper and said, "Remember the guy I used to date that helped me when Adam was kidnapped? I'd like to hire him to help us and it may be expensive."

"Yeah, I remember," she dropped the volume of her reply to match mine. "Great kisser, lots of muscle. Why are we whispering? Planning a little hanky-panky?"

"Get real," I hissed. "I'm planning on having my back watched so I'm not surprised again."

"Ooh, aren't we touchy?" she giggled. "What do you call expensive?"

I started ticking the tab off on my fingers. "Let's see, about $700 for last minute air fare and a car rental while he's here. Figure that brings it up to a thousand, easy. Your old unit is empty and I'd like to rent it, but the current owners only rent for a minimum of a month. That's another $3000 to $4000 and a daily fee and expenses. Geez, Sherrie, if he's only here for a couple of weeks it could end up costing you $7 or $8 Grand."

She dropped her voice even further and leaned toward the glass. "I steal that much in a good week from the stores. Do it."

I flicked my eyes toward the guard to see if he'd caught the incriminating statement. "Will you please try to remember why you're here and not give them any more reason to keep you locked up?"

She looked over her shoulder, then back at me and giggled again. "Sorry," she whispered.

I cringed and looked again at the guard. He pointedly tapped his watch and circled his raised finger. "I'm getting the high sign from your companion. Guess I'd better be going. I'll keep my fingers crossed for you tomorrow."

"Funny, isn't it?" she said. "All my life I've wanted to be at a big time trial. Little did I know that I'd be the glamorous defendant."

"You're really twisted, you know that? Only you could think this was a lark."

She smiled at me through the glass. "Hey, Cassie, aren't you always telling me about finding the silver lining? I'm taking your advice, for a change."

"Another first," I smiled back. "Love you, honey."

"Love you more," she said, pursing her lips in an air kiss. Her hand was moving the phone toward its cradle as she turned and said, "Let's go, handsome."

The guard rolled his eyes before the two of them disappeared through the door at the rear of the room. Moments later, he re-emerged to meet me in the hall and escort me back. He held the side door for me to leave the building and stepped through.

"Is something wrong?" I asked in the deepening twilight.

"Just seeing you to your car," he replied.

"Gee, Officer, I don't know if that will be necessary. I can really take care..." I stopped as I saw a shadow dart through the bushes along the road. Fear tingled up my spine and I shook my head. "Forgive me. I'd very much appreciate your walking me to the car." We stopped by the driver's side of the Beemer as I fumbled through my purse for the keys. I turned the key in the door lock and a loud honk immediately shattered the night. I dropped my purse as the headlights flashed and the horn wailed. Next to me, the cop extended his hand for the key, aimed the remote and quiet descended again.

"New car?" he asked.

"A friend's loaner," I explained.

"Must be some friend," he said, eyeing the car. "Good night, M'am."

"Goodnight. And thanks." I climbed into the car and he shut the door behind me. I waved to his back as I left the lot and headed for the Fishmonger to meet Gene. Trying to concentrate on what to have for dinner, I couldn't get past the image of a sweating tumbler of Chivas. Telling Gene about my day and the decision to install Jim Stillman as our next door neighbor could use a little liquid assistance.

EIGHT

By the time I reached the Fishmonger, the lot was nearly empty. I pulled the Beemer into the flood-lit parking lot, hit the remote lock and quick-stepped into the restaurant. Gene was seated beneath a fish tank where a solitary, miniature shark swam lazy figure-eights between the rocks. He spotted me and rose from the table to pull out my chair.

"Hungry, Baber?" he asked as I took my seat.

"You bet," I replied. "And after the day I've had, thirsty, too."

Before Gene could comment, a sing-song voice over my shoulder said, "Well, Sweetie, I can help with that. What'll it be?" Turning, I looked into a pair of chocolate brown eyes whose ridiculously long lashes batted at me from a drop-dead gorgeous male face under blonde-tipped short brown hair. The white jeans and tee were molded to a seriously cut body. Unfortunately, his feet were planted in a dancer's pose and his pinky extended at just the wrong angle from a glittery pen poised above a note pad. To straight, single women, this guy was the walking definition of wasted flesh.

"Chivas on the Rocks," I said.

"Oooh, honey, have we had a rough day?" he asked.

"You wouldn't believe," I said.

Our waiter headed toward the bar as Gene flicked his raised hand downward and lisped, "Nathan has been really attentive. Another few minutes, and he'd have asked me out."

I grinned at my husband. "Well, at least he has good taste."

"Another of your unemployed actor friends, no doubt," he said and raised his glass. "Believe it or not, the kitchen closes at nine, so you'd better look at the menu." He handed me a beat-up laminated card containing sea-food choices on the front and a variety of land animal entrees on the back.

Before I'd read through the appetizers, our waiter was back with the drink. "Go ahead, Gene," I said as I quickly scanned the entrée's. He ordered mahi-mahi, but I couldn't bring myself to eat Flipper after I'd played with him in the surf. "I'll have the jumbo shrimp appetizer as my meal, with a salad and bowl of clam chowder."

"So that's how you keep your girlish figure," he said as he swished away.

"I'll bet the older crowd eats that up," I said.

"Shoot me if I ever get that old," Gene replied. "So, Cass, tell me about your day."

"You first," I said, enjoying the warmth spreading from my throat to my stomach as I sipped the woody Scotch.

"Oh, I had a ball. What could be more fun than spending the day in a lawyer's office? How about being passed around the phone system at the State's License Bureau and a visit to the Clerk of Courts for Lee County?" He picked up a knife and mimed cutting his wrist.

"Poor baby. Find anything interesting?"

"Some. With Aggie's help, I was able to track several of the Walters' assets, as well as a string of business licenses for Tom that were on and off the books in record time."

I wrinkled my forehead. "Aggie?"

Gene waved his hand, "Lanahan."

"Well, well," I smirked. "Aren't we the little heartbreaker?"

"Oh, sure," he smiled. "My boyish charm does have a way with older women, but I suspect that if Aggie dropped her panty-hose in the office, the furnace would kick on. How were things at the house of crime?"

"Unnerving. If you can believe it, I think I was more nervous about being locked up than Sherrie was. She acted like she was the heroine in a crime novel." Gene listened attentively as I detailed my visit, including the power of attorney I'd acquired. I paused briefly when our salads arrived, along with a steamy bowl of thick clam chowder. Nathan ground fresh pepper over the salads and my soup while inquiring about the state of our drinks. Gene nodded and I shook my head as I sampled the soup and hummed my approval.

When we were alone again, Gene asked, "So, what caused the delay?"

I held up a finger as I swallowed a second spoon of chowder. "Well, I had some unexpected company at Sherrie's house." Gene dropped his fork at the first mention of the break-in, causing Nathan to swoop back. Gene dismissed him abruptly and I rushed through the story as quickly as I could, finishing with, "So, I left Logan to lock up and took Sherrie's clothes to the jail. That's about it."

He closed his eyes and shook his head from side to side. When he finally looked up, he said, "I swear to God, Cassandra, I'm thinking of locking you up with Sherrie for your own good."

"Ah, Gene, don't over-react. I'm just fine," I said as I patted his hand. "And I've got a plan."

"Well, as long as you've got a plan..." he glared under hooded eyes.

"Ok, ok," I said. "Just hear me out for a minute." He nodded and I told him about wanting to install Jim Stillman next door as protection and another set of investigating legs. I elaborated several rock solid reasons for my brilliant plan and waited expectantly for complete agreement. What I got was silence that stretched on and on. I cleared my throat and said, "Uh, Gene, it's your turn to continue the discussion."

"I don't know what to say, Cassie. My first inclination is to pack up and head back to Ohio as fast as we can. Jim Stillman doesn't exactly conjure up warm and fuzzy memories." He finished his salad in silence as I tried to think of something witty that would lighten the moment. I was fresh out of witty. Gene drained the last of his drink as Nathan arrived, flourishing a fish laden tray.

I smiled and small-talked Nathan away since Gene was still brooding quietly. I grabbed my first shrimp by the tail and swirled it through the cocktail sauce, hoping the heavy silence would become as uncomfortable for him as it was for me. *Dream on, Cassandra.*

Moving rapidly from persuasive mode to pissed off, I was mentally sorting through a number of statements guaranteed to project impatience and just the right amount of guilt as I watched him slowly demolishing his food without making eye contact. I leaned back and sighed audibly as I munched away on the cold shrimp. Gene finally looked at me.

"Don't start, Cassandra," he said. "What is it with you and playing detective?"

I stuck out my lower lip, hoping to affect the perfect Marilyn Monroe pout. "Well, the last time I became involved with an investigation, it worked out pretty well." His response was to lower his eyes and stab a piece of fish.

After being married for umpty-something years, most wives learn when to retreat. Though not always my forte, this did seem like one of those times, so I segued back to a discussion of the bureaucratic jungle. Gene never let a chance to rant against government inefficiency pass without comment, so I had him talking and venting again on a subject other than Jim Stillman rejoining our lives.

Nathan returned to ascertain our interest in dessert and/or coffee. "Neither, thanks," Gene replied. "Just the check."

"Pity," he said, turning away. He took two steps, paused and executed a perfect pirouette before adding, "We're down to the last two pieces of a scrumptious white chocolate mousse pie."

"Wait!" I exclaimed, suppressing the urge to yip and drool.

"Yesss?" he said, folding his arms with a knowing smile.

"Put them into a box and bring them with the check," Gene said as his mouth twitched into the beginning of his own smile.

"Oh, goodie," Nathan clapped as he walked away. "Looks like we're going to kiss and make up."

"Is he right, Baber?" I asked. "Are we going to kiss and make up?"

"We'll see. Let's talk about this new wrinkle in your nosy nature while we walk the dogs."

It would still take some serious selling to stay firmly planted in the middle of the action, but the odds were looking up. The stage would be set with fabulous dessert and a moonlight stroll on the beach. If I couldn't make some headway with that combination, we were older than I wanted to admit.

Nathan arrived carrying a large sack and a leather folder with the bill. "Enjoy yourselves," he said and bent provocatively toward Gene. "Let me know if you ever decide to switch hit."

"You'll be the first to know," Gene said, reading the check and putting some cash into the folder. He handed it to Nathan and held a hand in the air to indicate that no change was required.

I patted Gene's cheek possessively and said, "Sorry, Nathan. This one is mine."

"Don't gloat," he said and turned to Gene. "Come back and see me with or without the ball and chain."

****

The bridge was deserted at this hour, so we pulled into our lot in less than ten minutes. As our feet crunched on the gravel next to the building, we heard the usual barking from the dynamic duo. In an effort to keep peace with the neighbors, we quickened our pace as we rounded the corner and started up the stairs.

"Stop right there," a female voice commanded.

Gene raised his eyes to the porch and stared directly into the barrel of a sub-nose .38 police pistol. "Holy Shit!" he exclaimed as he leapt backwards and reached for me. Heart pounding, I looked up and saw a set of tiny teeth bared next to a sizeable ankle.

"Madeline! It's us!" I yelled as three dogs erupted into a deafening chorus.

The gun lowered and she whistled, "Thank goodness. I've had my considerable derriere squeezed into this plastic imitation of a chair for nearly an hour." The gate next to the pool house banged and my heart flew into my throat again as she called out, "All clear, Gladdie." A tent of pink fabric emerged from the shadows. Moonlight glinted off the metal of a semi-automatic Glock that Gladys dropped into her bag as she lumbered toward the porch.

Maggie and A.J. were throwing themselves against the glass doors in an attempt to reach the action. I walked up the steps on shaky legs and fumbled with the lock. When I finally slid the door open, all three dogs ran down the steps in a blur.

"Maggie! A.J.!" Gene shouted. "Stay!" A.J. turned at his father's harsh voice while Maggie and Snookie did a slow walk by the plants along the sidewalk, sniffing audibly. Gene scooped Maggie into the air with one hand and she huffed her displeasure at being interrupted. Snookie gave him a quick growl and then ambled back to the steps where she waited patiently for Maddie to pick her up.

"Care to tell us what you're doing?" Gene asked as Gladys stopped beside him. "Stop it, Maggie," he commanded the squirming dog. Her ears dropped and the wiggling was replaced with a soft moan.

A.J. was at my ankle, staring up hopefully, so I picked him up and said to the group, "Let me get the leashes and you can fill us in while we walk."

"Good idea, Dearie," Madeline said. "Coming, Gladys?"

"Of course," she replied. "Since I'm the only one without an animal, I'll walk a martini." She withdrew a silver flask from her bag and settled the long strap over her shoulder as she waited for us to harness the canines. The seven of us angled south across the loose sand, making our way toward the water line.

"Tell, us, already," I said. "Why were you two camped out at our place, brandishing guns and scaring us shitless?"

"Sorry about that," Madeline said. "We were having cocktails on the lani when we heard your dogs start barking."

"The moon was so bright tonight that we were sitting there in the dark," Gladys added. "I heard some noise and assumed it was you two coming home. I got up to shout a greeting from the corner of the lani, but I didn't see your car. That's when I tip-toed back to Maddie with my finger to my lips," she pantomimed, looking like an inflated, Technicolor Charlie Chaplin.

"And I spotted a guy snooping around your porch," Madeline continued. "He pulled on the door and your babies went crazy."

Gladys slapped her thigh and continued. "Before I could stop her, she yelled, 'Hey, Buster! What do you think you're doing down there!'"

"You should have seen him run!" Madeline giggled. "After what you'd told us this afternoon, we decided to hold down the fort and protect the kids until you returned."

Gene stopped walking and turned pointedly toward me. I smiled and shrugged. He shook his head in disgust and let Maggie pull him forward.

"You see?" Madeline continued. "I told you that we might come in handy."

"Geez, Madeline. I appreciate the thought, but I didn't expect you to be doing *Lethal Weapon 65* from the front porch." When we caught up with Gene, A.J. and Snookie joined Maggie's investigation of a piece of driftwood. The dogs did their sniff and pee and sniff again thing around the hapless bit of flotsam as their humans stood in silence, listening to the waves.

Gladys unscrewed the cap from the flask and took a healthy swig. "Hits the spot," she proclaimed. She dropped the flask into her purse where it met the concealed gun with a loud clank.

I did a small jump at the sound and said, "You could have been hurt."

"Oh, sweetie, not very likely," Madeline said. "He took off like a rabbit as soon as I yelled. Probably just a kid, nosing around. Besides, we had some pretty good insurance."

Gladys patted the side of her bag affectionately. "You'd better believe it. Nobody's gonna mess with me when Big Bertha's along for the ride."

"Happy, Cassandra?" Gene asked.

I shook my head and looked between the smiling faces of *Charlie's Geriatric Angels.* "I'm so sorry. I should never have confided in you." Me and my big mouth. Guilt was rolling over me as steadily as the Gulf's water lapped the shore. What if they'd been attacked like I had been hours earlier? What if they'd shot themselves or some innocent bystander? I was working myself into a really bad place when another thought hit me. What if it had been the same guy that mugged me and they'd shot him in the family jewels? I giggled beneath my breath and mumbled, "Would have served him right and made my day."

"Speak up, honey," Madeline said. "These old ears don't hear so well over the surf."

"It was nothing, Maddie. Just talking to myself"

"So, how was your day at the slam?" Gladys asked as I tugged on A.J.'s leash and turned for home. I looked into the dark at a couple of figures advancing toward us and saw Gladys rummage through her bag. I put a hand on her arm and we watched them face one another, linger over a long embrace and stroll toward the buildings hand-in-hand. She withdrew her hand and said, "Cassie? Your day at the jail?"

"It's a long story and it's getting late. I'll tell you about it tomorrow."

The words were no sooner out of my mouth than Gene grabbed my elbow and whispered, "Will you never learn?" Then he turned to the old girls and said, "C'mon, ladies. It's bedtime."

"Huh?" I muttered.

Madeline grabbed her friend and whispered something into her ear that made them collapse in giggles. To me she said, "Let's not keep the man waiting. If I had a hunk like that, I wouldn't be wasting my time with the likes of you."

We chatted about husbands, dogs and other benign things as the five of us followed Gene and Maggie's substantial lead. We paused near the water before splitting up and Gene came trotting out toward us. He extended a bag toward Madeline and said, "A little something to make up for spending your evening on our porch furniture."

"Oh, honey," she said. "That isn't necessary."

"White chocolate mousse pie," he replied.

Gladys grabbed the bag. "Never argue with a man bearing gifts." She gave me a conspiratorial poke in the ribs and whispered, "We'll have the white chocolate pie, you enjoy the banana cream." Oh, boy.

She cupped her hand to Maddie's ear to share the joke, causing them to laugh so hard that she erupted into hiccups. Gene looked at her and said, "You all right, Gladys?"

"Couldn't –Hic! – be – Hic!- Better. Well, maybe if you were parking your shoes under my bed instead of Cassie's, I'd be better."

Gene looked at me and rolled his eyes. Then, he turned to Gladys and gave her a peck on the cheek. Madeline leaned forward, tapped her cheek and was rewarded with a duplicate kiss. "Now listen, girls," he said. "I've told you not to talk dirty to me when the wife's around. She'll get suspicious." This brought on a fresh batch of giggles from Madeline and even louder hiccups from Gladys.

She did a silent lock of the lips and tossed the imaginary key over her shoulder, finishing aloud with, "Toodle – Hic! – Loo!" We watched as the two of them giggled their way over the sand bar and were lost in the shadows beneath their building.

"You old charmer," I said as I gave A.J. to Gene for de-sanding while I went to the nozzle by the walk to rinse my own feet. When I got back to the porch, the dogs were inside the condo and Gene was waiting for me on the porch. "I thought you were ready for bed?" I leaned over and gave him a hopeful, wet kiss that he returned with less enthusiasm than I'd have liked. "I'm getting mixed signals, here."

He reached beneath his chair to hand me my purse and the phone. "I'd call the Nolans first to hold the condo. Somehow, I think Stillman is used to late night calls."

****

At 8:30 the next morning, Gene gave me a perfunctory good-bye kiss as he left for Arthur's office and I headed across the sand for the dogs' morning constitutional. The warmth of the early morning sun and the pleasant attention my fur-balls garnered during our walk had eased the frost-bite from the chilly evening and morning with my spouse. I was watching a dolphin family feed in the shallow water when Maggie and A.J. started pulling against their leashes and yipping excitedly. They were answered with a lower pitched bark, followed by the now-familiar "Yoo-hoo!" from our porch. I jogged behind the dogs to the condo without stopping to clean them.

Gladys waved an apple turnover the size of a salad plate and said, "Breakfast, Cassie. Woman cannot live by sex alone."

"Then this woman is truly starving," I replied. She lifted an eyebrow and frowned in confusion. "Sorry to shatter your illusions of my wanton sex life, but Gene were less than receptive."

"Say it ain't so," said Madeline. "I was sure you were getting lucky last night. What went wrong?"

"Yesterday was less than sexy," I shrugged.

"And you promised to tell us about it," she replied. "Pull up a chair and fill in your deputies."

"I don't have much time, girls. And last night was your last tour of duty as sentries." Their faces fell so quickly that I rushed to explain. "No, no, ladies. You've got it all wrong. I'm heading to the airport shortly to pick up some professional muscle that will be staying next door."

"What's really going on, Cassie?" Madeline pressed. "Surely you have time to humor a couple of lonely old widows with tales of your exciting life." This was delivered in pitiful tones that echoed my mother's best guilt-inducing voice. Simultaneously, they pinned me with twin stares that evoked the same response as "The Look" with which Virginia Marianna routinely manipulated me. *Do they have a special class for this when you pick up your Medicare card?*

"Ok, ok," I relented. Both faces immediately broke into smiles as Madeline passed a Styrofoam cup and a bag of donuts. I searched the sack for the least caloric choice and watched Gladys tip a flask into her cup. "You're some piece of work, Gladdie."

"Yeah, yeah. So dish," she said as she sampled the spiked coffee and patted her tummy with a satisfied, "Ahhh." While the three dogs lounged comfortably on the still shady porch, I told them about my visit to Sherrie and the break-in at her house. They listened intently, stopping me occasionally with questions that bespoke their years of de-briefing cop husbands.

Madeline extended a paper napkin to me as I rose at the end of the story. "So, girls, I've got to get a quick shower and head for the airport to pick up Jim Stillman."

"This is the 'professional muscle' you talked about?" Gladys asked. "What does that mean exactly and how would a nice Mid-western girl like you know about such things?"

"Oh, boy. That's another long story. Let's just say he's an old friend that helped me out of a jam in the past."

Madeline extended a hand for my crumpled napkin. "So many mysteries. Does his arrival have anything to do with your hubby being less than amorous last night?"

I huffed affirmatively. "You could say that." I bent toward the snoozing dogs and quickly dusted their feet of the residual sand. "I'll introduce you when we get back."

Gladys pushed out of her chair and said, "C'mon, Madeline. I want to hit Publix this morning for some groceries. We'll have to hustle back to get all spiffy before meeting the next interesting man in this girl's life. I swear, Cassie, you've got more men around you than Carter's got 'Little Liver Pills'."

I patted her on the back as she started down the stairs. "I haven't heard that in years," I grinned. "Actually, I hate to admit that I'm old enough to know what you're talking about."

"A pup like you? Don't even talk to me about age," Madeline said. "C'mon, Snookie. Mommy's got to go to the store with Aunt Gladdie." I waved to my aging accomplices and hustled into the condo. Maggie and A.J. took up their positions in front of the open screen door to watch the beach come to life as I headed for the shower.

Emerging, I debated how much to clean up for my old boyfriend, Jim. Glancing at the clock radio on the night stand, I mumbled, "Not very much." If his plane was on time, he'd be touching down in thirty-five minutes. We were twenty-five minutes with no traffic or blue-hair drivers, so I was pushing it. The last time I'd seen him was during the investigation of a series of crimes involving my family and he'd definitely witnessed my raggedy worst. But this was Jim Stillman, with whom I'd fogged many a car window while in my misspent youth. Emergency grooming measures were called for.

I dried my hair and grabbed a handful of make-up to be applied with the aid of the mirrors in the Beemer. My wardrobe consisted of the shortest shorts I owned and a light blue, second skin knit top. I slid into sandals, sucked in my tummy as hard as I could and checked the results in the mirror. If I slouched at just the right angle, I could look thinner than I really was. I patted the dogs and trotted to the car. By the time I crossed the bridge, I was squinting into the visor's mirror to apply mascara while trying to avoid a rear-end collision. *Vanity, thy name is middle-aged woman.*

NINE

For nearly twenty years, I'd loved the easy access of this small airport. Since I was running late, I had visions of dramatically screeching to a stop at the baggage claim area to find a waiting Jim Stillman. *A girl's gotta make an entrance.* I pulled into a gas station on Daniels Road, a half-mile before entering the airport grounds and hit the power button to lower the top on the 330. As the ragtop receded, I fluffed my hair, applied a coating of peach lip gloss and looked provocatively over my sunglasses into the rear-view mirror.

"Oh, yeah," I said as I licked a finger and touched it to my image in the mirror like it was an iron's hot bottom. "Tsssss," I hissed. "Just hot enough."

I sped through the curves of the airport grounds past several ponds. White cranes were slowly examining the water's edge in hopes of having lunch without becoming it for a submerged alligator. At the fork in the road that used to lead to the terminals, I encountered a roadblock that directed me into the parking areas. Another reason to hate 9/11. I opted for the more expensive short-term lot, frantically scanning the packed spaces for an empty slot. I found one at the very end of the blacktop, facing away from the terminal. *So much for my dramatic entrance.* I did one more check in the mirror, grabbed my purse and jumped from the car. I slammed the door, took two quick steps as I dropped the keys into my bag and smashed into someone hard enough to knock my sunglasses from my face.

"Oh, my God, I'm so sorry," I said as I lurched for the glasses that had come to rest under another car. To retrieve them, I had to squat with one leg extended, feeling blindly in the general direction. My hand closed around them after patting the ground in several places. I shoved my sunglasses back on my face and apologized to the black jeans topping the polished loafers of my victim, "I'm late picking up a friend."

"Planning's still your long suit, eh, Cassie?" he replied. My eyes snapped to the aviator sunglasses that flashed opaquely in the sun above Jim Stillman's wide grin. A black leather garment bag was slung over one of his shoulders with a matching duffel bag dangling loosely from the other arm. "Nice outfit. If you hadn't dropped something yourself, I'd have done it just to watch you bend over in those shorts."

"Ah, Geez, Jim. Why do you have to sneak up on a girl like that?"

"Well, Cass, if you'd been on time, I would have walked out of the terminal and into your car. Of course, I'd have missed the peep show, so it all worked out for the best."

"Point taken," I replied and hit the remote lock for the Beemer's trunk. "Let's head to Alamo to pick up your car."

He dropped his luggage into the trunk, slammed it shut and eased into the passenger seat. As we rolled through the tollgate, he moved the seat back as far as it would go and casually wrapped an arm around the back of my seat. He was still wearing a light-weight black micro-fiber jacket over a black silk tee shirt in spite of the heat. The coat gapped slightly as he shifted his weight to reveal a webbed holster beneath his left arm. That explained the jacket. Between the breeze created by the convertible and the occasional cloud obscuring the sun, Jim Stillman looked as cool as if he were taking a fall drive through Ohio. I was praying my deodorant would hold.

The wind whipping through the open convertible gave me a brief respite from my overheated middle-aged thermostat. The line at Alamo's check-in counter was mercifully short and I soon pulled the Beemer behind a navy Expedition the size of a rolling hotel.

Jim pulled his bags from my trunk and tossed them into the back of the SUV. He turned, swept an arm toward the road and said, "Lead on, Cookie."

"If you get lost," I said, "just follow the signs to the beach and turn right over the bridge."

"Thanks, Mom, I think I can manage," he replied.

I know it's childish, but I just couldn't resist gunning the engine and roaring from the lot. The navy roof of his monster car stayed in my rear-view mirror as I wove through the slow parade of aging Cadillac's that were the most numerous model on the road. As we turned onto Gladiolus Blvd., the SUV suddenly accelerated and managed to pull in front of me. An arm emerged from the driver's window and pointed toward the right of the road. Jim pulled into the parking lot of a large green building with a huge orange perched on top of a sign that said *Sun Coast Harvest.*

"Problem?" I asked, pulling beside him as he locked his car.

"Stopping for supplies while I have a chance," he replied. "Care to join me?"

"Delighted," I said. He waited by the door and held it ajar for me to pass. Once inside, he left me to my own devices as he quickly wound through the isles with a plastic basket draped over his left arm. I grabbed a gallon of fresh squeezed juice from the rear of the store and paused at the bakery counter. I pointed toward an orange glazed cake for Madeline and Gladys and waited while the clerk slipped it into a white bakery box.

"That stuff'll kill you, Cassie," was whispered a few inches from my ear, and I jumped like I'd been stung.

"Damn it, Jim! Will you *please* stop that!" *I'm gonna tie a bell around his neck.* I put my juice on the counter while she rang up the purchases and added, "It's not for me."

"Of course, not," he smirked. "Try to slow it down to the speed limit for the duration. Let's not get any more attention from the local police than you've already managed." He handed the clerk a

$100 bill with a megawatt smile that made her blush. He stepped to the door, nudged it open with his hip and inclined his head for me to precede him. "See you soon."

I placed the cake on the passenger seat and the juice on the floor. The car accelerated sedately from the lot with Jim's SUV tight on my bumper. Twenty minutes later, we rolled into the condo parking lot and I motioned for him to follow. I pulled into the slot for #102 and pointed to my left at #101. Familiar yipping could be heard from the open window as I waited for Jim to unload his car. "Let's get you settled and I'll fill you in while we walk the dogs."

"It's your nickel," he replied.

A familiar brown snout poked through the railing as we neared the porch, followed by "Yoo Hoo!" and a duet of giggles. Stillman raised an eyebrow without breaking stride and stopped before the stairs. Gladys fanned her ample chest and said, "Be still my heart. C'mon up, Handsome. I've got your key." Jim looked at me with a raised eyebrow.

"Another chapter in the saga," I said. "Jim, meet Gladys, Madeline and Snookie."

"Which one is Snookie?" he asked, causing a fresh batch of giggles.

"Well, aren't you the one?" Gladys said. "Snookie's the dog."

"Sshh!   She'll hear you," Madeline said as she playfully smacked her friend's bare knee. "Your neighbor left the key with us so you could get settled right away."

"Thank you ladies," Jim replied as he accepted the key from Gladys and dropped his groceries in front of the door that was shuttered. "I'm going to get my bags," he said to me with briefly narrowed eyes and trotted down the steps on the opposite side of the porch.

Maggie and A.J. were raising holy hell from the other side of our door. I extended the cake box toward Madeline and said, "A little something to thank you for all your help."

"Thanks, Honey," she replied.   "That certainly wasn't necessary."

"Listen, ladies, Jim's had a long trip and I know he'll probably want to shower and get settled," I said.

"In other words, you want us to scram so you can have him all to yourself," Gladys sighed.   "Are you sure we shouldn't chaperone for Gene's sake?"

"What a dirty mind you have, Gladdie. I've got to bring him up to speed on plans for today and then who knows what he'll want to do. Jim's used to doing his own thing, regardless of what the logical approach might be."

"We can take a hint, dearie," Madeline said as she pushed herself from the chair. "C'mon girls. Let's console ourselves with whatever is in this delicious smelling box. We'll catch you later."

"Of that, I have no doubt," I replied.

Jim rounded the porch and stopped to let the three of them pass. "A pleasure, ladies," he said as he bowed from the waist.

"I bet you say that to all the girls," Gladdie replied as they waddled past him. She winked at me and silently mouthed, 'Yummy.' "Toodle, loo!" she called aloud with a wave.

I unlocked my door without opening it to prevent the dynamic duo from escaping. "I'm going to throw on a suit and leash up the dogs. If you need some time to freshen up, we'll walk north on the beach and you can catch us."

"It's a plan," he said and disappeared into the condo next door.

******

We'd rounded the point and were heading for home, but Jim was nowhere in sight. *What could be taking Stillman so long?* I was working myself into a snit when I spotted a tan body clad in black trunks talking to a woman in a micro-bikini. He leaned toward her and whispered in her ear. Even from a distance, I could see the pout as she flicked her mane of long, blonde hair and sauntered toward an empty chair, watching as Jim walked toward me.

I asked as he fell into step, "An old friend?"

He ignored the sarcasm and replied, "Maybe a new one. So, Cass, what's the ill-conceived and under-planned strategy for helping *your* old friend who's been so wrongly accused?"

"What makes you think I don't have a plan?" I asked.

"History."

"Well, smarty-pants, it just so happens that I've gotten a signed Power of Attorney from Sherrie," I replied and stopped short of sticking my tongue out at him. *Smarty-pants? Good grief, I'd just had a momentary regression to junior high.* Gathering my wits and adult vocabulary about me, I continued, "I'm *planning* to visit Sherrie's main office to have a look at her books. I want to make sure that Junior hasn't been raiding her inheritance. I'd also like to see how much is actually at stake financially in this family drama."

"You're just going to drop in, unannounced, wave a piece of paper at her staff and assume they'll give you access to all her very personal business? Sure, that's gonna happen," he said.

I stopped walking and turned to stare directly into the mirrored lenses of Jim's sunglasses as I said, "Yes, it will happen. Sherrie called her office manager to clear the way. And just how will you be spending *your* day and Sherrie's money?" Maggie began to moan at our feet while A.J. pulled at his leash and then danced back, overtly conveying *his* immediate plans. Stillman bent at the waist and scooped Maggie into the air with one hand. "Careful, Jim, she's not very good with strange men," I warned.

He turned her nose-to-nose and said, "That so, Maggie?" She responded by licking the tip of his nose. He lowered her back to the ground and resumed a leisurely pace as he said, "But I'm *very* good with strange females." A brief mixture of ancient feelings surfaced to remind me of our misspent youth. The familiar weight of my wedding ring reminded me of the difference between puppy love and dog-solid devotion as I fell into an easy tandem with Jim and asked, " Your plans?"

"I want addresses before you leave: your friend's home and business and the same for the stepson. I also want to know exactly where you'll be and for how long."

"Gee, Mom, I just told you that I was heading to Sherrie's office. As to how long I'll be there? Haven't got a clue. Do you still carry a pager?"

"Of course," he said. "I'll program the number into your speed dial," he added as we turned toward the condo. I stopped for the usual de-sanding of the dogs while Stillman took the small flight of stairs in two strides. "I'll be waiting for you to finish changing and getting the addresses I need," he added as he unlocked the condo's glass door and slid it open. He stepped inside and stuck his head back out saying, "Start locking your door, Cassie. At least you can slow someone down long enough for me to intervene if I need to." Before I could reply, his door closed, locked and the curtains drew shut.

I quickly dressed in a short, sea-green cotton shift and tan sandals, determined to be waiting for Stillman rather than giving him another chance for smug banter. With a quick glance in the mirror, I pushed pearl stud earrings through my ears and clasped on my watch. I pulled a sheet of paper from the note pad in the nightstand next to our bed and a pen from my purse. I knew Sherrie's address by heart, but had to resort to the local phone book for her business location. As I scanned the directory for Tom's information, I realized that Fort Myers didn't list Naples information, so I dialed directory assistance.

After three rings, an automated voice asked for the city and state needed. "Naples, Florida," I replied.

I paced back and forth during a much longer pause before a gravelly voice that suggested a two-pack-a-day habit responded with, "And how may I help you?"

"I'd like the number and address for the Beachside Bread Company in Naples and the residence of Thomas Walters, also in Naples," I said.

"One moment, please. Your listing for Beachside Bread is 239-884-3687. The address for that listing is 1250 Gulf Palm Lane," she managed between a series of low coughs. "The other listing is unavailable at the party's request. Thank you for choosing Sprint," she managed to blurt before a series of hacks served as the prelude to disconnection.

"Swell," I mumbled and snatched the paper. Grabbing my purse and keys from the counter, I headed for the door. "Be good, guys," I called to the sad faces on the couch as I slid the door open, then closed and locked it.

"Not bad," Stillman said, causing me to jump and drop my keys. He was sitting in a tilted plastic chair with his legs propped against the railing.

"What is it with you?" I snapped. "Do you get some twisted pleasure from sneaking up on people and scaring the crap out of them? Here are the addresses you wanted, except Tom's home. He was unlisted. I'll get that from Mary Lou when I see her. And what's up with that outfit?" The bottom of a short sleeve denim shirt hung loosely over a pair of khakis that topped brown Birkenstock sandals. "I thought head-to-toe black was your personal fashion statement."

He shrugged. "Camouflage. And who's Mary Lou?"

"Sherrie's Operations Manager," I replied as I glanced at my watch. "Gotta roll. When will I be seeing you again?"

"Don't sweat it. I've got your back," he said as he vaulted over the railing to land on the sidewalk below.

"Show-off," I called to his receding back. I tossed my purse onto the passenger seat and slid into the car. "Yowch!" I yelped as I grabbed the steering wheel to lift my exposed legs from the scorching heat of a seat that had baked in the Florida sun. Of course, the steering wheel was black and even hotter. "Shit!" I yelled, falling back onto the seat while trying to stretch the abbreviated skirt over my stinging thighs. Reluctantly, I pushed the button to raise the convertible's top and switched the air conditioner to arctic with the fan blasting on high. The traffic was mercifully light as I left the island and headed east on MacGregor Boulevard. This old street was still lined with the royal palms that Thomas Edison had begun planting when his winter home and lab had been in old Ft. Myers.

Twenty minutes later, I pulled into the parking lot of a typical strip center. Cream colored concrete blocks sported a turquoise awning to shade the glass windows from the intense tropical sun. In the middle of the strip, glowing in shades of orange and yellow, was a neon sign of a palm tree with a giant loaf of bread in its branches. After the frigid interior of the car, the heat felt delicious for the short walk to the office. I pushed through the glass door into a small entryway with wood doors on both sides. Large photos of mouth-watering goodies hung on the wall over a small café table, holding a large platter of cookies and napkins embossed with the company's logo. To the right, a door led into an actual bread store, emitting the kind of smells guaranteed to add five pounds just by breathing.

I walked to the table and chose a chocolate chip, oatmeal cookie, wrapped it in a napkin and opened the door on the left. A light oak desk that had seen some serious use was all that blocked the way to the inner sanctum. A woman with short salt and pepper hair was totally focused on her computer screen as I approached. I switched the cookie to my left hand and extended my right, saying, "Hi, I'm Cassie Grimes to see Mary Lou Gamboni."

She jumped up and pumped my extended hand. "Hi, Cassie. I'm Mary Lou. Would you like some coffee to go with your cookie?"

"No, thanks. It always amazes me how you Floridians can consume hot coffee when it's this warm."

"You get acclimatized," she replied, pulling a pink sweater more tightly around her shoulders. "How's Sherrie doing? I cannot *believe* what's happened to her. Have you heard anything about her bail hearing?"

"Not yet. I checked with Arthur's secretary on the way here and she said it's the last item on the docket for today."

"Poor Sherrie. She'll wear a hole in the concrete of her cell pacing away the hours."

I took a bite of the cookie and smiled as a large chunk of milk chocolate melted in my mouth. "Mmmm, that's absolutely sinful. You know my hyper friend pretty well."

"We've been together since she took over the business," she replied.

"Ah, yes, the business. Did Sherrie explain that I wanted to look over the books? Since you've been together so long, have you seen anything unusual in the finances that I should pay attention to?" I asked.

"Not really. I just handle the payroll and taxes for her and deal with the suppliers for the routine ingredients that are drop-shipped to the stores. Sherrie handles the over-all finances and property management herself. I don't even have the password for her computer," she said.

Ah, Sherrie, I thought. There's a bit of your father still lingering. "Not a problem, Mary Lou. She gave it to me, though I'm sure she'd rather have eaten razor blades. I'd like to poke around in her files for a while, both electronic and paper. You wouldn't have a key to the file cabinets, would you?"

"Are you kidding?" she laughed. "You don't think the queen actually does her own filing, do you?" She bent to the desk, pulled the middle drawer open and retrieved a key ring with a small version of the company logo jangling between multiple keys. "Follow me."

We walked through a rather Spartan office. The requisite copy machine sat in one corner with a couple of 60" folding tables on which were stacked neatly arranged piles of paper. Against the wall, several black metal file cabinets sat side by side with listings on the drawers like "Ingredient labels," "Discount Coupons," and "Suppliers." Mary Lou stopped in front of a locked door, isolated a key on the ring and unlocked it.

We stepped into an office where my friend's personality oozed from every corner. The walls were painted a cool yellow. A white lacquered desk with an executive chair upholstered in lime and white faced the door.   Two guest chairs of striped yellow fabric were opposite the desk.   Sherrie's "In" and "Out" baskets were the ridiculously expensive, hand-woven Longaberger brand, lined with pale yellow gingham. The "In" contained a stack that wobbled a good three inches over the edge with a variety of brightly colored post-it notes jutting here and there from the pile. The "Out" showed only gingham: a testament to Mary Lou's efficiency. A light green cordless phone sat on the right side of the desk and a cup embellished with lemons was on a crystal coaster to the left. A small solid oak file cabinet served as the base for giant philodendra that spilled from a white vase. On the matching credenza behind the desk, a row of pictures in crystal frames showcased both her domestic and wild menagerie. One picture had tipped over and lay face down at the end. I walked around the desk and turned it over. Smiling from the photo was Dave in a beautifully cut charcoal suit and Sherrie in dove gray silk, accented with a scarf of geometric patterns in black and white.

I turned toward Mary Lou and raised a questioning eyebrow.

"It depends on the mood," she answered. "Lately, it's only upright when Dave's on his way in or she's expecting one of the franchisees who's been around long enough to have worked with Dave."

"Not exactly an advertisement for marital bliss," I sighed. Mary Lou pushed at the Berber carpet with the toe of her sandal.

"C'mon, Mary Lou. Sherrie has absolutely no filter between her brain and her mouth. I can't believe you didn't know exactly how she felt about her marriage."

She looked at me and blew an unsteady breath from her inflated cheeks. "You're right, Cassie. I did know and Sherrie had a pretty mean mouth when she got wound up. But I can't believe she'd do anything to hurt Dave. Hell, when my husband ran off with his secretary, Sherrie loaned me the money to get an apartment and a lawyer. She's the most generous person I've ever met. You can't believe that a woman who feeds stray cats has it in her to murder someone."

"I don't. But most people don't know her like we do."

We heard the door open to the outer office and a male voice yell, "Hey, Mary Lou, where should I put these packages?"

Turning in tandem, we saw the familiar brown shorts and shirt of the package delivery service. I waved her forward, saying, "Go. I'll be fine in here."

She nodded and walked through the door. As she pulled it closed with a gentle click and I heard her say, "Hi, George. I've been waiting for those." I turned back to the credenza and returned the picture of Sherrie and Dave to its face down position. While I booted up the computer, listening to the soft whirling of the machine getting ready for work, a screen saver of brightly colored fish swam lazily across the monitor. From the right lower corner of the screen, a Great White Shark appeared and began to leisurely swallow the fish, one by one. When the shark was all by itself, he turned toward me and rudely belched. I laughed aloud and spun the chair 180 degrees. The row of photos reminded me to call good neighbor, Bruce, to feed the kitties. That gallery of pictures was the perfect example of the pure, tender heart of my Sherrie, except for one tiny exception.

"Oh, no, you don't," I said to the imaginary bad guys, as I righted the picture of the Walters in happier times. "I'm not giving you any excuse to read too much into this situation. OK, Cassie, time to do a little authorized snooping."

TEN

Several hours had passed in a mind-numbing search of Sherrie's payables. I tapped the mouse over the icon and produced hard copy. Even with Mary Lou's help to filter the records down to the most recent three years, there was still heavy work ahead to separate the wheat from the chaff. Cassie Grimes: Baking Pun-aholic.

At a little after three, Mary Lou breezed into the office following a quick rap-tap-tap on the door. "Could you sign these, Cassie?" she asked, handing me a stack of paychecks.

"No Problemo," I said and picked up a silver pen.

Mary Lou did a tsk-sigh combo and said, "Sometimes, I really hate people. Sherrie's locked up in jail, and the stores rang the phone off the hook this morning, worrying about getting their checks. A few had enough sense to ask about her, but there were just as many who thought *she* was inconveniencing *them* with Dave's disappearance and her arrest."

"Ingrates. Why feeding their family is more important than the queen's predicament, is a mystery to me," I said, scrawling my signature across the bottom of the checks as a thought hit me. "Hey, should we call your bank to tell them that a different signature will be on the payroll?"

"Already done," she said. "And the woman I spoke with acted like I was nuts to even bother. She said that as long as we didn't protest someone cashing it, which we wouldn't know until we got our next statement or our checks started bouncing, their system probably wouldn't notice. So much for bank security."

"Not surprising," I replied. "Big Brother is already too involved in my life, so I'm fine with that."

"I guess. But delivering them means I can't be here to help you."

"I'll be fine," I said. "I'm just waiting for the print out of vendor lists and payment history to take home with me; pretty boring stuff. Besides, Sherrie would have a fit if the stores didn't keep those cookies rolling. Just point me to the paper supply and do what you have to do."

"Sit tight," she said, returning to the outer office. A moment later, she was back with two reams of paper that she placed on the corner of the desk. "There you go. Well, Cassie, I'm outta here. I'll lock the door so you won't be disturbed. Just close it when you leave." The computer beeped a little exit music for Mary Lou and I turned back to its screen.

The printer was spitting out the complete list of invoices and payments for every company from whom Beachside Bread had received either product or service. Even with narrowing the list to the last three years, it made for some serious tree killing. The paper was stacking up as I scanned the screen for names that appeared often or in more than one category. There were hefty, monthly checks to Visa, covering an assortment of "business expenses." Yeah, right. Checks payable to Tom's company slowly trickled to zero. Wondering if these were from the multiple business failures that Sher had alluded to, I moved to the outer office to check the file cabinets for further documentation.

Hanging vendor files were alphabetized in Sherrie's own system; some by a company's name, some by the first names of individuals. The files were overstuffed with invoices for several years, the most current at the back. I recognized some of the data from the reports I'd been printing, but there was no hard copy for any business ventures with Junior.

"Now where would those be, Sherrie?" I asked aloud to no one. "Maybe in the credenza? A snooping we will go, a snooping we will go. Hi, ho, the dayreo, a snooping we will go," I sang to make some noise as I turned my back on the outer office whose window showed a nearly deserted lot as the work day came to a close.

After rubbing my weary eyes in a way that avoided smearing my mascara, I tapped the report key to open a window on Company Financials and printed Profit and Loss Statements and Balance Sheets for Beachside Bread and DaveSher Enterprises. OK, maybe I really didn't need to know these details, but I just couldn't resist the temptation of knowing exactly what my friend's little enterprise was worth. The Beachside Bread Company showed serious income balanced by a fair amount of out go. Sherrie was doing nicely for a business of that size, but not excessively so. The P& L for DaveSher showed a very healthy gross profit, too, but the bottom line shrank significantly due to Sherrie's salary. While her six-figure wages were impressive, I'd actually expected more considering the life style they led.

The balance sheet gave a clearer picture. The cash on hand was well into six figures, but impressive as that was, the assets delineated further down made me emit a low whistle.

"Whoa, girlfriend," I said aloud, "This is a few little buildings?" I moved the cursor to the line for property owned by the corporation and hit it for a more detailed explanation than the one line entry of $8 million and change. Their real estate holdings showed several condos that were rental units, two strip centers and a hefty share of a high rise office building. "No wonder Daddy could underwrite Tom's ventures." I hit the print button again, and swiveled 180 degrees to continue my search for the missing paper trail of the father/son escapades.

The drone of paper spewing from the printer was the chorus for my chant of "Where are you? Where are you?" as I rummaged through the files in the center of the credenza. "Double Damn," I murmured as I closed the doors on my fruitless search. When I turned back toward the desk I looked up into the eyes of a man striding toward me clenching his fists.

Lurching backward, I gasped and crashed into the credenza. Pictures skidded over the surface as the chair tipped, dumping me to the floor. "How did you get in here?" I squeaked, forcing my wobbly legs underneath me and trying to put the chair between us.

"I used my key," he growled. "What the hell do you think you're doing?"

Two and two finally added to four, giving the panic that threatened to close my throat some much-needed help from rising anger. I looked up into the dark eyes of a guy over six feet whose chestnut hair sported gray at the temples. His coral golf shirt and navy slacks were obviously expensive, but rumpled from a day spent in the heat. He shared his father's nose, but I'd bet the lines around his mouth and eyes were not from smiling, but from wearing a permanent scowl.

"I'm here on behalf of the business' *real* owner," I replied in a surprisingly even voice. "And this is most certainly *not* your company, yet, Tom."

"It will be when that murdering bitch gets what's coming to her. I'm here to take control until I get to watch them put her down like one of her strays."

That did it. Good sense was out the window replaced by righteous indignation. "In your dreams," I snarled. "Sherrie gave me Durable Power of Attorney to oversee the business until your father is found or we prove her innocence, whichever comes first."

"We'll see about that," he said as he started around the desk. "It might be a little tough for you to handle things from the hospital."

I was trying to push the chair aside to make a break for it while keeping my eyes glued to Tom. I darted a glance toward the only door offering a way out and broke into a smile.

"You think this is funny? I'm going to enjoy wiping that smile off your face," he said.

"Not very likely," I said, sweeping an arm grandly toward the door and waiting for his gaze to follow.

Leaning against the frame was Jim Stillman. Tom's head followed my gesture and he snarled, "You think he's going to stop me?"

"Bet your ass, I do," I said.

Tom Walters roared as he grabbed one of the guest chairs and raised it over his head. He charged toward the door where Stillman was still slouched as I screamed, "Noo! Jim!" I saw Stillman lift an eyebrow before he dived into a forward roll beneath the chairs' descent and kicked upward into Walter's outstretched body. The chair fell harmlessly to the floor and Walters collapsed, gasping for breath. As he rose, Stillman grabbed Tom's right arm, twisting it behind his back. He pulled him from the floor and shoved him into the wall with enough force to dislodge a large Impressionist print framed in gold.

"Got your answer?" Stillman asked with a shove that sent Walters sprawling again in the direction of the door. "It's polite to listen when a lady speaks."

"This isn't over," Tom Walters wheezed as he slowly stood. "I'll have charges brought against you so fast your head will swim."

"Slow learner," Stillman said to me with a shrug. He unbuttoned his shirt pocket and pulled out a mini-recorder. He hit the play button, adjusted the volume and turned it toward Walters. "I'm going to enjoy wiping that smile off your face," replayed to an astonished Walters. "See you around," Stillman said as his hand flicked toward the outer office

Tom took a measured step toward Stillman and stopped. He threw venomous looks over his shoulder as he reversed himself and stalked out of the office. We heard the outer door slam as I sat on the edge of the desk, folded my arms and demanded,

"What took you so long?"

"A simple 'Thank You' would be sufficient."

"But I could have been hurt," I whined.

"The operative word here, Cookie, is 'could,'" he replied.

I looked around at the mess in Sherrie's office and nodded. "Guess you're right."

"Find anything?" he asked.

"Yes and no." I straightened the stack of papers and stuffed them into the denim briefcase that Mary Lou had provided earlier. "I'm taking these reports home to read more thoroughly. I also found several entries from Daddy to Junior, but no files to tell us what for. Maybe you should check more into Junior's business."

"Maybe. Leave a note for Mary Lou about this," he said, taking in the room, "and I'll follow you back."

"Good idea," I said as I grabbed a post-it from the desk's middle drawer.

"I'm full of them," he said.

"Well, you're full of something," I agreed as I scribbled a brief explanation. I grabbed my purse and the note and walked toward the door. Stillman did a slight bow from the waist and waved his arm in an invitation to precede him. I reset the lock on the door and glanced back to find him taking a cookie and a handful of napkins from the entryway table. I repeated his bow and gesture, followed him out and jiggled the door to make sure the lock was set.

Stillman silently walked me to the little green Beemer and extended his hand for the remote key. I dropped it into his waiting palm and said, "Now what?" He spread a napkin on the ground and dropped a knee onto it. He produced a tiny flashlight from some unknown pocket and quickly checked the underside of the car. Satisfied, he stood and offered the key, but withdrew it again leaving my hand grabbing air. "Enough with the games," I said and he absently handed me the key. I hit the button, tossing the briefcase onto the back seat and said, "See you back at the beach. Got any plans for…"

"Shhh," he interrupted, "Listen." I shifted my weight to the other foot and complied as he slowly turned his head back and forth, scanning the lot and the street ahead.

"Bugs," I said. "Loud ones. So what? It's Florida. I just hope it's not an army of mosquitoes heading for dinner on my bare legs."

Jim shook his head. "Too many, too loud. Stay here." He turned on his heel and walked briskly toward the opposite end of the strip center.

"Don't think so," I called to his receding back as I flipped the strap of my purse over my head and jogged to catch up. The closer we got to the end of the building, the louder the buzzing became. We rounded the corner and followed the sound to a large shed standing next to a dumpster. The decibel level of the insects rose in direct correlation to the stench emanating from the storage/trash area. "Whew!" I exclaimed, pinching my nose. "Somebody needs to call the trash guys for an early pick-up."

Stillman retrieved latex gloves from his pants pocket and pulled them on. He heaved the sliding metal door on the Dumpster's side and it opened with a screech. I walked to him and stood on tippy-toes to peer over his shoulder as he swept a small beam of light from a key chain over its interior. Rusted metal and a few lonely scraps of paper were the only things to see. "Damn," he muttered and took the few steps to the shed's door that was closed and latched. Light glinted from the padlock that had been cut off and discarded in the grass. He flipped the hinged latch and nudged the door open. A swarm of angry flies made their escape as I backed up, swatting the air around my head. He merely turned his head, waiting for the rush to subside. He swept the interior with the small light, ending with the beam centered on a crumpled body whose back rested against the distinctive green of a John Deere riding mower. Stillman moved the light to the body's face and asked, "Recognize him?"

I forced myself toward the open door and stared at lifeless brown eyes in a head sitting awkwardly on a chest awash in blood. Stumbling backward, I bent at the waist and wretched bile and cookie onto the asphalt.

"Stay with me, Cassie," Jim said as he bent over and plucked a business card from the victim's open briefcase that lay a few feet away. "Carl Morgan, Paradise Food Service. Ever heard of him?"

I shook my head slowly from side to side.

"God, Jim," was all I could say, wiping my mouth with the back of my hand.   I was shivering uncontrollably in spite of the muggy air. Stillman took my arm, gently turned me from the shed and led me away from the gruesome scene. When we'd rounded the building, he sat on the curb and patted the space next to him. I sank slowly to the sidewalk, hugged my purse and began to rock unconsciously back and forth. Jim wrapped an arm around my shoulder and reached with the other hand into my bag. After rummaging through the jumbled contents, he pulled out my phone. I stared mutely ahead, trying to quiet my lurching stomach as Jim called 911. After clipped conversation, he flicked the cell closed and returned it to my purse.

"Now what?" I mumbled.

"Now, we wait," he said. And so we did, with Jim lost in his silent thoughts and yours truly doing her best to mentally erase the hideous scene that kept replaying inside my throbbing head.

****

"How many times do I have to say that I don't know that guy?" I said as I rubbed my forehead in frustration. Stillman was several feet away talking with another officer when a silver BMW's lights swept the parking lot and a voice I instantly recognized raised above the rest.

"You damn well better let me see my wife."

I'd left a message on Gene's cell while we waited for the police to arrive, needing the moral support badly and dreading the husbandly frustration that was bound to accompany his presence. Suddenly, the crowd parted and Gene bolted toward me with Arthur Goldman in his wake. He grabbed me into a hug as Arthur quietly talked to the officer who'd been taking my statement. The officer shrugged, closed his notebook and walked back to his green and white cruiser.

"How'd you manage that?" I asked Arthur over Gene's shoulder.

"Simply pointed out that if you weren't under arrest, that you were done speaking with the police this evening," Arthur replied.

"Cassie, we've got to talk," Gene said as he relaxed his embrace just enough to look down into my eyes without releasing me completely.

My face reflexively scrunched into a lemon-bite parody. Expecting the usual admonition about my nosy ways getting me in over my head, I said, "Ah, Gene, it's not like I could have seen this coming."

"Of course not," he sighed. "I was telling Arthur about some things I'd uncovered when your call came. This is more complicated than you think and we all need to be up to speed," he said as he nodded in Stillman's direction.

An uncomfortable silence caused me to shift uneasily from foot to foot when Arthur's soothing accent broke in. "Let's reconvene at the Perkins on the corner of Summerlin and MacGregor." Gene hit the remote lock on Sher's car, extended his hand for the keys to the little green Beemer and glanced at Stillman. Jim nodded and glided in measured rhythm to his car. Everyone was moving, but I was still rooted to the same spot. Gene gently pulled me forward and slipped a protective arm around my shoulder as we walked. He opened the passenger door and I dropped onto the soft leather seat.

As Gene turned left onto the nearly empty street, I finally found my voice. "So, what have you found?" I asked.

"DaveSher Enterprises owns several properties. But one new warehouse has recently been acquired. Documents had been filed by Kowalski, for a building jointly owned by Dave and Tom Walters and some guy named Carl Morgan."

"Oh, God," I groaned, putting my hands over my face as the image of Morgan's lifeless eyes and bloody shirt played against my tightly shut eyelids.

"What?"

I dropped my hands and stared resolutely at the double yellow line on the road ahead. "The guy that Stillman and I just discovered was Morgan. What the hell does that mean?"

"That we should go home," Gene answered.

"We can't go home. After tonight, we're involved in at least one murder," I said as I pointed toward the entrance to Perkins. "I might as well have a double latte. I probably won't be sleeping much tonight."

"Probably not," he said, breaking the car for the turn into a nearly deserted lot. "There's more, Cassie. This is way beyond the usual messes you seem to attract."

****

Arthur was chatting amiably from a booth in the restaurant's rear to a waitress in khaki shorts and a bright green polo with the diner's logo stitched on her chest. Her short dark hair was cut in one of the hip, messy styles favored by the young, allowing her to show off several piercings per ear. Stillman was on the opposite side of the booth, his back to the wall. As we approached, Jim and Arthur rose. Jim stepped aside, so I slid into the booth as Gene took the seat facing me. Our companions resumed their aisle seats just as the waitress returned with coffee.

My spoon clinked against the white ceramic mug as I added liquid creamer from one of those little plastic cups. It was the only sound coming from our table. Arthur finally raised his mug in a toast that swept the air and said,

"Shall we begin? Cassie, as I suspected, Sherrie's bail was denied." I was still so shaken by our gruesome discovery that my only response was to nod and sip the metallic coffee. Silence continued until Arthur took charge again. "Perhaps Gene would be so kind as to explain what he's found?"

"Sure," Gene raised his eyes, sweeping both Jim and me with a less than hospitable glance. "I checked any public record of the Walters' finances to see what might turn up. There was very little since DaveSher Enterprises is privately held. Then, I decided to do a title search. Most of their real estate is in Sherrie's name. Convenient, eh?"

"And just maybe a concession to the fact that Sherrie is my tender age and Dave is double parked next to a two by six by six foot condo," I said, glaring at him.

"Which she probably thinks he was overdue to inhabit." He returned the stare and upped the amps. "The only other property was the one I told you about, Cassie."

"In the car," I blurted when Stillman pinched my thigh under the table. "Something about a warehouse being jointly owned by Dave, Tom and Morgan."

"Right," he nodded. "Dad and Junior were listed as minority owners with 20% each. Carl Morgan owned 60%, under the umbrella name of CM Management, Inc."

"Hold on," I interrupted. "I know that name. They were listed in several categories under payables."

"Beginning when, my dear?" Arthur asked.

"I can't tell you the exact date, but no more that a couple of years," I replied. "Some vendors had been with them since Dave was a single guy. CM Management didn't show up until recently, but when they did, Beachside Bread did a lot of business with them."

"Maybe Dave started doing a little nest building for himself as Sherrie got more and more nasty," Gene said, fixing me with a look.

"Or maybe," I returned his look and added a nose crinkle for emphasis, "his kid came up with another 'sure thing' that he convinced Daddy to invest in. He stashed it in the company's payables after Sherrie insisted he cut Junior off."

"But, if Sherrie was the business genius you claim, wouldn't she have known something about CM Management?" Gene asked.

"Well, yeah, I, uh, yeah, uh, I..I.. guess so," I stuttered.

"Ahem," Arthur gently cleared his throat. "Perhaps the files in your car will yield more information, Cassie. There is also the matter of Mr. Morgan having been represented by Mr. Kowalski -- rather unsuccessfully, I might add – for burglary in the State of Ohio."

"Unsuccessfully?" Jim asked. Verbose, thy name is definitely not Stillman.

"Quite," Arthur replied. "It resulted in his being sent to the Mansfield penitentiary for a period of two to five years. Since the felony didn't involve a weapon, he was paroled after two and rejoined society with no recidivism."

"Were there problems in Florida?" Jim was really getting into the swing of things.

"One parking ticket," Arthur replied, "for five dollars on an expired meter in the Fort Myers Beach public parking area a year ago."

"So he's been here a while," I said.

"So it would seem," Arthur answered.

"We need to know more about this guy and how he ties to the Walters," Gene said. "Maybe those files can tell us." Gene nodded to Arthur who stood as the insistent whoop and wail of a car alarm brought silence over the restaurant. Two couples standing by the door both looked at each other and headed for the lot.

Our waitress was standing to the side with a coffeepot ready for refills as Gene slid across the seat. She rolled her eyes at the sound and spoke loudly, "More coffee?"

"Does that happen often?" I asked.

"Oh, yeah," she replied, as she poured for Jim. "What a great idea. Give people who are scared of remotes and computers a key smarter than they are and let the show begin. The hostess on the day shift has become an expert at turning the damn things off since the owners don't have a clue."

I continued to babble about Dave's sneaky ways and Sherrie's innocence, glancing occasionally toward the door. Both men returned to the hostess, but the wailing continued. I frowned at Stillman who was already on his feet. Just then, Gene pushed through the door and stalked toward us.

"Where's the briefcase," I asked.

"Gone," he said. "Arthur, someone slashed the top of your car to get it."

"What!" I yelled. "Why would anyone want…"

"CM Management," Stillman interrupted. "I'll be in touch," he said as he dropped a five on the table and headed for his car.

"But where are you going?" I asked his back, sliding out of the booth to follow. Gene stepped to the end, put a hand on my shoulder and pushed down.

"Hey!" I exclaimed.

"Arthur," he said, "Would you mind handling the police report? I'd like to take Cassie home now."

"Of course," he replied. "I'm afraid I don't have another car to offer, though."

"That's fine," Gene said. "We'll need a lift back to Beachside Bread. She's better off with me, anyway."

"Hey, macho man, I've got things I want to do, too."

"Hate your luck," he replied.

"I want to see Sherrie. It's her life we're talking about."

"Yours is more important to me now. You're in danger, Cassie. Or can't you figure that out?"

Arthur cleared his throat again. Either he's got a cold or he's allergic to warring spouses. "May I offer a suggestion? Gene can drop you at the jail in the morning. I'll join you for a conversation with your friend and then you can drop me at the office. My car will be at your disposal through my afternoon appointments. Is that acceptable?"

"Swell," I replied.

"Yeah, swell," Gene said in a much different tone. "It's very generous, Arthur, considering the result of your last auto loan."

"Hey, that wasn't my fault," I said.

Another cough from Arthur. The guy definitely needs a throat lozenge. "Insurance is often a needed commodity and I am adequately prepared. I'll take the two of you back to your vehicle, Gene." He waved us toward the door as he pulled the phone from his pocket and speed dialed the police. His clipped conversation ended before he began the return trip to Shers' office.

The little white Beemer was parked outside the yellow crime-scene tape so we attracted little attention. We thanked Arthur and climbed into our car for the drive home. It was a frigid affair, not just from the blasting air conditioner. When we pulled into the drive, I let myself out of the car and trotted to catch up with Gene's long strides. I tentatively slipped my hand into Gene's and said,

"They'll be desperate for a walk. Do you think, for the kids sake, we could declare a truce?"

"All right." He stopped on the porch and pulled me into a tentative hug, causing Maggie and A.J. to hurl themselves at the glass. "I'm worried about you, Cass."

"I know. Me too. Let's harness the crew and walk this off in the moonlight."

ELEVEN

I slept badly. Maggie and A.J. spent the night pacing the bed. At about 3:00 a.m., they ran to the door, dived beneath the closed curtain and barked maniacally. A fevered bark echoed from next door, to be answered from my two and so on until, I couldn't stand it anymore. Gene was still snoring as I pushed from the bed and threw a blue terry cover up over my head. I eased the door open a crack, quickly squeezed through and slid it shut again before the dynamic duo could follow. I leaned my back against the door, straining to hear what had caused the doggie alarm to go off. Inching to the end of the porch, I peeked around the corner. Nothing seemed out of place until a high pitched squeal of tires from next door indicated a car speeding away. I jumped on a wobbly table to get a better view, but the eight-foot high bushes that served as separation between the properties blocked my view. Seconds later, two large shadows emerged from the beach side of the Westward Arms, preceded by a much shorter one. I slid our door open and pushed the dogs back with my foot.

"Go back to sleep, hon," I called to Gene. "It's just the ancient juvenile delinquents next door. I'll be back in a minute." A loud snort was the only response he offered.

My bare feet were freezing as I jogged to the end of the sand bar and spoke loudly enough to carry over the surf.

"Hey, you two, do I have to call the cops to get some sleep?"

"Yoo-hoo!" rang out, followed by an audible "Shoosh!"

Snookie was doing an abbreviated dance on her tiny back legs, so I bent to pet her and prevent a trip to the doggie chiropractor. Behind her, Madeline's sturdy legs were planted apart while Gladys' equally chubby ankles wobbled uncertainly. After having given the wiener dog her due, I rose and said,

"So, ladies, what kind of trouble are you getting into in the middle of the night?"

Gladys suddenly lost her balance and started to crumble toward Snookie. Madeline clothes-lined her beloved pet, yanking her out of the way just before Mount Gladys smashed her into hot dog patte.

"For heaven's sake, Gladys. You're embarrassing yourself," Maddie chided.

"Ah, lighten up, Maddie. Yur rainin' on my parade. I juss had a perfecly wunnerful evenin."

"Which included cocktails, eh, Gladdie?" I said. Her slurred words were a perfect explanation for why she'd nearly squashed the dachshund. She started giggling so hard that I was laughing in unison as she slid from a sitting position to her back and began making sand-angels. Maddie was not similarly amused. She'd turned her back and was staring North with arms crossed, Snookie waiting patiently at her feet. I wiped tears from my eyes and stooped to help Gladys stand. OK, there was no way I could lift that kind of bulk unaided, so I did my best to push her into a sitting position and rose with a hand to the small of my aching back. Maddie remained unmoved with the breeze plastering her floral nightgown against her considerable backside and thighs. The thin cover up I was wearing was flapping too and I was starting to chill. Curiosity beat shivers, so I asked,

"Maddie, why weren't the two of you out in tandem as usual?"

She answered without turning. "I wasn't invited. Snooks and I were enjoying her constitutional, when Gladys got a call from the man she'd met at the Center. He asked her out for tonight and she didn't even notice how rude it was to make such last minute plans."

"Oh, fur Hevn's sake, Maddie. At our age, if we play har' to get, we'd never be got."

"So who is this mystery man?" I asked.

"His name is John. He's juss the cutest l'il thing. He took me to a secluded l'il nite spot where we drank Mango Martini's and talked about everything from big ban' music to big cars with giant tail fins. We'd switched to Mimosas when he took my hand, leaned into me and said, 'I never realized how much I loved those big rear ends.' Well, I was juss a l'il bit tipsy by then, so before I knew it, I said, 'You mean like mine?' and he said, 'Esacly like yurs.'"

I tried to picture a senior citizen chubby chaser puttin' the moves on Gladys. Yikes. "And then what happened?" I asked.

"He copped a l'il feel and said he'd like to show me how much he liked what he was seein', but he needed to plan ahead with a taste of Viagra."

That did it. Before I could stop it, I said, "Yeeww."

"Now, sweetie," Gladys said, "At our age thas to be 'spected. So he brought me home and we necked in the parkin' lot for a while."

Madeline broke her silence. "And Snookie's superior hearing picked up the sounds of horny, teen-age wannabies and started to growl. With what's been going on at your place, Cassie, I grabbed my gun and went to investigate. He wasn't even gentleman enough to walk her to the door. When I came out of the elevator, he peeled out of the parking lot like the hounds of Hell were on his heels. Well, Gladys was so smashed..."

"Was not," Gladys interjected.

"...annihilated, gone, loopy, sloppy, skunky drunk, that I tried to get her to walk it off. Obviously, she's beyond that, too."

Madeline turned her back again and Gladys said, "Jealous."

"What!" Madeline turned, hands on her hips.

"Jealous. Greenie-eyed monster's got you."

"Girls, c'mon now." Cassie Grimes, diplomat.

"Never realized she was such a slut," Madeline said.

"Never realized she was such a prude," Gladys replied. "Whassa matter, Maddie? Been so long since you got a tingle in your panties that you think the only reason for bein' wet down there needs a Depends?"

"Well, I never…" Maddie sputtered.

"Maybe thas the problem," Gladys replied, trying unsuccessfully to stand.

"Please, ladies, it's too late for this nonsense. I've got to get back to bed. C'mon, Gladys, I'll help you up." I was tugging with both of my arms on one of hers, when the hair on Snookie's back stood straight up. She leapt six inches into the air and barked furiously. The hair on my neck matched Snookie's as I reflexively let go of Gladys and we fell in a mound next to a seriously pissed-off dachshund.

As two distinctly male shadows emerged from the cover of the sand bar, Madeline thrust her hand into the pocket of her robe. When she pulled it out, the moon glinted off the barrel of the revolver she'd aimed at them. Jim Stillman raised his hands in unison with his voice.

"Whoa. We're here to offer whatever assistance we can to restore peace before you wake the entire beach."

"It's Gene and Jim, Maddie. Please put down the gun." She did.

"Cassie, for the love of God, please come inside," Gene called. "And you two," he shook his finger between them. "You're old enough to know better."

"One would think," Madeline said as she pushed the gun back into her pocket. "But then, there hasn't been much thinking tonight."

"Fun beats thinkin', is what I'm thinkin'," Gladys said, flopping onto her back and remaking the sand angels.

"Ah, fellas, we could use a hand getting Gladys up to bed," I said.

"Glad to oblige," Jim said. "Up we go, Sweetheart. My partner and I will walk you to your door." Gene and Jim crouched next to Gladys and lifted in unison as I pushed from behind. When she was wedged upright between the men, I draped a chubby arm over each set of shoulders and they maneuvered her toward the building with Madeline, Snookie and me moving ahead to catch the doors.

Maddie and the dog left the elevator, walked past the first white door in the aqua hall of the seventh floor and slipped a key into Number 702. We stepped into the condo decorated in various shades of beige, with framed prints of shells and sand dollars creating a beach theme typical of furnished rentals. Gene turned sideways to negotiate his giggling burden through her bedroom door, with Jim pushing from the rear. They turned Gladys so that her thighs were pressed against a bedspread of pelicans and fish and eased her downward.

Gladys made a half-hearted swipe at their retreating backsides and they quickly stepped out of range. Before collapsing on the bed, she managed to wink at me and say, "Ooh, Cassie, so many men, so little, uh, somethin'. I forget. Toodle Loo!" With that, she fell back, closed her eyes and began snoring softly.

"Thanks, and I apologize," Madeline said.

"Not to worry," I replied. "What happens on the beach, stays on the beach."

The three of us returned to the elevator, quietly descended and slipped through the path that was beaten in the sand bar. We parted at the walk and entered our respective condos without a word. The dogs tried to hit us up for a walk of their own, but I wasn't in the mood and Gene was downright surly.

"Sorry, guys, morning's going to be here soon enough. We'll walk then," I said and added, "Thanks, Gene. Say, Gladys had a mystery date tonight."

"And this would be important to me for what reason?" he asked.

"Just making conversation," I replied.

"Don't," he answered, as he pulled the comforter around his shoulders and rolled over. The red glow from the alarm clock showed only three minutes passing before Gene was snoring again.

I rummaged through the nightstand for emergency earplugs, shoved the foam pellets into my ears and turned off the light. Maggie and A.J. flopped disgustedly against my side as I groaned inwardly over the few hours left before the alarm rang. Prison visitation and sleep depravation. I had to get a new game plan for vacations.

****

The alarm rang moments later, or so it seemed. I smacked the snooze alarm, giving Gene a few extra minutes to shower and become more civil. After harnessing the dogs, I started down the stairs for our usual route. We reached the end of the sidewalk and I automatically turned toward the water. The leashes snapped taut as Maggie and A.J. pulled toward the parking lot.

"What's wrong, you guys?" I said. "You know the route."

They only pulled harder. I tried a light tug and Maggie dug in, lunging forward so hard she began to cough. Still, she refused to change direction.

"Fine, you win," I said. There was abbreviated landscaping between the parked cars and the longer building that ran perpendicular to ours toward Estero Blvd. I was too cranky from sleep deprivation to insist. If they wanted to pee on impatiens and hibiscus bushes, so be it. They both did their thing on the first hibiscus whose red flowers were just re-opening in the morning light when Maggie leapt over the curb and headed toward our old

Beemer. My head was turned toward A.J., still in pursuit of bush number two when I felt Maggie's leash tighten as she ran out of rope. I stared from my hand down the length of purple leash to where it disappeared beneath the car.

"Have you lost you doggie mind?" I said, giving a slight tug on the leash. Maggie responded by pulling in the opposite direction and whining. A.J. was now trying to belly-crawl beneath the chassis to join her. I stomped in frustration and said, "Dammit, you two, get out of there!"

"Language, please," said a voice behind me. I dropped the leashes and threw a whirling forearm toward the sound, which was caught neatly in Jim Stillman's right hand.

"Dammit, dammit, DAMMIT, Jim."

"And a good morning to you, too," he replied. "What's up with the walking popcorn balls?"

"I don't know. We always go in the same direction, but today they insisted on coming out here. Maggie decided to inspect the underside of the car and A.J. followed. Why?" I shrugged. A dog's mind can be a complex thing. "Maybe some discarded food or a lizard. Hell, I don't know." I picked up the ends of the leashes still protruding from the cars' bumper and said, "Come. Now!" A.J.'s furry butt showed immediately as he backed out. Maggie continued to moan without moving, but my patience was gone. I flexed my knees, crouched and forcefully pulled her toward me. When she cleared the bumper, I grabbed her and stood. The moaning continued, so I thumped her on the head with a forefinger and said, "Shut up!"

Jim was doing a one-handed push-up by the car, peering beneath. While visions of my hands wrapped around squirming white fur danced in my head and A.J. danced at my feet, Jim rose and said,

"No, Cassie, I think you'd better listen to her." He clapped his hands to dust off the sand from the asphalt and extended one to scratch Maggie's ear. "You are a very smart dog."

"Ok, now you've lost your mind too," I said. "I'm just not in the mood for this kind of...."

Jim raised a hand for silence. "Give her scrambled eggs for breakfast and I'll throw in a steak. How's that sound, Maggie?" She stopped moaning and stared expectantly at Jim.

"Why would I do that?"

"Because, Cass, there are wires running from a Beachside Bread Bag to the engine of the car. Take the dogs inside. I'll handle this."

"Oh, my God, who could have..."

"Go," Jim commanded.

"We don't have to tell Gene about this do we?" I asked.

"I'll get back to you," he said before dropping to the ground to look beneath his rental. Satisfied he electronically keyed his trunk, removed a leather tool kit and gave his wrist one more flick to send me on my way.

As I slid the glass doors aside, the sounds of our shower running gave me a brief reprieve. The smells of coffee drug me toward the kitchen where I enhanced a mug of Mr. Coffee's finest with the requisite sweetener and flavored artificial creamer. By wrapping my hands firmly around the cup, I managed to get the shaking under control as I sipped. Gene and I passed silently in the hall as he headed for his second cup with a pink towel wrapped around his waist.

I shut the bathroom door on the tense quiet, turned the shower back on and stepped in. The steam rolled uncomfortably around me, so I opened the window in the shower itself to vent the already rising heat. I adjusted the water's temperature to tepid for my final rinse and glanced toward the parking lot. Jim was facing the window with the offending bag in his right hand. He saluted with his left, smiled broadly and walked toward his condo.

I was still blushing furiously when I wiped the steam from the mirror with my own pink towel before tucking it under my arms to create a strapless, terry robe. Florida had always felt completely safe, so naked fit in nicely. Now, I felt vulnerable and shaken and guilty for the doubts that were creeping into my view of Sherrie. My longest friend was the vortex of a string of violent events whose threat was now sucking me in. Suspicious disappearances, threats, murder and bombs all led back to Sherrie. Was she the tragic target of circumstances spinning around her or had she helped set them in motion?

It's tough to slam a sliding door, but the sound of it shook me from my melancholy. I chugged the remains of my cold coffee and blew through my normal routine. Dried and painted, I studied the few options left hanging in the closet. I chose a pair of white Capri pants that I rolled to the length of Bermuda shorts and a yellow tank top with matching linen blouse. I tucked toes in desperate need of a pedicure into white flip-flops and patted sulking heads on the way to join Gene. On the opposite side of the porch, Jim sat in silence, looking at the surf.

As I locked our door, Gene rose. Men. They can't walk into a room without turning on the TV, but they can sit four feet away from one another and say nothing.

"So, Jim, I'm heading to the jail to meet Arthur and Gene's going back to his office. What's your itinerary?"

"I'll be around. Page me if you need to and I'll catch up." He was dressed in faded blue jeans and a black camp shirt that hung outside his jeans. As he stood, he reached beneath the shirt in the back and pulled out a small .38. He extended it toward Gene and asked, "Know how to use it?"

"There a reason for this?" Gene asked.

"Just a bad feeling," he said.

"Welcome to my world," Gene said, accepting the gun and slipping it into his pocket. It bulged awkwardly, but Gene would never untuck his shirt. The three of us walked to the cars and I shot Jim a nervous glance before Gene unlocked the door. Jim nodded slightly, the interior light flashed and we were soon leaving the parking lot just ahead of Jim. Once again, the interior of our car was icy. If I didn't leave Florida soon, I'd have pneumonia.

Since it seemed unlikely that Gene would be talking to me, I retrieved my cell and called Mary Lou.

"Beachside Bread," she answered.

"It's Cassie, Mary Lou. Did you find the note that we left about the mess?"

"And yellow tape all over the end of the building. What happened after I left?"

"Too much to explain right now. Do me a favor right away?"

"Sure"

"Zip the vendors transactions for the last three years and email them to Miss Lanahan at Arthur Goldman's office," I said.

"I'll do that right after I clean up this mess," she said. "But why? I thought you printed out those records last night."

"They were stolen."

"Oh, God," she moaned. "What next?"

It suddenly dawned on me that Mary Lou might be in danger. "Do you have a safe in the office?"

"Sure. Queenie checks it every day when she comes in."

"Do you have the combination?"

"Yeah. Why?"

"I want you to lock the doors and back up the files you're sending to Miss Lanahan. Then, lock the disc in the safe and get out of there."

"You're scaring me Cassie," she said. "What happened here?"

"Besides the mess around you, there was a body found behind the building."

"Oh, my God. Who was it?"

"A man named Carl Morgan. You know him?"

"Uh huh. Expensive clothes, drives – uh - drove a Porsche, came here more than any other rep. We dropped several old suppliers to buy his "gourmet ingredients." As if there's a designer sugar. Talk about a slick-tongued salesman."

"I've gotta go," I said as Gene braked for the light just before the jail. "Will you call Miss Lanahan and tell her what's coming? I'll be seeing Sherrie in a few minutes."

"Done. Then, I'm outta here. Tell her I'm praying for her and to call if she needs anything." The line went dead.

TWELVE

We pulled into an empty slot next to Arthur's silver sedan. Gene shifted immediately into reverse and stared straight-ahead, engine idling. The longer the silence continued, the angrier I became. Why was he mad at me? I hadn't caused this. OK, maybe I had caused our involvement, but Sherrie was – is – my closest friend. He should understand.

"Aren't you coming in?" I asked.

"I've got to get to Arthur's office for those files. Sherrie's dirty, Cass. I don't know how, but the shit is swirling around her like a sewage dump."

"You don't know that," I huffed. Of course, those same thoughts had swept through my mind in the bathroom this morning. I grabbed the handle and was half way through the door when a tidal wave of guilt swept over me. Sherrie was important to me, but was she so important that I'd keep lying to my true best friend? I leaned across the center console and kissed his cheek. More softly, I said, "This will all work out, Gene. I promise." He closed his eyes and nodded.

The car was already on the move when I stepped to the electronic eye that opened the doors. Arthur was waiting for me, dressed in his usual navy suit, white shirt and a stunning silk tie in geometric patterns of navy, dark olive and white.

"Good morning, Cassie," Arthur said. "Shall we go?" He nodded toward the dispatcher behind the bulletproof window and we crossed the lobby. Before we passed the palms in the center atrium, Officer Malloy stepped through the familiar door and stood waiting. Arthur paused to allow me to precede him.

I handed my purse to Malloy and said, "Good morning."

"M'am," he said as he extended his hand for Arthur's briefcase and added, "Mr. Goldman. Your package will be waiting when you leave."

"What package?" I asked as Malloy searched our things. I envisioned musty evidence boxes pulled from the depths of some storage facility, just begging to give up their secrets to the diligent search. OK, I watch a little too much TV police drama.

"The iris painting that we saw on our previous visit," Arthur said. "The artist was willing to negotiate a bit on the price and it will make the perfect birthday gift for my sister-in-law. Mad for purple."

Malloy returned our belongings, locked away his revolver and said, "Three to area six." Déjà vu, all over again. Had it really been only two days since I'd heard that the first time? I looked at the overhead camera and waved while we waited for Sherrie to move into the interview room.

"Hello," echoed around the room and Malloy badged the lock. Arthur and I took our seats at the table and moments later the interior door opened. Sherrie shuffled through in a gray polyester jumpsuit with Lee County stenciled on the left chest. Her face was clean except for the remains of her courtroom eye make-up which accented the dark circles beneath her eyes. She slid into the chair across from us and sent an angry look toward Arthur that softened only slightly when her eyes met mine.

"You look like hell," she said.

"Right back at ya," I replied. "Sorry about the bail, Sher."

"So much for high priced legal talent," she glared at Arthur. "How long will I be staying in this dump?"

"I'm not sure, my dear," Arthur replied. "This case is becoming very high profile after yesterday's developments. That tends to make the authorities irritable."

"Just because my bail was denied? I thought you expected this," she said. "My nails are a mess and just look at me. Cassie, can you believe I'm being forced to wear polyester? Me? And a terribly unflattering shade of gray to boot." She added a forced laugh that had the same effect on my mood that flatulence in an elevator would cause.

"Listen, Queenie, it's not always all about you. I was accosted by Tom in your office last night."

"See what I mean?" she said. "Now you know what an asshole he can be."

"I'm fine, thanks for asking," I snipped. "That's just the tip of the iceberg. We had to call the police again last night. Stillman and I found a body in the shack by your dumpster."

She paled slightly at this and, for a change, had no snappy retort. "Do you know who it was?"

I stared across the desk and instinctively took her hand. "Carl Morgan."

It hit her like a semi. Sherrie jerked her hand away so violently that the chair lurched backward, threatening to capsize. She gripped the edge of the table and started to keen,

"NO! NO! Nooooo!" she wailed as tears streamed down her face. "This can't be. We didn't do anything. Why am I being punished? Oh, Carl. Why? Why?" The sobbing became punctuated by racking breaths that preceded each outburst, building to a crescendo.

I was dumbfounded. Sherrie had cried when she heard that Dave was missing, but this was way more. What had been going on between Carl and her to cause such an impassioned reaction? I stared my question at Arthur, whose expression showed mild interest, but little more.

Gradually, the moaning was replaced by silence. Tears continued to stream down her face with her hand swiping periodically at her runny nose. I drew a deep breath and exhaled so

I wouldn't scream the questions flooding my mind. Arthur calmly snapped open his briefcase, withdrew a white handkerchief from its pocket and extended it to Sherrie. She wiped her eyes, removing what little mascara was left and swabbed her nose. When she lifted her gaze to mine, I was staring at a woman who'd aged before my eyes. The classic tale of Dorian Gray passed through my mind. I squashed the image and cleared my throat before addressing the friend I thought I knew.

"What's going on, Sherrie? What was Morgan to you?"

"He owns a company called Baking Gems," she sniffed. "You know how I like to get the very best." As Sherrie's wealth increased, her definition of "the best" became a matter of high cost. I usually experienced this idiosyncrasy while dining in restaurants where the wait staff fawned but the food was mediocre at double the price.

Arthur re-focused the discussion. "Your relationship with Mr. Morgan was purely professional?"

"Yes, darn it. Well, technically."

"Huh?" Cassie Grimes: queen of the brilliant rejoinder. I pushed back from the table and paced in an attempt to regain my vocabulary. "What do you mean, 'technically?' I'm having a Clinton-esque moment here, Sher. What exactly happened between you two?"

"Nothing, really. He became one of our main suppliers, so I saw him a lot. He was so funny and he really appreciated me as a business person," she said with her eyes glued to the table. "We could talk about anything. Do you have any idea how great it is to be with somebody who loves the same songs? Who talks about the same events that made a difference in your life? Who's interested in something other than pension plans and the golf channel?"

"Yeah, Sher, I'm married to one of those, though Gene is inordinately attached to ten o'clock police dramas, " I replied. "Get back to the 'technically' part."

"We got along so well," she said. "I mean, we'd be laughing together and he'd pat my hand. Then we'd hug as a greeting and that led to pecks on the cheek. Then he'd come by when Mary Lou was running errands and we'd steal a little kiss. Then the kisses led to tonsil hockey and some serious groping." She smiled at me, hoping her joke would draw a laugh. It didn't. Arthur shifted uncomfortably in his seat and I sat down. The smile faded and she said, "But I swear, Cass, we never actually had sex."

"Ok, now I get it," I said. I'd played the same game in high school to remain a 'technical virgin.' Often, with Jim Stillman. Good grief. History does tend to come back and bite you on the butt. No pun intended. "But if this guy was so great, why stop there?"

"I was married," she said. I raised an eyebrow. "I mean, I *am* married even though my lying rat of a husband was talking to that bottom feeder, Kowalski, about divorcing me. The irony is thick enough to gag you, isn't it?" She wiped her eyes again and straightened in her chair. "Oh, all right. Dave was planning his annual trip to see his navy buddies from 'the Big One'. I told Mary Lou that I was planning a separate vacation. Carl and I had been researching week-end trips to the Bahamas and then…Oh, Carl, why?" She buried her head in arms crossed on the table as the waterworks started anew.

I wasn't really surprised. Considering the age difference, I'd been expecting this for years. The sound track of my mind started playing the Eagles' tune. "You can't hide, your lyin' eyes. And your smi-ile is a thin disguise…" Suddenly, the electronic strains of a Russian folk dance played from my purse. I threw a look over my shoulder toward Malloy who nodded his permission. I frantically searched the scrambled confines of my bag and managed to answer before the third refrain put the caller to voice mail.

"Hello?"

"Cassie, it's Gene." Arthur was asking the top of Sherrie's head a series of questions designed to prevent any more surprises about her personal relationship to the deceased. I got up and walked the few feet to the corner of the room.

"Ah, Sweetie, I'm kinda busy here," I said in voice slightly more than a whisper.

"That's why I called. Aggie helped me search the files and there's something we think you should ask your pal, the brilliant business woman."

"Aggie again? Do I need to worry about you two?"

"Well, she would get a great senior discount at motels," he snorted. "Cassie, when Sherrie started buying ingredients from a company called 'Baking Gems'..."

"Carl Morgan's company," I interjected.

"Perfect. She was paying three times what she used to pay for basic ingredients, but the top line stayed about the same. Hence, no price increase to the consumer. And the bottom line was dropping dramatically. Did she ever talk to you about business being bad?"

"Not really. Her P&L looked pretty good to me."

"Not compared to other years. And, she was paying much less on estimated taxes because of the shrinking bottom line. So, Cassie, what do you think? Did Sherrie suddenly forget about profit or was something else going on?"

"Like what? You're losing me, Gene."

"Her payables match large payments to Baking Gems, a subsidiary of CM Management whose bank is located in the Cayman Islands. Her bottom line is shrinking like my shirt collars, but not her lifestyle or Dave would have been suspicious."

"What do your shirt collars have to do with this?"

"They're both laundry problems, Cass. Are you with me? Laundry. Pinpoint cotton or money, what's the difference?"

"Ah, shit, Gene. I don't believe this."

"Ask her, Cass."

"Ok," I said and snapped the phone closed.

"So, you're fairly confident that you and Mr. Morgan were discreet enough not to attract anyone's attention," Arthur said.

"I'm sure of it," Sherrie replied

I took my seat, put my forearms on the table and leaned forward, "Tell me again about your business relationship with Morgan."

"I told you. He sold the best of the best ingredients."

"And your bottom line was dropping like my aging chest. Did making money suddenly become unimportant to you?"

"C'mon, Cass, you're in business for yourself. Carl helped me get certain tax advantages."

"So Gene found out. Your estimated tax payments are much smaller, but then again, so is your bottom line. Dave didn't get the least bit suspicious? Even swapping top shelf Rum for Captain Morgan's wouldn't be enough."

"Hell, Cassie, he didn't pay attention to anything anymore. That forgetful old fart…"

"…was anything but from what I saw on that tape. Sheryl Marie Drexler Walters, you're lying to me. There is no way you'd let the profit slip away without a fight. Not with your habit of expensive beach bags," I said. I stared pointedly at her and watched as the allusion to what lay tucked in a safety deposit box sank in. "What was really going on besides dry humpin' in the back room?"

"Sheryl," Arthur said. "Attorney/client privilege is more than just a concept."

"Ok, but I don't really think it was all that bad," she began. "Carl dropped in on the day I'd mailed a hefty check to the IRS for estimated taxes. I was bitchin' and he said that's why he kept his company's finances in Grand Cayman. I told him that Dave, Mr. 'Buy American,' would never allow us to do that. So, he made a suggestion."

"I'll bet."

"Because I was such a good customer and he had great connections in the Caribbean, he'd bill me the standard retail price for product and I'd pay him the standard amount that would end up in his account off-shore. Of course, banking being discreet there, he could also make withdrawals without the IRS breathing down his neck for business expenses. I got a 'good customer' rebate in cash, my taxes dropped and my *private* reserve increased.

"God, Sherrie, I can't believe you're that stupid."

"C'mon, Cassie. It's no different than my slipping a couple bucks in my pocket for a cookie that doesn't go through the register. Either way, I get a little something that Uncle Sam doesn't touch."

"Technically, you're right. Either one is tax evasion. Any record of the rebates? No? Do you get it now? You were helping Carl Morgan to launder money. Just how did you get these little customer incentives?"

The color drained even further from her pallid skin. "Every so often, Eddie would show up with a box of some new product, lined with my favorite shade of green. Hell, Carl was so generous;

he even helped Eddie start a discount buying service for expensive perfumes and cosmetics. You can't believe the deals I got on *Joy* perfume or French mascara that retails for $80 a tube at Neiman Marcus."

"You do realize you were probably accepting stolen goods, don't you?"

A sheepish grin pulled at the corners of her mouth. "Well, the thought did cross my mind. I've got to confess, Cassie, it was exciting to live on the edge every once in a while, compared to the constant boredom of my real life."

"And who is this Eddie?" Arthur asked.

"I don't know. A friend of Carl's who'd fallen on rough times. Carl said he'd known him since they were kids."

I felt the tumblers click into place. "Do you happen to remember what he drove?"

She shrugged her shoulders, tipping her head to the right. "Some cheap American sedan. It was red, I think."

"Taurus," I said and stood. "I need some air, Arthur." I grabbed my purse from the floor, pushed back from the table and looked toward Malloy. He nodded.

"I'll join you shortly, Cassie," Arthur replied.

"Cassie, wait," Sherrie said. "You know that I couldn't hurt a soul. I thought I was falling in love with Carl."

"You were once in love with Dave, too," I said. "You put my life at risk to cover your ass."

"Cassie, please, I didn't mean to hurt you. You said friends love each other no matter what."

As the door buzzed open, I said, "This is an 800 pound 'what' sitting on my chest. I'll get back to you." I walked through the door without looking back.

"Know your way out?" Malloy asked.

I could only nod.

Arthur found me sitting in the lobby, staring at a spot between my feet on the tiled floor. Without speaking he put a hand beneath my elbow and drew me to my feet. The station's automatic doors slid open and we were wrapped in the damp warmth of a South Florida morning that promised the normal sauna day. He hit the car's remote and opened the passenger door. A wave of much hotter air hit me, so I waved him around while waiting for some of it to vent before taking my seat. He did the same on the driver's side, carefully hung his suit jacket from a hook on the ceiling over the rear window and we both climbed into the car. Even though the Beemer's giant engine pushed meat locker air from the ducts, my discomfort stayed somewhere between twitchy and excruciating.

THIRTEEN

On the way to his office, Arthur chatted in his faux-British accent about the case. I responded with polite grunts and monosyllables. The pressure of discovering that my "honest" friend's lies had nearly cost my life, made my head feel like a water balloon attached to a fire hose. I knew Sherrie hadn't set out to hurt me, but I felt betrayed none the less. My internal compass was twirling so wildly I had motion sickness. Finally, Arthur parked in his reserved space, turned to me and raised an eyebrow.

I met his eyes and asked, "Is your offer for the car still good?"

"Of course, my dear," he said. "Where shall I tell your husband you're off to?"

"I'm heading to the beach for some surf and exercise therapy. Tell Gene, I'll call him on the way."

"Very well," Arthur said. We simultaneously reached for the door handles. He retrieved his briefcase from the back as I walked to the driver's side. He held the door for me and paused before closing it after I took my seat. "Cassie?"

"Yes?" I leaned out of the still open door.

"This too shall pass. Give it some time," he said and shut the door before I could reply.

The midday traffic was light on the short drive back to the beach. I drove on autopilot, taking out my frustration by weaving effortlessly around the other drivers without feeling the increased speed.   I flew through the intersection at Summerlin and MacGregor, oblivious to the heavier traffic. I was still at highway speed when the four lanes narrowed down to two that were clogged with cars heading for their own R & R on Ft. Myers Beach. I slammed on the breaks, laying rubber and stopped inches away from the bumper of an SUV with an inflated green alligator, a black and white whale and a gray dolphin protruding from the rear window.

The soundproof large sedan forced me to read the lips of a red-faced woman leaning out of the window. I concluded that she was highly displeased with my driving, so I smiled and shrugged. She switched to sign language for a final rebuttal by pulling her head back into the car and extending a naked arm through the window.   The one-sided conversation concluded with three emphatic thrusts of her middle finger into the air. As the line of cars began to roll forward, I read the single sticker on her bumper: "Jesus is my co-pilot." Hmmm. I took that as a sure sign that He had a sense of humor.

My cell phone erupted again in that cheery folk dance as I joined the line of cars inching toward Estero Island. I fished it from my purse and answered, "Hello?"

"Headed to the beach, Cass?" Gene asked.

"Stuck in traffic on the bridge at the moment. You?"

"Arthur's got me digging through Kowalski's background. I'm on my way to the police station to hook up with Logan. Arthur made nice with his boss, so Logan is going to do some cop-to-cop courtesy calls to the Akron area. See if he can get a better line on Kowalski's pre-Florida career."

"Swell."

"You're really spending the day at the beach? I think I'll page Stillman to keep an eye on you."

"I don't need a babysitter, sport."

"Right. Listen, Cass, it would be nice to know you're safe for a few hours."

"I'm just fine," I said. Except for that car bomb I'd neglected to mention. Somehow, this didn't seem like the right moment to share that little tidbit. I sighed. "I'm planning to walk the dogs and do some laps in the pool. That should help adjust my attitude."

"Arthur told me you didn't take what happened at the jail very well," he said. "I'm sorry, Cassie."

"Go ahead, Gene. I know you're dying to say 'I told you so.'"

"It'll keep. I know you're beating up on yourself, right now," he said.

"You're right."

"Say that again, with feeling," he said.

"Youuu – Arrrre – Right."

"That's better. Cass, keep your cell phone handy. I'll call you soon."

"Will do," I said and snapped it shut.

Due to the line of exhaust belching vans and convertibles heading for a day of skin cooking, surf and sand, it was afternoon when I finally pulled into our lot. The usual barking greeted my arrival as I rounded the building and found Madeline and Snookie in the diminishing shade of our porch. I was not in the mood.

"Cassie, I'm so glad you're home," Madeline said. "I'm worried about Gladys."

"Listen," I said. "Anybody would be sick as a dog, no insult intended Snooks, after a night like she had. I'm sure she's dealt with a hang-over before."

"Doesn't get them," Madeline replied. "She was up by nine, chirping like a silly schoolgirl. She had a date with Mr. Wonderful for brunch. Snookie needed her constitutional, so I was out when he showed up."

Maggie and A.J. were barking and jumping against the glass doors, reminding me that they were in need of a constitutional of their own. Snookie stretched at her mistress' feet and rolled onto her side so that Madeline could rub her tummy with a chubby foot.

"So, why are you worried?" I asked, easing into the condo and sliding the screen closed.

"I don't know. Maybe I *am* jealous that she's getting all the action and I'm left to fend for myself. Still, with everything that's happened around here, I'd feel better if I knew more about this guy. Cop-wife paranoia, I guess."

The dynamic duo waited expectantly as I pulled off my clothes and hung them in the closet after a quick sniff of the armpits. The laundry basket was overflowing, but I dreaded using the communal machines that took $2.00 per load for marginal cleanliness. I struggled into a black one-piece suit guaranteed to "make you look ten pounds thinner." It may have shaved off five pounds, but the thick, girdle-like spandex didn't slide easily over my glistening skin. Maggie moaned her impatience at my feet while A.J.'s head swiveled between me and the door. Our visitors were still on the porch as we emerged, leashed up and ready to walk. Fabulous.

"Mind if we join you, Cassie?" Madeline said.

Rather be punched in the kidney was my thought. My mother's voice pushed its way into the dialog in my head. *Be nice to old ladies, Cassandra. If you're lucky, you might be one yourself, someday. Good grief.* "Of course not, Maddie," I said. "Come along." *Nice touch, Virginia Marianna. Perpetual telepathic guilt.* Geez.

For a change of scenery, we turned south toward the high rise condos. This slowed our progress considerably since the popcorn balls and wiener drew quite a crowd. The dogs accepted their homage good-naturedly as hand after sun screened hand reached toward them and gushed baby talk. Even Maggie was gracious until a plastic shovel wielding toddler dressed in a bloated diaper left the shade of his mother's umbrella and hurried in our direction. Maggie dug her front feet into the sand and growled. Madeline scooped Snookie into the air at the same time I lifted Maggie. But A.J. is mad for kids. The little tyke was still waving the shovel, yelling, "Goggie! Goggie!" when he came within leash range. A.J. happily knocked him to the ground where he could cover his face with doggie kisses. Fortunately, the kid thought this was aces, so when his mother hurried toward us, she heard only laughter.

"Sorry about that," I said, stroking Maggie's snout with intermittent squeezes to quiet the hostility.

"Oh, he loves dogs," she said.

A.J. was now sniffing the kid from head to toe. Perhaps his love of small children had something to do with food remnants and other things dogs sniff that humans use air fresheners to eliminate.

Over loud protests, Mom grabbed junior under the arms and marched him to a beach towel beside a bag overflowing with disposable diapers. We dropped Snookie and Maggie back to the sand and continued toward the pier. We were nearing the public beach where teens and twenty-somethings were less interested in dogs and more interested in drinking, smoking and groping. I was now looking at my feet to avoid the beer cans and cigarette butts that were discarded in the sand in favor of underage mating rituals. Walking barefoot through garbage bothered me and I worried about the hazards to little paws.

"Hey, Maddie, let's head back, ok?"

"It's OK with me, Cassie. I'm starving," she said. I squashed a sarcastic retort about her being far from malnourished as we attempted to turn the dogs around. Unfortunately, Snookie was straining against her leash, trying to pull Madeline toward one of the high rises being renovated. Maggie insisted on joining her, so Madeline and I were tugging on taut leashes when we both heard the approaching whistles of the foam and feather missiles that had replaced Frisbees as the tossing toy of choice this season. Simultaneously, we dropped the leashes to stoop and cover our heads as several whizzed by with one thumping Madeline on her bright pink backside.

"Yow!" she protested as a skinny kid in baggy Hawaiian print trunks ran toward us.

"Sorry," he called as he scooped it up on a dead run and rejoined his friends.

"Oh, shit," I said as I sprinted after three dogs that were running toward the construction site with leashes trailing in the sand. "Maggie! A.J.! Stop! Stay!" A.J. pulled up and grinned happily as I grabbed his leash. Maggie ignored me, running awkwardly through the uneven, looser sand.

"Snooookie!" Madeline called from behind. "Where - are - you?" she yelled between audible gasps for breath.

The inhospitable terrain slowed Maggie enough for me to grab her leash. The only sign of Snookie was the trough left in the sand from her low slung belly. The furrow led us to a dilapidated construction shed sitting atop four cement pavers in the sand next to the parking lot of broken asphalt. When we reached the side of the shed, we saw a brown skinny tail, a leash and a cloud of sand being furiously dug out by the burrowing dachshund. Maggie immediately joined in as A.J. pulled in the opposite direction, barking happily at Madeline's approach. I switched both leashes to one hand and pulled at Snookie's leash with the other. Budging a determined, buried wiener dog was no small feat.

Madeline dropped to her knees in the sand and grabbed the wagging tail. "Snookie, come out of there. You are a very bad girl." We heard a yelp emanating from the underside of the shed as Snookie's back scraped the wood siding. Madeline was now holding the tail with one hand while scooping sand away from the firmly lodged dog with the other. "Oh, baby. Mommy didn't mean to hurt you. What's gotten into you?"

Still holding the leads on my two, I bent over to dig on the opposite side of the offending tail. Above us, a male voice boomed, "Now there's a picture."

Bright sun bounced off the mirrored lenses of Jim Stillman's sunglasses. He was standing behind us with his arms crossed and a huge grin splitting his face.

"Help us, will you?" I said. "This crazy dog won't give up the dig."

"Interesting," he said as he walked to the front of the shed.

"I'm not in the mood, Jim," I said. Madeline continued to coax her unwilling dog from the hole she'd dug. I straightened my back and pulled my dogs from their digging to follow Jim. The shed was padlocked. Stenciled on the door in black paint was 'CM Management.' I tugged at the unyielding lock and kicked the door in frustration.

"Patience," Jim said. "I'll be right back." He jogged around the building and returned seconds later with a bolt cutter. Fixing the jaws around one side of the metal pin securing the lock, he pushed the long arms closed. Jim pulled the severed lock free, tossed it to the ground and opened the door.

The interior heat hit us like a blast furnace. At the back of the shed lay a mound of green and yellow striped fabric. Jim blocked my way as he removed his sunglasses and stepped inside. I pushed my shades onto my head and thrust my head into the shed's darker interior in time to see him bend down and reach for what I assumed was someone's neck.

"She's breathing. I assume you don't have your cell phone."

"No pockets, smart guy. Besides, I didn't think I'd need it," I said.

"Temper," he said, as he backed out and flicked his open.

I passed the leashes to Jim and ducked into the shed, squinting to adjust to the dimmer interior. "Oh, God," I groaned. Gladys was slumped against the back wall with blood caked in the hair above her right temple. Lowering my gaze, I watched the reassuring rise and fall of her ample chest. The brightly colored caftan she was wearing was low cut to accentuate her darkly tanned size double G's. I frowned. There was a small white corner protruding from her cleavage that Jim must have missed. Using my body to block his view, I pulled out a sweaty business card and shoved it deeply between my own adequate knockers. I squeezed her hand and backed carefully from the shed. Jim immediately handed the leashes to me as I watched Madeline and Snookie waddle toward us.

"You are such a very bad girl. Mommy is not happy," she said to the sand-covered dog. The look on my face must have spoken volumes. "What?"

"Actually, she's a very *good* girl," I said. "Thanks to Snookie, we found Gladys. She's hurt, but I'm sure she'll be fine."

Madeline immediately gave the dachshund's leash to me and entered the shed. "Oh, Gladdie," she called. "It's me. Speak to me, Gladdie."

"Ohh, ohh," Gladys groaned. I stepped closer to eavesdrop. "Madeline, my oldest friend, is that you?"

"I'm here, Gladdie. Tell me how to help you," Madeline said.

"Maddie, dear Maddie," she rasped and paused. When Madeline leaned closer, her clear voice enunciated, "Get me a drink and make it a double."

A team of EMT's hustled to the shed, closely followed by cops in sweat-stained dark green. After insisting that Madeline leave, the parameds enlisted the help of the local police to hoist Gladys' groaning girth onto the gurney and carry her toward the waiting ambulance. We followed them until they slammed the rear doors shut.

"Can't I go with her?" Madeline asked.

"No room," said a young man in a white tee embroidered with the Lee County Fire Department logo. Now that was an understatement.

"At least tell me where you're taking her," she said.

"Lee Memorial on Summerlin," he replied. "You can meet us there."

"Stay here, please, m'am," one of the officers told Madeline, including all of us with his glance. "We've got some questions."

We nodded our agreement and watched them trot back to the shed for a little detecting, no doubt. Madeline leaned against one of the cruisers, cradling Snookie against her chest.

"She'll be fine," Madeline said and beckoned with her finger. "Pssst, Cassie."

Jim cleared his throat. I put one foot on the asphalt before remembering they were bare. I pulled it back into the sand and motioned for Maddie to join us.

"Sorry. These northern toes can't take the heat," I said. "What's up?"

"That car at the corner of the lot," she said, shifting Snookie to one arm so she could point with the other.

Jim nodded as if he knew exactly what she meant. I saw nothing but the main building, so I handed control of the dynamic duo to Madeline and tip-toed quickly over the scorching surface of the parking lot.

"Ouch, ow, damn, ow, ow, ow, ow," underlined each step. I rounded the corner of the building and stopped in the shade provided by the wall. A dark blue '66 Monte Carlo in cherry condition was parked sideways in the far corner of the lot. It was the only vehicle within sight without a light bar on the top. "Yow! Ooh! Ouch! Ow,ow, ow," I repeated as I hopped back to the foot-friendly sand. Maggie, A.J. and Snookie were lying down with their tongues extended and their eyes squeezed shut. "OK, nice ride. But other than its mint condition, what's so special about that car?"

"It belongs to the mystery man," Madeline said, returning two leashes to me. "That's the car I saw peeling out of our parking lot last night."

"No sign of the driver," Jim said.

"How do you know that?" I asked. The corners of Jim's mouth twitched in answer. "Ok, smart guy. Answer this. Why would he want to hurt Gladys? He's only known her a few days."

"Decent question, Cookie," Jim said. "I didn't see a purse. Robbery, maybe?"

Madeline shot a pointed look at me. I tilted my head and scrunched my brow as I tried to understand her meaning. Her purse was gone. That meant money, a snack or five, her ever-present flask and…It hit me so hard I winced with my whole body. Two white heads and a brown one rose momentarily. Six dark eyes opened, looked at me, and closed again as their heads returned to the cool sand.

"Don't tell me that she was carrying, too," he said.

We nodded as a siren announced the arrival of another police vehicle. Moments later, my old nemesis, Logan, rounded the building and was met by one of the officers. They spoke in quiet tones and Logan walked toward us.

"Ms. Grimes. Once again you're in the middle of a crime scene," he said.

"It's not like I planned this," I said. Logan threw a look over my head. I turned and saw a couple of uniforms sprinting toward the water to restrain the crowd of beach walkers who had gathered.

"The officers believed your story about discovering the injured woman," he said.

"Actually, it was my Snookie that discovered her," Madeline interjected.

"And you would be…?" Logan asked.

"Madeline Jackson from Akron, police widow and best friend of the victim," she said.

"You?" he looked at Stillman. Jim looked toward Logan for permission to put a hand in his pocket. Logan nodded and Jim silently passed him a business card from which Logan read, "Security and Private Investigation. You carrying?"

Stillman nodded again and handed a license to Logan. Logan examined it, frowned and returned it.

"If you're finished, we'll be on our way," Stillman said.

"I've got one more question for the woman that's single handedly inflated our crime statistics."

"Hey, I haven't done anything wrong," I cried.

"And yet, you've been at the scene of several violent crimes since you arrived."

"Unlucky coincidence," I said.

"Crap magnet," Stillman offered with a characteristic lip twitch. Logan nodded and moved the corners of his mouth.

"Ms. Grimes, do you recognize the car parked in the front of the building?" he asked.

"It's a Monte Carlo," I said. "But if you're asking me if I know who owns it, I don't have a clue."

"You're sure?" he asked.

"Completely ignorant," I said. Logan and Stillman simultaneously coughed into fists covering their mouths. Behind my sunglasses, I rolled my eyes. "Only in this *particular* instance. Madeline thinks it belongs to a guy that Gladys, the victim, has been seeing lately. Why do you think I should recognize the car?"

"Because it's registered to David Walters," he replied.

"Oh, my God! That means Dave's alive," I said. "It proves my friend is innocent. I can't wait to call Arthur so he can get her released."

"It proves nothing, Ms. Grimes, since Mr. Walters is still nowhere to be found."

"But, shouldn't you run fingerprints from the steering wheel? Check for DNA? Do something cop-like?" I asked.

Logan's face was turning red. Somehow, I didn't think it was sunburn. "Let's continue this at the station."

"Are we under arrest, sir?" asked Madeline.

"Not at the moment," he replied.

"Then, we'll be going. I've got to get to the hospital and these two have things to do," she said, giving a small tug on the leash attached to the prostrate wiener dog. Snookie pushed to her feet, panting rapidly. Maggie and A.J. also rose and pulled lethargically against their harnesses with their tongues nearly touching the sand.

"We've got to get these dogs out of the sun," I said. "You know where to reach me."

"Wherever another body turns up," he said and walked toward the group of cops standing outside the shed.

We turned for home, dragging three heat-exhausted canines in our wake. I stopped to pick up Maggie. Jim scooped A.J. into the air as Madeline struggled to lift Snookie's dead weight.

A few minutes later, we stopped before our condos and returned the dogs to the ground. "Maddie, would you leave me a message when you hear about Gladys?"

"Of course, Dearie. Where are you off to?"

I shrugged. "Don't know yet. Give her our best."

She turned toward her building and Jim handed over A.J.'s leash.

"What's your husband doing?" he asked as he walked up the steps to his unit.

I continued with the dogs toward the faucet. After lying in the sand, their fur was embedded with grit. "He said he was checking up on Kowalski with Logan. Hey! Logan was just here. I could have asked him what they found out."

"And I'm sure he'd have shared that information with you. I'm going to hook up with your ball and chain and head to Kowalski's office. I've got some questions of my own. Stay out of trouble until we get back," he said. Before I could say another word, he'd unlocked his door, stepped inside and vanished behind a sliding glass door and a sweep of curtains.

Maggie and A.J. were straining toward our door. I wanted a little less of the beach in my living room, but they were hell bent on getting a drink. The three of us worked through our warring priorities, with me winning, marginally. When I opened our door, they bolted toward the kitchen. Seconds later, I heard the clatter of an empty water dish on the tile and Maggie emerged from the kitchen. She stood on her back legs and barked her displeasure loudly enough to create an echo. I filled her dish from the faucet and adjusted the top of my swimsuit. A wrinkled business card dropped to the floor. When I read the address, I knew where I was going.

FOURTEEN

As I turned off the shower, I heard an engine in the parking lot come to life. I cranked the window open in time to see the taillights of Jim's SUV flash before he turned onto the road. I grabbed a still-damp towel from the rack and dried as I walked naked to the thermostat and cranked up the air conditioner. A slight detour through the bedroom allowed me to prop the phone's receiver between my chin and shoulder to call Arthur's office while squeezing my eyelashes into a fashionable curl. Now if my balance held, I'd further compress the time to re-enter the world. If not, either the phone would crash on the tile or one eye would be hairless. Welcome to life on the edge with Cassie Grimes.

"Arthur Goldman, Attorney at Law," said Miss Lanahan in her cool, professional voice. "May I help you?"

"It's Cassie Grimes. May I speak to my husband?"

"Gene just left to meet your Mr. Stillman," she said. "You're lucky to be married to such a charming, considerate man."

'*My* Mr. Stillman,' followed by a tribute to Gene? Hmmm. "Just like winning the lottery," I replied. "Could I speak with Arthur? I need to make arrangements about his car."

"I'll see if Mr. Goldman is available. Please hold," she said. *Mr. Goldman? I pictured a silver haired afghan hound squatting to mark her territory.*

"Hello, my dear. I understand you've had another interesting afternoon," Arthur said. "How's your friend?"

"No news yet, but she was asking for a drink as they loaded her into the ambulance. I'm optimistic. I can't believe she was dating Dave while the police were looking for his dead body. Sherrie should be thrilled."

"Sheryl hasn't heard the news yet, my dear. We're not entirely sure who was driving that vehicle. Until we have proof of that, it would be premature to discuss this with her."

"Who else would be driving his car?" I asked.

"There are many possibilities," he said. "Speaking of automobiles, I do need to have mine returned. With the afternoon waning, when should I expect to see you?" he asked.

I stepped from the bathroom and the setting sun flashed through the glass doors. "I'm sorry, Arthur. I didn't realize it was getting so late. What am I going to do without a car?"

"I've given that some thought," he said. "I'll have Miss Lanahan call a rental company to deliver a vehicle to the office and, then, I'll meet you to exchange cars."

"Ah, Arthur…" I began, knowing the cost of rentals and the state of our finances.

He interrupted. "Of course, the bill will be added to your friend's mounting invoice. Why don't we meet at the Walters' home? I assume recent events have prevented your visiting her menagerie?"

Whew! Saved again. I tried to cover my relief by switching into Earth Mother mode. "I'm ashamed to say that I haven't given her animals a second thought. I'll be there within the hour, traffic allowing."

"Right, then. I'll see you soon," he said and hung up.

I applied mascara to curled lashes and dusted my face with powder and blush. I grabbed the last pair of clean pants from the closet (black shorts that weren't "hot pants" but were far more abbreviated than golfer sedate) and a sleeveless coral V-neck tee. The drawer still held clean skivvies, so I dressed and walked toward the kitchen, stopping to retrieve the business card from the counter. Maggie and A.J. were out cold on the tile.

"Hungry, guys?" I asked. They raised their heads momentarily at a phrase normally met with great enthusiasm and dropped them again. "Ok, still tired. Mommy's got to leave for a while, so I'll put out some food just in case." I opened a can of Alpo Gourmet Turkey and Bacon, divided the mystery squares of meat into two bowls and chopped them into smaller pieces. I set the bowls on the floor and bent down to pat the sleeping dogs. A.J. turned subconsciously onto his back, but Maggie didn't move at all.

"It's ready when you are," I said, snatched my purse and Arthur's keys from the table and tip-toed out the door.

****

I was soon walking through the Walters' garage. A wave of apprehension washed over me as I grasped the handle of the connecting door. Flashbacks of my last visit caused me to retrace my steps from the garage to the drive. I looked across the street toward Bruce's house and saw a beautiful brunette dressed in a bright pink spandex running ensemble jog across the street and into the drive.

"Claudia?" I asked, extending my hand. "I'm Cassie Grimes, Sherrie's friend from Ohio."

She grasped it firmly, sporting nails that were manicured in a shade of pink that matched her outfit. "Nice to meet you, Cassie. Any news about Sherrie? Or Dave?"

"Not really," I dodged. "Seen any unwanted activity over here?"

"Quiet as a funeral. Oh, God, that was insensitive," she said, blushing furiously.

I blew a puff of air through my teeth. "Sherrie's the poster child for insensitivity. She'd enjoy the irony. I'm here to put in my shift at the animal soup kitchen."

"Great. I told Bruce if we hadn't heard from you by tonight, I was going over. But, here you are, so I'll get on with my run. Nice to meet you," she said with a wave and trotted into the street, dark brown ponytail bobbing with her stride.

"Do a couple miles for me, would you?" I called to the tight buns bobbing in sync with her hair, adding quietly, "Show off. Get a grip, Cassandra." This time I walked briskly through the garage and opened the door without hesitation. Scarlette and Scooter slid to a stop at my feet as I closed the door and dropped my keys on the credenza. They howled their displeasure at the disruption of their normal routine. "So call the Humane Society if you think you can find a better deal," I said.

In a very non-feline manner, they followed me into the kitchen. I retrieved the empty dishes from the floor and gave each a double serving of canned, fishy something. When the full plates returned to their places, all I saw were cat butts and flicking tails.

I gazed absently through the window as I rinsed the cans. Gray tabbies were sprinting across the open ground, heading toward the pool cage. I rummaged through Sherrie's cabinets, extracting several large bowls that I carried to the deck. I spread the bowls apart on the brick pool deck and filled them from the bags beneath her grill. I dumped the contents of bowls one and two by the door for the kitties, and took three and four into the grass further from the house for the raccoons and squirrels.

With uncharacteristic caution, I locked and double-checked the cage door and the French Doors connecting the house to the pool. Plates with scraps of food were where I'd left them, but Scarlette and Scooter had disappeared. "No, please," I said to the air, "Don't gush your thanks at being fed. With any luck, your mommy will be home soon and you can tell her how badly I mistreated you." That made sense, right? Of course, nothing else had made much sense since I'd left Ohio, but I am basically an optimist.

I carried the bowls back to the sink and stacked them on the counter, tossing the rinsed cans into the recycling bin. As I dried my hands, the cats emerged from the bushes and began eating the food nearest the pool. Further out, Papa Raccoon led the family to their dinner as squirrels darted toward the waiting chow, stuffed their cheeks with seed and beat a quick retreat up the tree before the raccoons challenged them. Lost in thought, I spent several minutes watching Sherrie's wards enjoying their dinner. All was peaceful until the sound of a slamming car door dispersed the zoo faster than a clap of thunder will send my dogs running for cover. I walked toward the living room and saw a white Chrysler 300 parked in the drive. Arthur's hand paused inches from the doorbell as I opened the door.

"Good evening," he said, grasping my hand and raising it to his lips for the customary kiss. "All is in order here?"

"Pretty much," I replied. "I was just cleaning up."

"Where to now, Cassie?" he asked.

I hesitated and decided on the truth. "To Naples. Gladys had a business card for CM Management. The address was on the same street as Tom Walters' office."

"Do you think that's wise?" he asked. "Gene said your last meeting was less than cordial and normal business hours have concluded."

"That's why I'll be fine," I said. "Chances are, Tom's office will be closed and I'll just cruise by the other address to check things out."

"Things?" he asked.

"You never know what you'll find," I replied. "Besides, there's still plenty of daylight left and I'll call both Gene and Jim to tell them where I am."

He raised his eyebrows. "I have your word on that?"

"Of course," I said. "I'll grab my purse and the keys to your car and meet you in the drive." After locking the front door, I trotted to the credenza by the garage entrance, eager to be on my way. My scalp was tingling with the feeling of finally being on the right trail. Dave Walters was alive and the card he'd given to Gladys linked him to Naples, Morgan and CM Management. It would be tough to indict Sherrie for a murder that hadn't taken place. If I could just get a line on where Dave was hiding, I could turn everything over to Logan. Then, Gene and I could enjoy our beach hideaway for a little while longer.

I hit the button for the garage and ducked out of the closing door. Arthur was standing by his silver BMW, his suit coat draped over his arm. I dropped the keys into his outstretched hand and gave it a small squeeze.

"Thanks, again, Arthur."

"My pleasure," he replied. "Don't forget your promise."

I pulled my cell phone from my purse, sweeping it toward him. "Would I lie? I'm hoping Sherrie will be feeding the crew by tomorrow. See you then."

****

True to my word, I left messages on both Gene and Jim's phones as I drove to Naples. The ride from the senior Walters' abode to Junior's exit took less than thirty minutes. I turned onto Old US Route 41 from I-75 South. Multiple office/warehouse combinations lined the nearly treeless road because of the proximity to the interstate. Downtown Naples' swanky shops and restaurants were closer to the Gulf so that the residents of the million-plus-dollar homes could enjoy their winter retreats away from ambiance busters like semi's and manual labor.

I turned right onto Gulf Palm Lane and rolled to a stop across from the sign designating the various businesses on that street. Beachside Bread was listed near the top with a notation of *1250*, but CM Management was not among the others. There were, however, empty spaces on the marquee. I retrieved the card from my purse and read *1350*. The last business listing showed a street number of *1390*. Hmmm.

A familiar palm tree holding a loaf of bread hung over an office space in the center of a row of individual stucco buildings. Parked at the Naples headquarters for Beachside Bread was a dandy light blue Mercedes convertible. I passed that drive in favor of the one behind it. Feeling invisible in the white rental car, I cruised slowly past the identical buildings whose numbers were in descending order. In the middle of that strip, I saw no large sign, but did manage to read *1350* stenciled in black on the top of the glass door. Beneath it, in small block letters, was "CM Management."

The lot was deserted and the closed venetian blinds at *1350* showed no light or movement. I parked at the end of the row and watched through my rearview mirror for any sign of activity. Nothing. In fact, my car was the only one in sight. After a few minutes, I turned left and left again. I pulled the rental car into the middle of several cars parked in front of *#1220*, whose sign read "Island Tool and Die." When I left my car, the sound of machines on metal assaulted my ears. Evidently, business was brisk enough that a second shift was running, with the rear of the warehouse area emitting enough sound to travel over the entire strip. As I walked past, the only visible person through the glass windows was a heavy-set woman with salt-and-pepper hair, alternating between typing on the keyboard of a computer and flipping paper over in a stack to its left.

I stopped in front of The Beachside Bread Company and quickly stepped into the air- conditioned interior. Unlike the Spartan interior of the parent company, this office was a page out of *Luxury Business Designs*. A large receptionist station of curved oak with a green marble top protected a collection of polished oak desks. Matching green metal file cabinets complimented the station and the lighter tile floor. I snatched a manila file from the station as a surgically pretty woman with shoulder length blond hair emerged from one of the back offices. She was poured into a peach camisole and matching, second-skin Capri pants.

"Can I help you? I'm about to close," she said as she pushed her hair behind one ear with a hand sporting a large, channel set diamond and wedding ring combination.

I gave her sincerity, overlaying urgency. "Gosh, I hope so. I'm late for an appointment… I'm lost…and I have to use a restroom in the worst way."

"Who are you looking for?" she asked.

"The address I've got is 1250 Gulf Palm Lane," I said, waving the folder.

"That's our address."

"Are you sure?"

"Duh. I'm Mrs.Walters, the owner. What's the name of the company you're trying to find?" she asked, unconsciously jingling a massive diamond tennis bracelet. Well, well. Not all of the money Tom had squeezed from Daddy and Sherrie had gone into bad business deals. The missus sported some serious bling as well as a wrinkle free face and perky breasts.

"CM Management," I said, watching closely for her reaction. I hit the mother lode.

Her blue eyes began to fill before she could answer. "Their office is right behind us, but you can't possibly have an appointment there," she sputtered.

"Oh, man," I said. "I made this appointment weeks ago. My plane was delayed so I didn't have a chance to change. I can't believe Mr. Morgan would stand me up."

She scanned the receptionist station and found a box of tissues. She quickly pulled two from the container and dabbed at her eyes. "Then you must not know. Mr. Morgan was found… was recently…he was murdered."

I gave her astonishment. "Oh, my God. That's terrible. I'm so sorry. Did you know him well?"

She nodded, blinked and dabbed, and then looked at me. "He was the best thing that's happened to me in a long time. For the first time in years, I was as giddy as a school-girl. Hell, I don't know why I'm telling you this."

"I've got one of those faces," I said with a shrug. "Sometimes it's easier to talk to a stranger. You know, like having a conversation with the person sitting next to you on a Trans-continental flight."

"I guess. It's an old story. Your husband takes you for granted, no matter how much you go through to stay attractive for him. He works long hours and comes home late without explanation. Then, along comes a man who appreciates you. He says you're beautiful and actually listens when you talk. I'm not proud of it, but Carl made me feel alive again."

I'd switched into actress mode with the first lie. As such, I managed to keep my expression sympathetic and neutral as I shoved my left hand into my pocket and wiggled my wedding band off. "Don't I know it. Men can be such pigs."

She sniffed and nodded.

An uncomfortable silence was developing as I thought about how many branches of the Walters family tree old Carl had successfully lopped off. Still in character, I remembered that I'd already given myself a way out.

"I'm sorry to sound so selfish, but I could really use that bathroom," I said.

"Sure. Last door on the right before you hit the warehouse," she said, making her way back to the corner office.

I locked myself in a small restroom that held a toilet and sink. It was painted a pale yellow with a small arrangement of silk daisies sitting next to an aerosol air freshener on the white counter. I took advantage of the facility and washed my hands, drying them on a fringed yellow towel embroidered with the company logo. I automatically checked my reflection in the mirror and whispered, "You're one lucky broad, Cassandra."

I was opening the door when a soft chime sounded and I heard the younger Mrs. Walters call out, "We're closed!"

I slowly pulled my door closed. A male voice that sent chills up my spine said, "Not until I say we're closed. What are you still doing here, anyway? Who's watching the kids?"

"They're at Gina's house. I was about to lock up when…"

"Save it. You should be home making a decent dinner for them," he said.

"I will, honey, I just have to…"

"Beat it! I've got a private meeting in a few minutes and I want you out of here."

"But, Tom, there's still…" The sound of a brutal slap reached me in the bathroom and I clamped my hand over my mouth to keep from screaming. The door chimed again and then, there was silence.

Geez, I'd gone from luck to deep shit in fifteen seconds flat. I kept my hand in place until my breathing quieted, praying Tom wouldn't discover me. But how would I get out of here without that damned doorbell giving me away? There was nothing between me and the parking lot at #1220 besides open space and concrete.

What must have been minutes seemed like hours as I stood with my back pressed against the metal door. There were no sounds coming from the outer office, but I hadn't heard the chime of Tom's exit. I prayed my luck would return, he'd leave and I could make a get-away without being detected. A doorbell rang again and my hopes soared. They quickly plummeted when I heard voices raised in anger.

"Eddie, what the fuck!" Tom yelled.

"Easy does it, Tommy boy," he said, sounding much closer than the front door. "I've got a surprise for you out back."

"Fine. Great," said Tom. I could see the shadow of his shoes through the small space at the bottom of the door. I returned both hands to my mouth and held my breath. *This was becoming a habit.* "Now put that stupid gun away."

Eddie laughed. "What's that the NRA says? Guns ain't stupid, people are."

In front of my hiding place, I heard the door that led to the warehouse open and click shut before I removed my hands and breathed. The air duct in the bathroom let me eavesdrop as the men walked through that space. I kicked off my sandals and climbed onto the toilet to hear more clearly.

"Here," Eddie said. "Open the trunk."

"Dad!" Tom cried. "Jesus Christ, Eddie, have you lost your mind? Help me get him out of there."

"Don't think so. Dear old Dad forgot the plan. He was supposed to keep under wraps 'til we could finish the frame on his wife. But the old sonovabitch got frisky and started playin' tonsil hockey with some cow on the beach."

"So you beat him up?" Tom said. "Christ, Eddie. He's old. You could've killed him."

"Nah. He was still breathin' when I tossed him in the trunk after takin' care of the old broad. Hidin' her fat ass was no piece of cake, I tell you. I drove down the beach a ways and doubled back on foot to take care of his car. Sweet ride. But when I got there, cops were swarmin' around the shed where I'd stashed her, so I had ta leave.

"You killed her?" Tom said.

"Don't know. That was the plan, but I couldn't make sure. I had ta get off the island to put some distance between us and the Ft. Myers' Heat."

"What do we do, now?"

"We ain't doin' nothin'. Plans have changed. Won't be long 'fore the cops come here lookin' for CM Management."

"Why would they do that?" Tom asked.

I stood on tiptoes and pressed my ear against the grate. I could feel the sweat trickling down my back as I speed-dialed Gene and whispered, "It's me. Hold on."

Eddie was answering, "....bum luck. Shed had the name on the front. And after Carl bit the big one, even the FM Greenies'll be able to put two and two together."

"You killed Morgan?"

"Nope. Actually, I 'spected to ride that pony a while longer."

"Listen, Eddie. We can work this out. I'll take Dad and disappear for a while. My wife will cover for me. I'll make sure of that."

"You're a sap, Walters. She's been screwin' you for months," Eddie said.

"She wouldn't dare," snarled Tom.

"No? She's been bangin' Carl in the back of the CM warehouse, right under your nose."

"I'll wring her scrawny neck," Tom said.

"Tommy, Tommy, Tommy. That's not my plan. Somebody's gotta be around to inherit the money. Flexibility. That's the key. I had ta make a few adjustments; but, so far, the only mistake I've made was with your Mom's nosy friend."

"She's not my mother," he said.

"Whatever," Eddie replied.

"What mistake?" Tom asked.

"Something went wrong with the rig to blow her ass up."

Suddenly, my bare feet slipped on the toilet cover and I fell. The vase holding the silk daisies crashed to the floor and my cell phone flew out of my hand. I could hear Gene's voice. I reached behind the sink, grabbed the phone and whispered. "I'm in trouble. Shut up and listen." I managed to stash the phone behind the toilet before they were pounding on the door.

"It's locked," Tom shouted.

"Not for long," Eddie replied.

It had to be dumb luck, my particular brand of the stuff. I slid on my butt to the place where the door's hinges fastened to the wall. Seconds later, a deafening explosion ripped through the small room and the door was yanked open. I could see Tom's snarling mouth open and close, but I couldn't hear a word. My eyes locked on a gun pointed at me and flicking up and down, up and down. I finally got the message and stood. I was staring into the bruised face of the man who'd attacked me and chased me down Sherrie's driveway.

"Damn it!" I yelled. "I can't hear a thing! Hell, TOM, I should have known you'd be mixed up with the ass-hole who broke into Sherrie's house."

Eddie responded by lifting the gun toward my head. My legs were turning to liquid. I struggled to keep standing as Eddie smiled, stepped back and gestured with the gun toward the warehouse.

As I stumbled barefoot through the door, I yelled, "At least let me help your father. That is, if this guy didn't kill him when he locked him in the trunk after beating a defenseless woman."

Then, I was walking through the door and my precious link to the outside world was still on the floor behind the toilet. I forced myself not to look in that direction as the gun's barrel jabbed my back, causing me to stumble out of sheer terror.

I sent a silent prayer to the patron saint of clumsy, nosy women. *Please, please! Let Gene and Jim have heard this and be on their way.*

FIFTEEN

The small warehouse was stifling. Two giant stainless steel ovens stood on one side of the room, pulsating heat. Large plastic barrels of ingredients were arranged on the opposite side, with long tables in the middle for mixing, kneading and whatever other culinary chores went into delivering fresh baked goodies to the Naples area. Toward the rear were racks filled with bags and labels for packaging. The walls of concrete block ended in a triple wide door to admit delivery trucks, with a small exit door to its' right.

Parked in front of the sealed rear of the building was a red Taurus with an open trunk. I ran past Tom toward the car, my bare feet slipping in a fine dusting of flour. I slid into the rear bumper and looked inside.

"Dave," I said, placing a trembling hand against his neck to feel for a pulse. "God, Dave, are you alive?" He opened one eye and moved his index finger to his lips for a split second, then pretended to be unconscious again. I drew a deep breath and turned to face Tom Walters and his felon pal as they walked toward me.

"Was it worth it, Tom?" I asked, rubbing my ears.

"Shut up! I never intended for him to hurt Dad," he said.

"And yet, your father is unconscious in the trunk, covered in blood and bruises. Another one of your brilliant schemes gone wrong," I said and shifted my glance to Eddie. "Listen, Eddie, nobody's dead yet. You've still got a few options. Be smart."

He exposed the ragged, yellow teeth I remembered in what passed for a smile. "That so? I'd say 'smart' is bein' on the right side of a gun. The only mistake I made was not cappin' you the first time."

"But here we are. You can't possibly believe you could murder us all and get away with it. Besides, you just said the cops will be here any minute."

"So what? You won't be here."

"What?" I squeaked; panic snaking from my acidic stomach to my throat. If Gene had heard all my shouted clues via the cell phone, he and Stillman should be on their way.

"Give Tommy boy a hand with dear old Dad. We're gonna take a short walk," he said, keeping the gun trained on us as he backed toward the small door. He rotated the lock and pushed the door open. The sound of screeching metal assaulted us and I realized it would completely cover a cry for help.

Dave groaned as Tom faced the trunk and wrapped a flaccid arm around his neck. He circled Dave's upper body with his left arm and lifted. I grabbed his right arm, threw it over my shoulder and we both struggled backward. As his legs cleared the car, Dave moaned again. He squeezed my shoulder, but managed to remain limp as we pulled him from the trunk. We turned and carried him toward the open door, his dragging feet tracing two lines on the concrete floor of the warehouse.

Eddie transferred the gun to his left hand and fished something from his pocket with his right. He extended his right arm through the open door for a moment and then returned a remote door opener to his pocket. He shifted the gun to his right hand again and stepped back into the warehouse. He waved the gun toward the open door and commanded, "Move!"

Dave still hung between us, his head bouncing on his chest. To get through the small door, the three of us had to turn sideways, so Tom led the way, dragging his father behind him with me supporting him from the rear. Dave's feet thumped over the door jam and I stepped through. Directly across the alley, the black hole of an open garage door yawned menacingly. I froze.

The hard barrel of Eddie's gun smashed into my kidney. "Move it, bitch."

"Ow!" I yelled. My brain was screaming at my feet for action. My feet weren't co-operating. Maybe it was because they were beneath a set of knees that had begun to shake uncontrollably from bearing Dave's weight and from my accelerating fear.

Dave's hand suddenly dug into my arm. His head came up and he twisted toward Eddie. "You sonovabitch!" he yelled and threw his weight against me. The three of us hit the closed garage door of Beachside Bread and went down in a pile, yours truly on the bottom, jammed against the hot, unyielding metal. I saw Eddie jump through the door and pull it closed with a slam.

"Get up!" he yelled, "Into CM and quick or I'll shoot you right here!"

"Jesus, Eddie, stop! I'm moving," Tom wailed.

At the bottom of the pile, I pushed a hand into my pocket and wrapped my fingers around the business card that had spent time between both Gladys and my boobs. I shoved half of it under the garage door and made a big show of pushing Dave up and struggling to stand.

"Dammit! You broke my back," I moaned as I crab-walked on hands and feet across the alley, my butt thrust in the air and purposely fell on top of Dave and Tom, smashing them to the ground again.

Eddie stepped between Beachside Bread and our three bodies with his back to the door and his gun pointed toward me. "Worthless bitch. Can't you do anything right?"

"Having a gun pointed at me can be distracting," I said. That crack earned me a literal kick in the ass. We scrambled across the remainder of the alley into a dark warehouse. The shapes of machinery and industrial shelving were shrouded in shadow. Eddie walked to the left of the open door and flicked on the light switch. Two rows of overhead fluorescent lights illuminated tiers of boxes from floor to ceiling and a small forklift. I watched as the door slowly closed. It hit the concrete floor with a bang and I silently prayed that the one thing I'd done right was to place that card where Stillman and Gene would find it.

****

Dave had given up all pretense of being unconscious. He put his arm over Tom's shoulder again and staggered toward the shelving. Tom lowered him to a sitting position with his back resting against a large carton emblazoned with a red diamond whose center was bisected with the words "Baking Gems." Tom sank next to his father as I backed away from them inch by inch until I bumped into the forklift and stopped.

"What are you going to do with us?" I asked, rubbing my ankle and stalling for time.

"Kill you," he said. "Just have ta figure out a few of the details."

"Eddie, for God's sake, listen to reason," Tom said. "The cops are close to locking up that bitch for good. Instead of a four-way split, it could be three. We're talking more money than you could ever imagine."

"Shit, man, I can imagine me livin' with your filthy rich old lady, playin' with those titties you bought her. And if she doesn't want to share, a little reminder of what happened to Daddy's wife should bring her around. Hell, now that I think about it, I'll just blackmail the bitch. Let her know how suspicious it'd look if anybody knew she'd been bangin' Carl. Yeah, that fits like a glove and I'll be getting' all the strange pussy I want."

I fought down a gag reflex as the image of Eddie's yellow teeth exposed in the throws of passion flashed through my mind. *Keep stalling, Cassie.* "So, Dave, you're up to your eyeballs with these rocket scientists. If I'm not going to make it out of here alive, I'd sure like to hear the whole story first," I cut my eyes toward Eddie. "C'mon. What have you got to lose?"

"Not a damn thing," he said. "Why not? Tell her the old plan and I'll work out the details of a new endin' while yer talkin.'"

Dave touched the side of his bloody nose and winced. He drew a ragged breath and grimaced a second time, moving a shaking hand to clutch his ribs.

"God, Dave, you should be in a hospital," I said, moving to his side. "I thought you were smarter than this. Why would you get mixed up with this guy?"

"This guy wasn't around at the beginning," he replied. "Tom came to me with a proposition. I was tired and this seemed like the perfect way out."

"Tired?" I said

"Of my life with a whining, cold woman. I gave her everything she has and what thanks did I get? She spent my money on therapy sessions, crying her eyes out and criticizing me. *Me.* The one who drug her out of a ratty little apartment and into a life she could only dream about."

"And you got a woman half your age to hang on your arm and stroke your ego. Oh, yeah, and someone who worked with you side-by-side for years and built your little business into real money," I said.

"With what I taught her. She owes it all to me. All of it."

Tom interrupted, "And that gold digger tried to turn my dad against me."

"Why was that?" I asked. "Because she put a stop to Dave investing is a string of failed business deals?"

"I had some bad luck," Tom replied. "I was lied to. Every one of those deals should have made a bundle. If my partners had half a brain, I'd be set."

"Right," I said and rolled my eyes. "Every scheme bit it, but it was somebody else's fault. How convenient."

"Not every one," Dave said. "CM Management was thriving. I'd given him a little money from private funds to get started. He repaid me within three months."

"Whoa, there," I interrupted. "Private funds? I thought all your money was tied up in a trust."

"Sherrie's not the only one who knows how to put money away for emergencies. Who do you think taught her how to make a cash business work to her advantage? Don't forget, Cassie. I was in business for myself years before your friend ever came along."

"And tricked Dad into giving her my money," Tom said. Dave shot him an angry look.   "You know what I mean; my inheritance." Dave grimaced and shook his head.

"That makes sense; you being the next Donald Trump and all," I said. Tom lunged upward quickly enough that Eddie waved him back to the ground with the gun. I took another tiny step to the side and asked. "Why CM Management, Dave? Why now?"

He tapped the cardboard box he was leaning against. "Baking Gems, for starters. We were investing in a profitable commodity that tied to our product line: Vertical Integration. Morgan also gave me a reason to finally make a change."

"And that was…." I prodded.

"Proof that Sherrie was unfaithful. I wasn't about to let her make a fool of me."

I thought, *no, you can do a perfectly good job of that yourself.* What I said was, "What kind of proof?"

"A tape. When Sher pushed me out of the day-to-day functions at the stores, I needed something to do. I was already managing the properties at DaveSher Enterprises and Morgan needed someone with my considerable experience," he rasped, paled and paused.

So, Morgan knew how to flatter men as well as women. Each time Dave cleared his throat, his skin became a lighter shade of gray. I nervously scanned the room and spotted a water cooler by the door to the offices.

"Eddie, could I get him a drink?" I asked, already moving in that direction

"Make it quick. I've got things to do," he said, pointing the gun at my back and swiveling his head between the men and me.

I dashed to the inverted five gallon blue bottle, grabbed a paper cup from the dispenser and filled it to the sound of "Blurp. Blurp." With my back to my captor, I swept my eyes over this end of the room for anything I could use to improve my chances. All I saw was a plastic file holder nailed to the wall and dust bunnies. The needle on my chance-o-meter still wavered between slim and none.

I only spilled a little as I trotted back to Dave. He took the cup with a tight smile, leaned back against the cartons and sipped with his eyes closed.

"Thanks," he croaked. "Carl was spending a lot of time at our main store and finally pulled me aside to tell me that he'd seen Sherrie acting pretty chummy with a couple of clients. With the way she'd been treating me, I wasn't surprised. I decided to confront her, still hoping that he was wrong and it was just some silly thing she'd get through. I knew I was slowing down, but, hell. She owed me a little loyalty, didn't she?"

"Damned right," Tom interjected.

"That's when Carl suggested a test that would show me if his suspicions were right."

"Test?" I asked, incredulous. "For your wife of twenty something years? Did you ever consider talking to her, Dave?"

"She'd have lied," Tom said.

"Maybe. She's certainly not the only one in this family doing that," I said. *If you get me out of this one, God, I promise I'll never lie to Gene again. Well, at least not about the important stuff. Oh, boy.*

Dave broke into my reverie. "I'm not proud of it, Cassie. But what else could I do? Carl offered to come on to Sherrie and record the whole thing with a mini-cam hidden in his briefcase. When I saw the tape of him making out with my wife and planning a trip to the Bahamas, I knew it was over," he said, the parts of his face without bruises flushing a bright red. "That's when I planned to disappear and leave her holding the bag."

"Jesus, Dave, what's wrong with this family? Have you ever heard of a neat little thing called 'divorce?' The spouse is gone, nice and legal, and your share of the assets puts you in Fat City for the rest of your life."

"And watch her take up with a younger man on my money?" he said. He shook his head back and forth with a surprisingly venomous frown.

"So this is really all about pride and greed? You're not as smart as I thought you were," I sighed.

"Really? I convinced your two-timing friend that I was a befuddled old man. Funny how ready she was to believe that.

Morgan's lawyer set the wheels in motion to change the will and my son took me for a routine blood test."

"Where he had a bad spell," Tom chimed in. "I had to take him to his doctor right away and the tubes of blood they'd just drawn suddenly appeared in my pocket."

I pinched the center of my nose. "So the cops found your deserted car at Lover's Key with a bullet hole in the window, your actual blood on the front seat and no body. Tom gives the tape from Kowalski's office to the cops, your wife goes to jail and he gets all of your money. That's very trusting of you, Dave; especially in view of Tom's excellent record for fiscal responsibility."

"Why wouldn't he trust his own son?" Tom asked.

"I don't know Tom," I said. "I'm sure you've been completely honest with him. Like how you were cooking the books about Baking Gems and slipping the money into your own pocket?" It was a stab in the dark, but I doubted that Morgan would pass up an opportunity to work the same scam on Tom that he had on Sherrie.

"What's she talking about?" Dave asked.

"Dad, really, it was nothing. A little side deal," he said.
Bingo.

Eddie, who'd been pacing around the warehouse throughout the story, rolled the barrel of his gun in a circle and said, "Wrap it up. Yer outta time."

I swallowed hard as sweat traced the line of my spine from my bra strap to my waist. I was running out of clever fast and I had no desire to hear Eddie's demented finish to the story. Where were Gene and Stillman? I strained to hear sirens. I heard only silence.

"So why not disappear as planned," I asked, searching for a way to defend myself. All I could see were floor to ceiling shelves, packed with box after box of 'Baking Gems.' I drew a frustrated breath and said, "So, Dave, why didn't you stay invisible?"

Years rushed onto his face. His eyes lost their fire as his spine compressed and his jaw went from a determined thrust to flaccid. "We were double-crossed.," he mumbled. "Tom picked me out of the water in an inflatable and rowed me to his car. We deflated it, packed it into the trunk and let the tide erase our footprints. We were ahead of schedule when he dropped me outside the hanger at a private airfield in Bonita Springs and took off. The place was deserted and I was afraid of being seen, so I hunkered down behind a shrub."

"Must have been just before we drove up," Eddie said.

"I watched Eddie and Morgan get out of the Porsche and talk briefly before Eddie slipped into the hanger. I can't tell you why, but something seemed weird. I decided to stay put and see what happened. Morgan leaned against the car for a while, checking his watch. Fifteen or twenty minutes passed and Eddie came out, carrying a gun in his hand. They climbed in the Porsche and took off. That's when I decided to really disappear."

I looked at Eddie and said, "You were going to kill him that night, weren't you?"

He nodded. "Carl tol' Daddy we'd be hidin' him in the Caymans. He shouldn't talk to Junior in case the cops started sniffin' around. Not to worry, we'd keep Sonny-boy in the know; us bein' partners and all," he pulled his lips back from the yellow teeth. "Dad was gonna skydive without a chute over the Atlantic. We'd have time to burn while the bitch went down for murder and we sucked a bunch a money outta Tommy's inheritance through CM. Man, it was beautiful," Eddie said, his smile fading to a snarl. "But the old geezer got jiggy and went in the wind. Left too many loose ends."

"You bastard," Tom said and lunged toward Eddie. Eddie swung the gun like a club and clocked Tom across the forehead. He dropped to his knees.

"So much for honor among thieves," I said. Tom crawled back to his place against the cartons, blood oozing from a gash over his eye. "That explains everything except where you went, Dave. And why you came out of hiding."

"Old man's folly," he said, crumpling his cup and tossing it aside. "I holed up in one of our condos on Sea Oats Drive. The tenants called me a few days ago, asking for an early out on their lease. He said his new job started immediately and asked could I clean out the Frig? Nobody knew about it since I thought I'd be long gone. I got cocky about how I'd given these guys the slip and set up my cheating wife. Hell, why not slip out for a little fun where no one would ever look for me?"

"Uh huh," I giggled in spite of myself. "Why would anyone look for an eighty year old at a Senior Citizen's Center?"

"Never been to one," he said. "I kidded myself into believing that having a young wife kept me young. Sherrie and I went to the club, out to dinner, the movies or anyplace that people her age hung out. In my mind, I was frozen at 55 and she was catching up. I didn't count on meeting somebody who lit my fire again."

"Gladys?" I asked.

He nodded. "She was more woman than I was used to."

Eddie said, "She's a whale. I almost got a hernia hauling her into that shed."

"You ass hole," Dave said. "The only thing she was guilty of was having a good time with me. We got loaded together and I got clumsy. Is she gonna be all right, Cassie?"

"Yeah, Dave, she'll be fine," I said and saw Eddie's eyes narrow. I quickly added, "She wasn't much help to the police. Said she didn't see her attacker and didn't remember much after he whacked her on the head."

"Lucky for her," Eddie said. "Here's how the rest of the story's gonna go."

SIXTEEN

Ok. I was curious; terrified, but curious. Eddie ordered Tom onto the forklift using his gun for emphasis. Tom moved slowly and gave Eddie a really bad poker face. It telegraphed the calculation of his chances to start the heavy machine and end our immediate problem.

Eddie waved his gun like a schoolteacher's finger. "Don't get cute, Tommy," he said. "You'd be dead long 'fore you got to me."

Tom's face collapsed in disappointment. "All right, all right. What do you want me to do?"

"Pull out one of them big boxes on the bottom," he said.

Tom turned the key and the engine hummed to life. He awkwardly wheeled the unfamiliar equipment toward the cartons, raised the heavy metal fork and stabbed the side of a box. White powder spilled to the ground when he withdrew the tongs. He threw a look toward Eddie and shrugged a question.

"Moron," Eddie said. "Drop the fork and slide the tongs into the wooden palate under the box. Lock it and back up." He cut his eyes to Dave and said, "Guess rich kids don't learn how to do real work."

After a couple of failed attempts, Tom managed to pull the palate forward. The back of the wood scraped loudly across the concrete. Eddie flinched at the sound and I swiveled my head from side to side, desperate to find a way out of this mess. On the last pivot, I stared directly into Eddie's weasel eyes.

He smiled that 'before Crest' smile of his and said, "Nice try. You ain't that fast." He looked back at Tom and drew his finger across his throat. Tom killed the engine and climbed from the seat. Eddie flicked his gaze between Tom and me.

"Open it." I sighed audibly and he shifted the gun toward me. "Purty please," he puckered his face into a pout. What a comedian.

At gunpoint, Tom and I attacked the top of the taped carton with our hands. Nails broke and fingers bled until it opened to reveal an inner plastic bag, knotted with a large wire tie to keep its' white, powdery contents dry.

Eddie kept the gun aimed toward us and turned his head slightly. He stared at Dave; his lips compressed in a thoughtful frown, and then looked at me.

"A little less than half should do it," he said.

"Huh?" I responded. Like I said, I was fresh out of clever.

"Start shovelin'. Daddy's a small guy. He'll fit."

"Omigod, you can't be serious," I looked frantically between Dave, the box and a gun whose proportions seemed to grow by the minute. "He'll suffocate in there."

"Only if he gives me a hard time. If he's a good boy," he grinned, "he'll climb in and I'll tap him quick in the back of the head. Nighty, night, Pops."

Tom started crying, "Oh, Dad, I'm so s-s-s-sorry. I never thought you'd get hurt."

Dave shut his eyes and drew a ragged breath. Tom continued to whine as I removed the wire tie and blindly plunged my hands into the powder. I flung it behind me in a motion reminiscent of Snookie digging away on the beach.

I discovered that sugar was as heavy in your hands as on your hips. The only sound other than my grunting was Tom's sniveling and it was getting on my last nerve. My arms were shaking with the effort to control my emotions and continue the task. With each snuffle, I fantasized about pulling my arms from the powder and slapping Tom silly. It'd probably be the last thing I ever did, but it would be worth it.

"Yer a pussy, Tommy," Eddie said. *Who'd have thought? Common ground. Maybe this was the beginning of a very brief Stockholm Syndrome.* "Guess your old man's got the only set a balls in the family. Hey! I just had a thought."

"Miracles happen," I said. *Good bye, Stockholm. Hello, Smart-Ass.*

"Keep diggin' baby, or you go before Tommy," Eddie said. "Here's the thing. Dad's gonna be easy, arencha, Pop?" Dave nodded. "Good, good. Tom, here, is gonna take one in the jewels with these in his hand." Tom turned up the wailing a notch as Eddie reached into his left pocket and pulled out a pair of red thong underwear. "Recognize 'em, Tommy? I'm gonna enjoy boppin' the missus as much as Morgan did. But, before that," he cut his eyes to me, "you and me are gonna party."

I gave him venom laced with ice as I held his gaze. "You'll have to kill me first."

"Not a problem. You'll stay warm for a while," he said.

That's when I saw it. A figure dressed in black was silently moving behind Eddie over the top shelf of boxes. I turned my back to him and thrust my hands deeply into the sugar, grabbing two handfuls of the stuff.

In my peripheral vision, I saw Stillman spread his arms and drop through the air. I pivoted, threw the sugar with all my might and dived hard to the floor, screaming, "Warm this, dickhead!" My arms wrapped around my head reflexively and I held my breath.

A shot rang out and I screamed. The pain that throbbed through my body seemed to originate from my elbow and knee. No gunshot wounds. Yet. I opened my arms and raised my head from the concrete. Stillman was atop Eddie, who flailed as if his life depended on it. Stillman jammed a knee into Eddie's back, grabbed the hand with the gun and slammed it to the ground. The sounds of metal and bone smashing concrete echoed through the warehouse and the pistol slid beneath the skid. Eddie roared as Stillman twisted the same arm behind Eddie's back and pulled him to his feet. In one fluid motion, Stillman stepped hard to the side, dipped his shoulder and lunged into Eddie's back. The momentum spun Eddie like a top. He slammed face first into the steel beams holding the two by four slats of shelving. He collapsed in a steady flow of blood.

"Cass, you ok?" Jim asked as he released his hold, still watching for signs of consciousness from a flaccid Eddie.

"Could be worse," I admitted, "Of course, you could have been quicker." I pushed to my feet and brushed the sugar from my clothes. Dave slid over to his son and pressed his hand over the one Tom was using to hold his arm. Blood seeped between their fingers as Tom continued to moan. "You were almost too late," I added.

"Cookie," he said as he snapped handcuffs on Eddie, "almost doesn't matter with anything but bombs. Save the nagging for your husband. It's over."

Suddenly the sound of the machine shop screeched through the quiet. The small back door flew open and Dave yelled, "Hey!" Jim and I both looked toward the door, expecting Gene. My mouth dropped as a large man stepped from the shadows, an Uzi dangling from his right hand.

"On the floor, with your arms over your head, palms to the floor," he said to Stillman as he brought the gun up to belly level.

Jim complied. "You think a moron like Eddie could come up with this? Or that face, Morgan? The jerk actually thought his scam was about sugar and flour. There's a lot more at stake, here, than baked goods, "he said.

"Drugs," I said, recognizing the face of Greg Kowalski

"Among other things," he said. "That's the beauty of a large organization. I take care of you and one quick call brings a clean-up crew. Thanks to the silencer and the tool shop, I'll slip quietly back to my office and no one will be the wiser."

He slowly brought the machine gun toward the center of his body while moving his left hand up for a two-handed grip. The left hand never made it. A loud bark echoed through the warehouse, followed by Kowalski pitching forward. A pool of blood was already spreading on the floor as Stillman rolled toward him and pulled the gun from Kowalski's hand. Gene threw his gun aside and ran across the space to wrap me in a tight embrace.

"Thank, God," he whispered into my sugar coated hair and began to tremble.

"That was some entrance," I said, stroking the back of his neck. "Dirty Harry would be proud."

"Shut up, Cass. I just killed a man. I don't regret it, but 'proud' isn't what I'm feeling right now."

The sounds of sirens and flashing blue and red overlay the noise of metal being ground into parts. Suddenly the constant din of the machine shop stopped, leaving only the cop sounds.

"Police!" was shouted from just outside the door.

"Door coming up!" Stillman responded. "All secure! Don't shoot!" He punched the button next to the small open door and the garage entrance creaked upward. One of the officers stepped forward as Stillman handed him his weapon, handle first. They talked quietly for a few moments before he pointed across the room to the gun Gene had discarded. Another cop was waved forward. He snapped on plastic gloves and retrieved the gun, dropping it into a plastic bag.

"Clear!" the first officer, shouted over his shoulder. One by one, the sirens went silent, leaving only the red/blue, red/blue strobe bouncing off the surfaces of the warehouse.

The five of us walked through the open door. An ambulance blared its arrival, adding its red flashers to the light show. One uniformed officer walked behind Dave and Tom as they shuffled forward. Paramedics met them with gurneys, insisting that both climb aboard. Bandages were wrapped and IV's were started as police priorities vied with medical ones. For the moment, medicine won.

Gene and I were separated from Stillman, who spoke quietly with an officer, by the bumper of his car.

"Tell us what happened," our cop demanded.

"I was..," I said.

"She was..," Gene said.

We stopped, looked at one another and smiled.

"Ladies first," Gene kissed the top of my head.

Arthur emerged from the back of the crowded alley. An arm blocked his way as he approached us and waved.

I nodded in his direction and said, "The three of us would like to continue this conversation in the presence of our lawyer, Mr. Goldman."

"The three of you?" he asked.

"That's right. My husband and Mr. Stillman are both employees of Mr. Goldman. I'm a family friend."

"Of who?" he asked.

"It's complicated," I answered.

"Yeah," he said. He gave a terse wave toward Arthur who gathered Stillman in his wake before joining us.

"Perhaps your station would be more conducive to these conversations," Arthur suggested. "My client and employees will be glad to speak with you there, but not before."

"How'd you know where to find us, Arthur?" I asked.

"Professional courtesy," he said. "On his way here, Gene called Officer Logan, who should be here shortly. Logan was kind enough to call me after he notified the Naples police to provide whatever assistance they could."

The officer spoke briefly into his radio, punched the button and said, "Let's go."

The three of us were allowed to ride together in the back seat of the same cruiser. Naples' higher tax base allowed us to climb onto the modified back seat of a blue and white Volvo X90 rather than the Ford Crown Vic's that the Ft. Myers' force used. I was the uneasy estrogen meat in the sweaty, testosterone sandwich of my husband and former boyfriend. They were staring straight ahead and the silence was killing me.

"Well, that worked out pretty well, didn't it?" I said

They looked at one another over my head.

"You're a strong man," Stillman said.

"More than you know," Gene replied.

"Hey!" I began. Simultaneously, both men's hands covered my mouth. I swiveled my eyes to make sure Gene's was directly on my face. I snaked my tongue between my lips and licked salty skin. Gene sighed and nodded at Jim. Both hands dropped and I had the last word. "Don't ya just love it when a plan comes together?"

****

The next day was a flurry of activity for Arthur, and a day of relative relaxation for us. He had to deal not only with the legal bureaucracy of Sherrie's release, but also with referring Tom and Dave to other legal beagles who could sort out the sorry mess they'd made of their lives. They were going to need all the help they could get. Even though Dave had been missing for only six days, the story of the "Runaway Husband", was picked up by the cable news channels. Logan got some air-time as did an assortment of officials from Naples. Arthur had phoned to tell us Sherrie's release would be broadcast, live, at 4:00 p.m.

Gene and I had awakened to the demands of Maggie and A.J. The events of the last few days brought us both to the same conclusion about our condo.   As we walked along our familiar beach, Gene sighed and said, "Well, I guess we should see a realtor."

"The sooner, the better," I said and burst into tears.

"I'm getting mixed signals, Babe," he said.

I pulled up my sunglasses and wiped my eyes. "I know it's the only thing that makes sense, Gene. But I don't have to like it."

He put an arm over my shoulder and we resumed our stroll. In the shallows between the sand bar and the beach, a lone dolphin surfaced and submerged, surfaced and submerged, in the familiar pattern of a lazy meal. The dynamic duo were oblivious to the show. A.J. spotted a toddler clad in a diaper and sunbonnet and was straining against his leash. Maggie sniffed a dead fish in perfect contentment, refusing to move. With Gene and I attached by his embrace in the middle, we were the center in a furry taffy pull.

We soon turned our backs to the water and trudged toward the condo. After the usual routine of cleaning the dogs, we climbed the stairs just as Jim was locking his door.

"Got a date?" I asked.

"Yep," he said. "Flying out at 3:45 tomorrow, so I'm O.V. 'til then. There's a bill under your doormat."

"OK," I said, swallowing irrational jealousy as Gene nodded.

We stepped into the cool air of the condo without a backward glance. I went to the kitchen with the pups to fill the water dish. Gene went into the bedroom and pulled the Ft. Myers Beach phone book from the drawer of the nightstand. He flipped through the pages and dialed. After a few quiet comments, he paused for the reply.

"Three o'clock would be fine," he finally said and hung up.

"For what?" I asked.

"Realtor visit," he replied.

"Are you nuts!" I screamed.

"Let's rock," he said as he pushed me aside to retrieve the meager cleaning supplies under our kitchen sink. The subsequent frenzy filled the air with the scents of Windex and Comet and the sounds of an old vacuum. By 2:15, we were both in the shower, careful to kick the dirty water toward the drain to avoid another tub scrub.

I was brushing my teeth when I heard the screech of tires on the asphalt behind the building. I spit, rinsed and finger-fluffed my hair. I dashed to the bedroom to pull something from the hamper just as Gene was sliding the door aside. Maggie stood on the bed and barked. A.J. flew to the front and leapt against the thighs of our visitor.

A tiny woman with very short red hair pulled her ankle length green skirt up enough to bend her knees and extend her right hand as an invitation.

"Aren't you the friendly one?" she said.

I scooped the still growling Maggie from the bed and walked toward her. "And here's the socially challenged one. Cassie Grimes," I said, waving Maggie from my right arm in a parody of a handshake while trying to smooth the wrinkles from my dirty clothes.

"Agnes Williams," she said. "What a charming place. May I?" she indicated the chair with a leather portfolio.

"Of course," Gene replied.

She opened the folder, balancing it on her lap while attempting to scratch A.J.'s head.

"I took the liberty of running a few multiple listings for similar properties based on the information you gave me." She passed the papers to Gene who thumbed through them and emitted a low whistle.

"Are these realistic?" he asked.

"Absolutely," she replied. "There's only so much waterfront left."

I positioned Maggie between the arm of the couch and me and extended my hand. I was leafing through the information as I asked, "So, Agnes, what's your suggestion for an asking price here?"

She named a price and added, "Your bottom line should be within $20,000 of that figure." The number didn't reside in "Fat City" but it was definitely in the vicinity of "Serious Cash." We spent several minutes discussing the details of selling our paradise get-a-way. The whole thing seemed surreal. At least the detachment kept me from crying like a baby. We finally signed the contract for Agnes to represent us and she waved a cheery farewell. She paused with her head still jutting from the partially closed door and said, "I've got all your numbers. I'll call as soon as I have any information. We can do the closing by fax and courier service." Whoosh, click and she was gone, leaving the reality of our situation in her wake.

I was a jumble of emotions, fluctuating between excited and nauseous. Maggie relaxed her guard dog persona when Agnes left and stretched across my lap. Gene scooped A.J. from the floor and joined us on the couch. He reflexively picked up the remote from the coffee table and started to channel surf.

"Could you give it a break?" I asked. He ignored me. "Hey! Wife speaking here."

He pointed the remote toward me and mimed pressing the Mute button. I tossed Maggie to the floor and lunged for the offending changer. He held it as high over his head as his arm would reach. A real wrestling match could have ensued, but we were interrupted by the familiar sound of "Yoohoo!" A quick double tap on the glass door followed by a "Woof" caused us to stop. Madeline had her hands pressed against the glass in a chubby telescope.

"Swell," Gene said. I rose, straightened my clothes and walked to the door.

"Hi, Maddie," I said as I slid the door open. With her ears and tongue flapping happily, Snookie trotted toward Maggie and A.J. while her mistress took two short steps and flopped into the chair. "Guess your roommate's still not up and about."

"Are you kidding?" she said, pulling the halter top away from her bosom and fanning with the other hand. "She went shopping bright and early. Somehow Fox News picked up her involvement as the other woman tied to 'the Runaway Husband.'"

"No way," I said. "How's she taking that?"

"Positively thrilled," Maddie said. I cut a glance toward Gene who was, once again, rolling his eyes. "I'm embarrassed and she's calling all our friends in Akron. Have you guys been watching the news?"

"Not really," I replied. Gene had resumed channel surfing to avoid the necessity of talking. I glanced quickly at the images flicking by in psychedelic sequence and heard *"Live from Ft. Myers, this is...."* The screen quickly morphed into a fishing segment, followed by a belligerent defendant on *Court TV*.

"Hey, go back to the Ft. Myers' report," I said. "It's almost four."

Gene complied and the three of us leaned forward. A man with flowing white hair smiled perfect teeth toward the camera and said, "Thanks, Mollie. This is Brad Jenkins, coming to you live from Ft. Myers. I'm standing outside the jail where we're waiting for Sheryl Walters' release, after having been cleared of the charge of murder when her husband was found, very much alive. Lee County officials tell us that both Dave Walters and his son, Tom, are under scrutiny for fraud, filing false reports and a variety of other charges for their part in the senior Walters' disappearance."

"This is also tied to the deaths of two other men, right Brad?" Mollie the talking head asked.

"That's right, Mollie. Carl Morgan was found murdered a few days ago. A lawyer, Greg Kowalski, was also killed in a Naples warehouse where Walters and his son were discovered. Three Ohio residents," he said, looking down at his notes, "a Mr. & Mrs. Grimes and Mr. Stillman, were also at the scene, but they were cleared by the police and released shortly after the incident."

"You're famous, too," Maddie interjected.

"Uh huh," I said as Gene blew air through his lips like a tired horse.

"Mollie, it looks like Mrs. Walters and her attorney are about to come through the door. Let's listen to what they have to say."

Sherrie walked uncertainly toward the reporters, dressed in the same crème pant suit she'd worn a few days ago to court. Lights flashed and microphones were thrust toward her. Dressed in his usual dark suit, Arthur Goldman walked beside her with a hand holding her elbow. Without saying a word, Sherrie's head swiveled back and forth as reporters shouted questions.

Arthur held up a hand and walked forward.

"Ladies and Gentleman, on behalf of my client, I'd like to express her gratitude for the diligence of the authorities both here and in Naples, in putting a quick end to this gross misunderstanding. All charges have been dropped and she asks you to allow her some privacy to recover from the trauma. As you can imagine, being accused of murder and unjustly incarcerated have been terribly difficult. But, thanks to the tireless efforts of local law enforcement and some very good friends, Mrs. Walters will be home shortly. That's all for now."

He walked purposely forward with his arm now around Sherrie as he guided her toward his silver BMW. There was an overlay of commentary as we watched his car pull away from the lot.

Gene flipped to Fox News when the live shot ended. On the screen, dressed in a powder blue matching top and skirt was Gladys. Her tan skin was glowing in a way that could only be achieved through the magic of a make-up stylist. She was seated in a studio, giggling. The stylist had managed to arrange her hair to camouflage any evidence of the blow to her head.

"Honestly, dearie, how many women my age can say they're at the center of a sex scandal?" Gladys said to an off-camera interviewer.

"No one with any sense," Maddie said to her image on the screen.

"So, you weren't aware that your, ah, gentleman friend, was really Dave Walters, 'the Runaway Husband?" asked a perky twenty-something brunette.

"Of course not," Gladys replied. "I'm not that kind of girl."

"Of course not" the reporter said, pursing her lips to avoid laughing. "And what are your plans now?"

"Nothing more definite than a cocktail on the beach at sunset. My friend and I will be heading back to Ohio, soon. But we'll be back. This was the best vacation I've ever had."

Gene turned off the TV. "Now there's an ad that the Chamber of Commerce will want to run," he said.

"She looked great, didn't she Maddie?" I said.

"She looked like an old fool," Maddie said.

"Come, on. She could have been killed when Eddie attacked her. She deserves a little survivor euphoria."

"You're right. She's a pip, isn't she? Having her as a best friend is never dull."

"I know what you mean," I said.

Madeline pushed up from the chair. "C'mon, Snookie, let's go get the drinks ready for Gladys and leave these folks alone. When are you two heading back to Ohio?"

Gene answered, "Tomorrow night."

I was speechless. We hadn't discussed that at all. What was the hurry? I needed to talk to Sherrie. I looked out of the door at the setting sun and a huge lump lodged in my throat. "But, Gene," I began.

"Give Gladys our best," he said, squeezing her arm as he escorted her to the door.

"But, Gene…" I repeated.

He shook his head for silence and dropped his gaze to the floor before raising it to meet my eyes. "I hate long good-byes," he said.

SEVENTEEN

Early the next morning we walked the dogs in silence, each of us lost in our own thoughts. When we returned, we did a small load of laundry while we packed. Clothing and toiletries were easy, but I agonized over a small shell here and a glass manatee there. Since we were selling the condo, furnishings and all, we had to make a detailed inventory down to the last washcloth for a potential buyer. We excluded the seascapes and abstract paintings I'd painted specifically for the condo. I wasn't willing to risk a difference in artistic taste that might doom something so personal to a garage sale or – ack! – the dumpster. I planned to ask Sherrie to ship them when the unit sold, feeling she owed me that much.

Just before lunch, I headed south on Estero Boulevard to retrieve the beach bag. Jim followed in his rental car. The teller admitted us to the vault, whose individual boxes had a mausoleum quality today. She inserted her key and the one I'd handed her into the twin locks, opened the door and left us alone. Jim pulled the bag from its niche and waited patiently while I closed the vault and returned my key to the teller, who explained that a refund would be forthcoming. I thanked her and we walked to his car.

I slid into the already hot seat and Jim placed the bag-o-cash on the floor between my legs. He cranked the engine over and flipped the fan to high, bathing us quickly in cooler air. I retrieved Jim's bill from my purse and read it again. I pulled bills from the bag and used my lap as a table to count and cross-stack ten piles of ten, one hundred-dollar bills. I re-shuffled them into one neat stack and handed it to Jim.

"That's more than the bill, Cookie," he said.

"She owes you," I said and sighed. "So do I."

He twitched the corner of his mouth, took the money and put it into a zipper compartment of the black cargo pants he was wearing. From another pocket, he pulled a pen and changed the total on the bill to match what I'd given him, scribbling "Paid in full" across the top before reaching across my lap to stuff the invoice into the bag of currency. His hand just grazed across the tops of my bare legs before he brought it up to caress the back of my neck. A small squeeze sent ripples of electricity through my body acute enough to cause the nipples to harden against my yellow tank top. I crossed my arms and his mouth twitched again. Oh, boy.

Jim opened his door and rounded the car. The fabric of the beach bag scraped against my thigh as he quickly pulled it from between my legs and held the door for my exit. This tingle was much smaller than the previous one, thank goodness. He walked me to my rented Chrysler, threw the bag into its trunk and paused.

"Gotta run, Cass," he said. "It's been real."

"Surreal is more like it," I answered. "Thanks again, Jim."

"It's what I do," he said and brushed a strand of hair from my eyes before he walked away without a backward glance.

I followed his car until it turned right to go over the bridge. I went straight for another quarter mile and turned into our parking lot. The dogs did their usual greeting of jumping and yapping as if I'd just come home from the war. Well, maybe I had: another victory for love over lust.   I walked down the hall to the steaming bathroom where Gene was showering.

I stood next to the commode and yelled, "Hey, sweetie, I'm gonna take one last walk before we go."

"Get everything handled with Stillman?" he asked.

"Yeah," I said and blushed at his choice of words. Glad I'd left the shower curtain drawn. "He's headed to the airport."

"I'll load the car while you're gone," he called as water splashed over the top of the shower curtain, misting the top of my hair.

"OK, thanks," I said and headed for the door. Maggie and A.J. danced excitedly in my wake. "No, guys. This time, I'm going alone."

At the top of the steps, I paused, kicked off my sandals and closed my eyes. The sun and steady wind from the Gulf wrapped me in a sensuous cocoon that flowed over my skin like a living thing. A lump constricted my throat and moisture formed at the corners of my eyes as a sense of impending loss swept over me. I drew a breath rich with brine through my nose and exhaled it slowly through puffed lips as I shook my head and opened my eyes.

I walked down the steps and angled across the familiar sand, praying that a dolphin would wander by. The familiar outline of Sanibel Island took on a clarity that made it spectacular beyond logical explanation. I studied it as I walked, resting in the green/blue water and was rewarded when one, two, then three dolphins leapt from the water in the channel separating it from Estero Island. In perfect rhythm, I watched as three dorsal fins alternated to the surface and disappeared toward the western horizon.

I took that as my cue to turn south and head for home. 'Home.' That pesky lump threatened to reappear so I increased my pace. *Maybe I was coming down with a cold? Maybe I was the world's biggest liar.* Just ahead, two teenage girls with micro-bikinis stretched over flawless skin that was, in turn, stretched over lean muscle, flipped towels to the sand and cranked up a portable CD player. I immediately straightened my posture and sucked in my stomach in a painful attempt to narrow the chasm between youth and middle age. It made me feel marginally better, but let's get real. Even if my name was Arnolda Schwartzenager, I couldn't eliminate the disparity

"As if I'm not feeling bad enough," I mumbled. The CD player was pushing out Sheryl Crowe's summer anthem, *I'm Gonna Soak Up the Sun.* They were giggling and bouncing toes painted in silver to match the toe-rings both sported.   As my steps automatically took on the rhythm of the beat, I struggled to focus on the plus column in the balance sheet of my life, rather than the minus column that would soon include this stretch of beach.

Just then, I turned toward the condo and saw Gene standing on the porch, watching my approach. Well, well. As I trotted through the looser sand, he slid open the door, grabbed Maggie and A.J.'s leashes and looped them around the rails. I rinsed the sand from my feet and he locked the door. He met me on the sidewalk, holding the dynamic duo on a short leash and extended my purse and sandals toward me as he said, "Ready?"

I tossed the purse over my right shoulder, slid into the flip-flops and took his free hand.   He smiled down at me sympathetically.   I beamed absolute certainty back at him and nodded emphatically. Struggle over.

"Let's roll," I said and the four of us walked to the cars, already idling with the air conditioners turned up. By the time the dogs and I were situated in the Beemer, Gene was turning the rental out of the lot. I followed him in mercifully sparse traffic across the bridge without a backward glance.

A.J. had his nose aimed at the cool air blasting from the vents. Maggie was napping with her head resting on the handles of the peach beach bag that Gene had transferred to the passenger side floor.

"You all right, princess?" I asked.

She raised her head, yawned her indifference and dropped it once more. There wasn't a moan or a whimper. Nothing. I was curiously irritated. After coping alone for seven hours of tantrum on the initial leg of the trip, I secretly wanted Gene to do his husbandly duty and share the misery on the trip home. But Maggie didn't stir until we stopped behind Gene at the guardhouse for Highland Estates. Gene stuck his head through the passenger window as a surprisingly thin guard with brown hair walked toward his car, eyes glued to the clipboard he carried. They spoke briefly and Gene pointed toward me. The guard nodded and returned to the hut. The gate went up, Gene pulled through and I received a cheery wave as I followed on his bumper, both dogs barking happily in response.

I parked in Sherrie's drive behind the white rental. Gene hopped out of the car and the dogs erupted.

"I'll take them for a tour of Sherrie's bushes while you see her," he said.

"You're not coming in?" I asked.

"Don't think it would be a good idea, Cass," he said.

I watched the dogs pull him toward a hydrangea bush and said, "Oh, right. Don't want to start a fight."

He allowed his sunglasses to slide down his nose and stared pointedly at me. "Yeah, that's it exactly." Hmmm. Could be that he wasn't talking strictly about the animal kingdom.

I pulled the heavy bag from the car and shut the door with a thrust of my hip. The garage door was up so I walked through the still empty space for Dave's Cadillac. I hefted the bag against my chest to get a better grip, kicked the door three times as a knock and waited. My heart was thumping loudly inside my ribs. I hadn't spoken with Sherrie directly since that awful day at the jail. I'd left a message on her voice mail informing her that we were leaving, saying I'd stop by with the bag. Now, as the doorknob turned, I realized I hadn't a clue about what to say to my oldest friend.

****

Sherrie was in as bad a shape as I. She opened the door and walked quickly away: no greeting, no hug. It was the first time in years, except for the peculiar decorum required when incarcerated, that she hadn't kissed me on the mouth in welcome. If you don't have really good girlfriends, it would be hard to explain how much I missed it. I was thoroughly pissed off, but the prospect of Sherrie leaving my life made my heart ache so violently that I stopped in my tracks.

"Get a grip, Cassie," I mumbled as I turned into her bedroom and threw the bag on her waterbed. It created a small tidal wave, spewing cash from the open top onto her comforter. I watched the undulating mattress as two voices battled inside my head. *"Pride!" shouted one. "Friendship!" replied the other. Geez, I was getting seasick.*

I walked toward the kitchen wondering if this trip was not only the end of our second home ownership, but also of a very significant friendship. To Hell with pride. I vowed to do my part to leave the door open for reconciliation. A large wicker basket sat on the kitchen counter. Sherrie was busily wrapping aluminum foil around sandwiches and baked goods before placing them inside. When she heard my footsteps, she turned.

"Gourmet cheese and veggie sandwiches for the ride. I packed some slices of beef and cheese for the dogs in separate baggies. You haven't turned them into vegetarians, too, have you?" she asked.

"Carnivores to the core," I grinned. "Stop that for a minute and come here." I wrapped her in a bear hug, boob to boob, and squeezed with all my might.

"Stop it, Cass," she said against my ear. "You'll puncture a lung with those things."

I laughed and stepped away. "So, how did it feel to be the headline on the news?"

"Not all that great," she said. "The freakin' phone has been ringing off the hook."

"Dave's still not home?" I asked.

"No," she said. "He's staying at the condo while this gets sorted out. He asked that I not do anything until his legal problems are resolved."

"You agreed?" I asked.

"Yeah, but I'm not sure what to do then," she said. "Can you imagine how embarrassing it is for 'the other woman' to be a geriatric whale? How could he do this to me?"

I considered my reply. The solid ground of our friendship had just been rocked with a 7.0 on the Richter scale. Should I give her platitudes or my real thoughts? I had to risk it or we were doomed to polite air kisses for the rest of our lives.

"Honey, he wasn't the only one sucking face with someone else," I said.

"At least Carl was good looking," she sniffed.

"So, it's not the betrayal that bothers you? Your pride is somehow wounded because she wasn't a babe? Could be that Dave was operating under the John Rogers Dating Credo," I said.

"Who the hell is John Rogers?" she asked, tossing a banana and orange into the basket.

"A friend of Gene's," I replied. "He always dated women who were overweight, ugly or older, believing that they'd be really grateful."

"Yeeeww," she said.

"Kept him off the streets," I replied. "Seriously, Sher, this should open the door for some real evaluation about your marital status."

She closed the top on the basket. "I'm scared, Cass."

"Of course, you are," I said, rubbing her shoulder. "But whatever happens, I can't be any worse than being convicted of a murder you didn't commit. Dodging that bullet was huge."

"Thanks to you," she said.

"And Gene, and Jim Stillman, and Arthur, and Logan," I said, bending my fingers.

"You pay your friend?" she asked.

"Ten G's. The bag is on your waterbed. You ought to do something about that soon."

"I guess the shoe closet is out of the question, now," she said.

"You'll think of something," I said. There was a loud knock on the garage door. "I've got to go, Sweetie. Gene's waiting with the dogs."

"You're selling the beach place." It was a statement, not a question.

"No choice," I said and turned.

Sher picked up the basket and walked behind me toward the garage entrance. "Wait a minute, Cass." She detoured into her bedroom and put our road food next to the beach bag, creating another wave pattern in high denomination bills. She shoved the cash into a small mound and picked up as much as she could manage with one hand.

I grabbed her other arm and spun her around. "Don't," I said.

"I want you to have this," she said. "I know how much you need it."

"I need you more," I said and gently turned her to face me. I grasped the wrist holding the cash and gently shook it over the bed. "I don't want your money." There was a confetti-like shower of Franklin's until her hand was empty. I slid my hand from her wrist to lace my fingers through hers. "It's probably gonna be a while before I get down here to see you again. But I'm always just a phone call away."

"You know I don't call people," she said and kissed me on the lips. I kissed her back and stepped away when tears began to blur my vision. "Love you," she said.

"Love you, more," I said as I picked the basket from the bed. I blew her one last kiss with my free hand before turning the knob.

A gray streak brushed past my legs and headed toward Sherrie. She stooped to pluck Scooter from his figure eights against her ankles and I walked through the door. Maggie was happily sunbathing with eyes squinted against the sun, her tongue barely protruding from her mouth. A.J. was straining against his leash toward a rock on which a chameleon was slowing morphing from green to brown.

"What's that?" Gene asked.

"Road supplies, compliments of the Baking Queen," I said. "I'll follow you to Hertz."

Gene loaded the dogs into the backseat of the Beemer. I put the picnic basket on the passenger seat, turned over the engine and backed quickly from the drive. Before we made it to the first stop sign, Maggie and A.J. were trying to climb across the console to raid the great smelling package. I spent the short drive to the rental return pushing the dogs back and saying "No!" in as many variations as I could devise.

I pulled to the side of the blue tinted glass building, trimmed in yellow, as Gene left his car and trotted inside to the return counter. I left the engine running and walked around the car to the passenger side. By putting the seat all the way back, I could just manage to wedge my feet into a small space between the gearshift and the basket on the floor. Moments later, Gene plopped down next to me, did a quick U-turn and left the lot. A quarter mile after making a left on Daniels Boulevard, we turned onto the entrance for I-75 North.

The car merged with the other migratory Northerners and Gene cut his eyes toward me. "You all right, Cass?" he asked.

I turned from the window, shifting enough to peek around the seat. Maggie and A.J. were pressed against one another, staring out of the rear window. I put my hand over the one that Gene had resting lightly on the gearshift knob, "You betcha, Baber. What could be better than a road trip with you and the kids?"

"I'm talking about the condo," he said.

"I know," I squeezed his hand.

"You do make quite an exit, Cass," Gene said.

"Just be sure you're always waiting in the wings."

"Always," he said and turned up the radio's volume. My head was soon bouncing as I dozed. I awoke with Maggie snoozing on Gene's lap and A.J. on mine in time to see the sign for Valdosta, Georgia. I expected one final throat lump at the finality of it all. I swallowed only contentment.

EPILOGUE

Three months after the long drive from Ft. Myers, I was sitting at my desk with a rock & roll station cranked up high enough to vibrate the walls.   At nine thirty this morning, the FedEx truck had delivered the closing documents for the condo's sale along with a cashier's check. After a mad dash to the bank, I was not only writing out checks for the entire balance of several credit cards, but also answering the phone for the first time in weeks. It was a rush to be able to say, "The check is in the mail." without the phrase being one of the three biggest lies ever told.

Gene was at the grocery store, buying ingredients that sported recognized names instead of the generic brands we'd lived on to squeeze a few extra pennies from a dwindling reserve. Prior to the news of the condo's sale, we'd eaten like college students while Maggie and A.J. continued to eat like the royalty they thought they were.

Gene spent several frustrating mornings talking with "Human Resource Managers" who were younger than some of his socks. In the afternoons and evenings, he worked on labor intensive home projects and creative cooking. My days were spent calling customers to pump some revenue into the business and painting over earlier, subtle canvases with wild colors and themes. We were financially healthier than we'd been in a long time, but flush we weren't.

In mid-afternoon, the dogs exploded in a barking frenzy. I turned the volume down on the radio and went to investigate. Gene pulled into the garage, as the UPS truck followed him into the driveway. I watched as the driver unloaded two large boxes and two smaller ones. He set them inside the open door and quickly pulled away. I was blocking a bid for escape by Maggie and A.J. as Gene entered the house with three bulging plastic bags in each hand.

"OK, OK. Give me a minute," Gene said. He dropped the groceries on the counter and squatted to pet the dogs.

I kissed the top of his head. "Planning to have a party?"

"A party for two," he shot in my direction. Both hands were feverishly petting Maggie as he crooned, "How's a good girl? Did A.J. give you a hard time while I was gone? Mommy, too? I'll spank 'em for you." A.J. got a running start and jumped against his back, rocking him forward. He grinned up at me and said, "Make that a party for four."

"Any more food in the car?" I asked.

"Nope. But UPS stacked a delivery in back of your car."

"No sweat," I said. "I'll move it." Gene was still caught up in the love fest when I returned, carrying the two smaller boxes. I elbowed the sacks aside and dropped the boxes next to them. I pulled out the box cutter I'd stuffed in my pocket and sliced carefully through the tape.

"What's in the box, Babe," he asked as he opened the refrigerator door and began unloading the groceries.

"This week's selection from the Queen," I said. Sherrie had initiated no phone calls since our departure. But, every Friday, UPS delivered a small box labeled with their red overnight sticker. Today's contents included a loaf of Healthy Nine-Grain, four Applesauce Bran Muffins and six Peanut Butter/Chocolate Chip Cookies the size of salad plates.

Following a lengthy, honest discussion about the serious flirtations they'd both had, Sherrie and Dave hired Arthur to work out the details of a surprisingly amicable divorce. With the help of good lawyers, Dave and Tom received relatively light sentences. They had to pay large fines as restitution for the man-hours spent in a fraudulent missing person's case. They were also on the hook for two year's probation that included community service, but their 'fifteen minutes of fame' were over. Greg Kowalski's passing wasn't significant enough in Southern Ohio to achieve bird-cage liner status.

Sherrie had thrown herself into work and increased her therapy. Thanks to Dave's dalliance with Gladys, Sherrie finally dumped her guilt over Morgan. She also used some of the cash stash and one of the properties that she received in the settlement to start a no-kill rescue center for cats. Now, when her picture hit the news, it was to publicize "Scarlette's Half-way House for Cats."

The other package had a label from Cedar Point Amusement Park in Northern Ohio. I slit the top and removed a thick envelope resting on tissue paper. Nestled in the tissue were five pounds of individually wrapped Salt Water Taffy in a variety of flavors and colors.

I nudged Gene with my hip while slipping a bright pink candy into my mouth. I groaned in pleasure at the burst of sweet strawberry with an underlying tang.

"God, I used to love these things," Gene said, grabbing a fistful and tearing off several wrappers. "Who sent them?" he asked and stuffed a taffy rainbow into his mouth.

"Duh no," I managed around the drool. "Maybe the letter will tell us." I turned over the plain brown, 5" x 7" envelope and squeezed the splayed metal clasps together to open the flap. I swallowed and said, "Get a load of this!" A cardboard matte engraved with the Cedar Point logo held a typical tourist trap photo. The bodies of two muscle-builder guys and two bikini-clad girls were painted on a large wood display with cutouts for the heads. Smiling atop the female bodies were the round faces of Madeline and Gladys. A somber, unrecognizable male face was next to Madeline. The fourth person was mugging shamelessly for the camera. I did a double take and focused again on none other than Dave Walters.

"Well, I'll be damned," Gene slurred around his candy.

"Looks like Dave's found an alternative therapy," I said.

"Good for him," Gene quipped.

"Good for everyone," I answered. "Hell, I guess change is good for us all."

On my way back to the office to wrap up the bill-paying orgy, I stopped at the bookcase. I pulled Webster from the shelf and scanned through the first few entries for Change\ *vb*. I paused on the last two; **6:** to undergo transformation, transition or substitution. **7:** to give up one thing for something else in return. Well, well, well.